PENGUIN BOOKS
ACROSS THE LAKES

Amal Chatterjee was born in Colombo, Sri Lanka in 1965 of Sri Lankan and Indian parents. He studied in India and the UK and now lives in Glasgow and Amsterdam.

Across The Lakes

AMAL CHATTERJEE

PENGUIN BOOKS

Penguin Books India (P) Ltd., 210, Chiranjiv Tower, 43, Nehru Place, New Delhi 110 019, India
Penguin Books Ltd., 27 Wrights Lane, London W8 5TZ, UK
Penguin Books USA Inc., 375 Hudson Street, New York, NY 10014, USA
Penguin Books Australia Ltd., Ringwood, Victoria, Australia
Penguin Books Canada Ltd., 10 Alcorn Avenue, Suite 300, Toronto, Ontario M4V 3B2, Canada
Penguin Books (NZ) Ltd., 182-190 Wairau Road, Auckland 10, New Zealand

First published by Phoenix House 1998
First published by Penguin Books India (P) Ltd. 1998

10 9 8 7 6 5 4 3 2 1

For Susan

For Susan

CHAPTER ONE

✦ ✦ ✦ ✦

The Dhakuria Lakes are the lungs of south Calcutta. Once upon a time they marked the boundary of the city, beyond them lay the railway lines and beyond those the fields and villages. Now of course they have all been absorbed into the metropolis and today, when you cross the Dhakuria Railway Bridge, you enter the new districts of the city, beginning with Jodhpur Park and going all the way up to Garia. About the only difference you will notice is that beyond those railway tracks cycle-rickshaws ply, while on the Lakes' side there are none – or should be. Some daring cycle-rickshaws do venture down the back streets, all the way up to Rash Behari Avenue but there they stop, afraid of encountering a policeman or a khaki-clad Home Guard and losing their vehicles, their livelihood.

Enter the Lakes from the Gol Park end. Walk down Southern Avenue, past the Ramakrishna Mission, past the various auto-repair stalls. And there, on the left, is a road that leads in. Not far on, a rusting barrier with a piece of wire netting hanging from it stops adventurous cyclists unless they duck through a tear. Pass the high walls of the Lake Swimming Club, turn left and ahead are the quiet tree-shaded expanses of water you seek.

In the evening the Lakes come to life, a place of *adda*, casual gossip, trysts and quiet rambles. Coxed fours, coxless pairs slice the still water, startling the huge fish, while overhead flocks of birds ebb and flow. On the banks, *chawallahs* and *jhaalmoori* men offer tea and puffed rice mixed with onions, chillies and spices to the idlers and lovers. Pass them by (if you can resist) and head along the shore towards the stadium which appears ahead as you turn one last bend. No, don't go so far. Beside you there is a high wall, and behind it the Dhakuria Rowing Club.

The club premises are not very impressive by the standards of Calcutta. The buildings, lawn, garden and drive would fit into a football field, and not a full size one at that. Still, it occupies a large, almost substantial area for a city in which space is in such short supply. If you decide to visit, be prepared to identify yourself as a member, or be ready to name one as your host, because the *durwan* is very particular. If you manage to satisfy him, you will be rewarded by the sight of the sprawling club buildings to your right and a gravelled driveway ahead of you. The latter leads to a lawn unsuccessfully hidden behind a carefully manicured hedge. An oasis within an oasis, the lawn, which reaches down the water's edge, is a peaceful place free of the vendors, lovers and walkers that populate the public spaces. Here a select company while away the time, seated at white tables, shielded when the sun is high by large umbrellas bearing the club's own logo of two crossed oars.

To enjoy the privileges of club membership you must fulfil two primary criteria – money (not the kind needed for the posher institutions, but sufficient to keep this one reasonably private), and a proven interest in rowing. An 'interest', not skill, is insisted upon. Of course, to join one must attend a certain number of lessons, but many who have completed the course would risk capsizing if they so much as plunged their oars into the water. The club is primarily a meeting place, the rowing team little more than an appendage like a college football team. This is not a place for business either, here one whiles away the evening, nursing a drink or a cup of tea, casually discussing whatever takes one's fancy. Leisure is the motto, you might say.

The evening of the New Year's Day Meena arrived home, Putul sat on the lawn of this very institution. Slight, in his mid-twenties, good-looking in a fifties film sort of way, he himself had been home for just a fortnight. After three years away, working hard on his doctorate, he felt he now deserved an extended rest. 'Recuperating,' he called it. Sailen Kaka, his father's brother, and his guardian, had indicated he would welcome Putul's presence and assistance in running the family business, but Putul was still managing to side-step the issue. After all, he had promised his professor – offered, actually, but why explain? – an article on the effect of liberalisation on the steel industry. Not that he had so much as put pen to paper. So far his aunt, his surrogate mother, was protecting him – 'The boy needs to do this paper thing, it is important to him, no? Why have we sent him so far otherwise?' – and his uncle had no stomach for family disagreement.

3

But it wouldn't last for ever ... The young man leaned forward and tapped sharply on the table bell. Nothing happened for a while, then – 'An indecent interval later,' he said to himself – a bearer with a faintly surly expression on his face wandered over.

Putul ordered a Limca and the man shambled off. Putul idly wondered why the management never attempted to 'straighten out' the staff. That man's jacket bore stains that looked at least a week old. And his tennis shoes had seen better days, much better. Putul sighed. He should have ordered a snack too. By the time the man brought the drink, took the order and returned, the Limca would be flat.

Meena! She half saw him before he saw her, hesitated, then turned away. But it was too late. He started up.

'Meena! Hey, Meena!'

She turned back.

'Putul,' Meena said. 'Fancy running into you here.' Her voice conveyed no surprise.

'Come and join me,' Putul urged. Then, remembering himself, he hastily added, 'That is, unless you have somewhere else to go.'

Meena looked uncertain. 'I'm waiting for Arun.' She looked round for her brother. 'I suppose he'll find me.' Putul's heart gave an unaccustomed leap. He had quite forgotten that Meena was fairly attractive. When they had met in Scotland he had found her rather daunting. But now her slight five foot nothing frame was definitely – well, *almost*, desirable. Pity she was a cousin ... Now her brother Arun was what cousins should look like, ordinary. The bearer materialised with Putul's drink. Putul sent him back for a pot of tea and a plate of fish fingers.

'So, Meena,' he began, 'when did you get back? I wasn't expecting you for a while.'

'Oh, my scholarship was for just six months – finished last week. Actually, I arrived this morning, on the ten o'clock flight.'

'This morning? You must be jet-lagged.' He could think of nothing else to say.

'Jet-lagged? No, I don't have time for that – there's just so much to do!'

Putul pondered this. 'I still claim jet-lag myself,' he said. 'You should try it, it's a good excuse.' Meena nodded. She looked bored. The conversation, barely started, was already flagging, he needed to say something, to say it quickly, 'And what did you think of England? Ooops, *Scotland*.' Relief when she smiled in shared recognition.

'Cold! It was minus twenty when I left – I could hardly believe it!'

'Amazing, it never fell that low while I was there . . .' A silence followed. Putul tried again. 'So here we are, back in Calcutta, *bekaar*, unemployed, two of the millions . . .'

'Unemployed?' She looked surprised.

'Well, only sort of,' he conceded. 'The family business, you know. My uncle is pretty keen, but car parts and all that . . .' He made a face.

'Would you rather do something else?'

'Yes. Nothing at all!' Putul chuckled. Meena smiled politely.

'Oh, I am a lazy one,' he said cheerfully. 'Nothing suits me better than doing nothing.'

It had been a long day, Meena said, she wanted to go home. She should find her brother.

'So soon?' Putul expostulated. 'The tea hasn't arrived yet . . .' But she was already out of her seat.

'Well, if you must.' He half rose. 'We must get together

again, sometime soon. To chat about Scotland, you know, reminisce and all that . . .'

'We must.' She was gone before he had time to suggest an appointment. Not that he had anything certain in mind. She wasn't really his type . . . He sank back into his chair, whistling softly through his teeth. As if on cue, the bearer reappeared with the pot of tea and fish fingers, banged them down on the table. Putul pursed his lips. Should he send them back? No, it wasn't worth the aggravation. He had a whole evening to himself, they might occupy him – after all, the sun hadn't even begun to set. He sighed and signed the chit. Doing nothing required imagination sometimes, he told himself.

Of all the lousy things to happen – in Calcutta for barely twelve hours and whom should I bump into but that idiot, Putul. He's one of the idle rich. I can't think of better words to describe him. God knows how he survives, how *they* survive. Each generation more idle than the last . . . There I was, looking forward to a quiet evening by the Lakes, catching up on all the news with my brother, and instead I ended up having an inane conversation with an idiot.

He's a cousin, not a first cousin, but a cousin all the same. His father was my father's . . . never mind, it's all too difficult to explain, let's just say we have a great-great grandparent by marriage in common. And his father and uncle and my father went to the same school so they were closer than most cousins – something I regret. When I was leaving to go to Europe his aunt, who had brought him up after his parents died, asked me to get in touch with him. Said it would be nice for both of us. I usually do try to be accommodating but that time I didn't really feel like it.

6

I've never had much time for him and I think he feels the same way about me. We're as different as can be. OK, I occasionally bumped into him or into mutual acquaintances, but we were completely different. Yes, we both went to missionary-run schools but his was the preserve of rich children who were dropped off at the gates by their fathers' drivers. My school, on the other hand, had rather less expensive taste in students. Sure, some of the girls who came from better-off families were dropped by cars, but the majority – including myself – got there by public transport, school bus or rickshaw. Come to think of it, the girls in my school who *did* come by car were driven by their parents, not by drivers, company or private!

And that is just the beginning, there's lots more that sets us apart. Take swimming, for instance. I learned down at the Lakes, while Putul went to the Swimmer's Club. His club had a huge, chlorinated pool, open air in a very posh sort of way. While mine was open air simply because it didn't have a roof. Simple as that. And there's the sorts of things we did in our spare time – he played tennis and met his friends at the rich folks' clubs, while I and my friends made do with visiting each other at home, going for walks together, that sort of thing.

Well, under the circumstances, you can imagine that when I got to Glasgow I didn't seek him out immediately. To tell the truth, I avoided him for as long as I could. But eventually my guilt began to get the better of me. How would I face his aunt or my mother when home? So, I called him at his flat, and was quite surprised that he sounded genuinely pleased to hear my voice. He seemed most extraordinarily anxious to meet me and to 'show me around'. I tried to get out of it but he wouldn't be put off easily, and insisted I visit him for a meal. I couldn't refuse so I asked, as I'd been warned was customary amongst students there, whether I should contribute something to the meal. His response surprised me.

'Come on, we Indians don't entertain that way!'

That 'we Indians' struck me too. I have never thought of us as alike. This claim of kinship, even at a national level, was most puzzling.

I was surprised to find he lived in a university flat, sharing a kitchen and other facilities with four others. I would have thought the room rather small for him, yet he appeared very comfortable in it. Even odder, he'd actually learned to cook a bit. Rice, dal and a meat curry – I did see a tin of Patak's Korma Sauce in the corner by the cooker, but it was still more than I had expected. In fact, when I walked in and saw him in front of the stove I stopped short, open-mouthed for a second. What would his schoolmates and his family have made of it? He was practically domesticated! His was a strange metamorphosis from one whom the world revolved around into a painfully shy, frightened bookworm who did his own housework.

I only spoke to him once after that, he 'phoned the day before he left. Our next encounter was when he was back in his element at the Rowing Club that New Year's Day, where he was, once again, an insufferable spoilt little rich boy.

Putul yawned. The sun was streaming through the chinks in the shutters. The tall grandfather clock in the corner showed eight thirty. His aunt, Swapna Kakima would have been up for over three hours by now. He was mildly surprised at how eight thirty, which would not have seemed particularly late a month ago in Scotland, had now become 'late'. He rolled out of bed, pulled on a dressing gown and made his way down to the dining room.

His aunt was expecting him. Almost immediately a servant bustled in with a pot of tea. Putul poured himself a cup and turned to the newspaper which lay still rolled up from delivery on a side table. He scanned the front pages and yawned. Politics. He flipped to the sports page. Ah, cricket, the Test series. He hummed contentedly.

'Putul, one egg or two?' His aunt called from the kitchen.

'One, Kakima, just one – as usual,' Putul was deep in the selector's choice.

'What about toast?'

'Two slices, Kakima, as usual.'

'Don't read while you are eating.'

'I'm not eating yet, Kakima,' he said mildly, replacing the paper all the same.

'You will be soon,' her reply came pat. 'And what are you going to do today? Laze around again? You should help your uncle . . .'

'You know I'm working on that article, Kakima . . .' he replied without hesitating. He was getting used to this.

'Article, sharticle!' she retorted disdainfully. 'Even if you are working on it – which I don't see you doing – what good is it going to do for you? It won't help fill your belly, will it?' She came into the room and slid a plate of toast in front of him.

Putul smiled. 'Kakima, *you* fill my belly. And if you won't I can always live on my inheritance, can't I?'

'Nonsense, Putul!' she huffed, returning to the kitchen. 'Your father would be horrified to hear you! Don't make fun of his memory!'

'I don't mean to,' he replied soothingly.

'But you do!' She was used to carrying on conversations from the kitchen. 'And when are you going to see your Boro Dadu? He has been expecting you for weeks now. I told him

9

you were tired and busy but I cannot keep saying that, can I? You must go and see him. He is very keen to see you again.'

Her nephew sighed. 'All he'll do is ask me who I am and then start rambling on about something or other. He doesn't know who he's talking to and I'm not sure he cares, Kakima.'

'That's his right, Putul. You should respect your elders more.'

Putul shrugged. 'I'll go this afternoon.' He reached for the paper but just then his aunt reappeared.

'And don't forget to drop in on your Raja Kaku when you go, and Priya Pishi, and . . .'

'That'll take me all day – no, all week!' he complained.

'So what? They are your family, you must pay them respect.'

'I'll go, I'll go . . .'

'And . . .'

'"And" Kakima!' He stuck his tongue out at her.

It was an old game. 'I won't stand for any of that, young man. Keep your civil tongue inside your head! And leave that paper where it is.'

Breakfast proceeded sedately. Putul dawdled over his tea and eggs, rising from the table only when his aunt insisted. Back upstairs, he indulged in a long post-breakfast shower. It was not behaviour his aunt would tolerate in anyone else, but Putul had worn her down over the years and now she rarely remarked on it.

An hour later, showered and dressed, Putul summoned the car to take him to the club. There were very few people around, just the usual retirees and a couple of others. He found himself a corner armchair without difficulty, ordered a beer and settled down to read a magazine. An hour later he was still there, engrossed in an article about the relative strengths and weaknesses of the teams in the Test series. Then, without warning, the magazine was snatched from his hand.

'Putul! I thought so, *shala*!' A chubby bespectacled figure stood over him. Expensive suit, silk tie. Leather briefcase with combination lock. Fair, almost ruddy cheeks. Bottle Ginwallah, real name Bobby Ginwallah, 'Haven't seen your ass in ages – when did you get back?'

Putul retrieved the magazine. 'Bottle. I should have known you'd find me here. Your manners haven't improved since I last saw you.'

'You think you are some epitome of etiquette?' Bottle snorted. 'You're a skunk. You slink back into the country to hide behind a pathetic magazine and then have the gall to tell me how to behave? Hey, you!' He grabbed the sleeve of a passing bearer. 'Another bottle of beer – this sahib owes me one.' Putul nodded. 'And make it snappy!'

'So, Putul, my boy,' he turned back to Putul, 'what brings you home? Run out of money and come to touch the uncle? Or back because they don't want your type over there? Can't say I blame them.'

'Nothing half as exciting. All that happened was I finished my degree and, having had enough of the cold, I came home.'

'Home, eh? Good, good, I can't stand it when you *vilayatis* say "back to India". You seem to have kept your head – or else you know me well enough to know how to please me. Which you should, seeing as we've known each other for so long and I'm your elder and better!' He slapped Putul on the back. Putul did not object, they went back a long time.

'Only just. Or haven't you noticed?' Bottle waved airily. Putul continued, 'So tell me, Bottle, what're you doing these days? I've never seen you this smart, you good-for-nothing! Whatever it is, it must pay quite a fortune to keep you in suits . . . unless you have only one, that is.'

'Only one suit? Come on, *yaar*, a suit doesn't cost a fortune yet. I earn a respectable salary – not by your *phoren* standards, but enough for a few suits.' He sighted the bearer again. 'Hey, bearer! Where's that beer? And get us some snacks too – some peanuts, chips, anything – jump to it, man!' The bearer scuttled off. 'God, the service is lousy here!'

'You should try the Dhakuria's service,' Putul said meditatively. 'They're amazing!'

'That good, huh?'

'No, that *bad!*' Putul laughed. 'Those guys can take a month to get you a cup of tea!' He shook his head in mock despair. 'Come on, Bottle, answer my question? Gone into politics or something, have you?'.

'Politics? Me? No way! I'm a gainfully employed humble employee.'

'Employee? You in sales or marketing or whatever you call it, ay?' He didn't wait for an answer. 'Go on then, sell us something. Plastic tea cups or whatever your bosses send you out to peddle . . .'

'Sorry, don't sell plastic tea cups. Can't stand them, disgusting little things.' The young man pursed his lips and looked at his watch. 'Look, I'm supposed to be meeting some colleagues for lunch, *yaar*. We're going to the Dining Room – want to join us?'

Putul allowed himself to be persuaded, extracting from his friend an undertaking to pay for the beer and the meal. Not that he couldn't have afforded it himself, he just liked the challenge.

The light, almost spice-free cooking of the club's 'Western' kitchen suited Putul's faintly anglicised tastes and, unsurprisingly, that day's menu was perfect for him: steamed *hilsa* with mashed potatoes and vegetables, preceded by a consommé and followed by ice cream. He enjoyed it as much as the company of Bottle's colleagues, all of whom welcomed him cheerfully. He joined easily in the conversation that accompanied the meal, animated chat of nothing in particular: the latest American film, the relative merits of James Hadley Chase and Alistair Maclean, the varieties of new cars now available. All laced with ribald jokes and sexual innuendo. Comfortably glowing alcohol in the warm afternoon, Putul felt confident enough to ask, 'No work to go to anyone?' No one was listening. He tried again, 'Are all you guys in sales like Bottle?'

This time he got a response. A man in a blue shirt glared across the table, incredulity on his sweaty face, 'In *sales* like Bottle? Shit, *yaar*, you really don't know your arse from your elbow, do you? I don't sell *things*!'

Putul drew back and gulped his beer noisily, filling the gap, 'Yeah, I know Bottle isn't a salesman, not really . . .'

The blue shirt exploded. 'You don't know *shit*! I'm not a salesman! Not a fucking anything *wallah*! Who . . .'

Putul goggled. Blue shirt was on his feet, leaning into the table, ham fists clenched. Hands – Bottle's, other's – reached up and hauled him rudely down into his seat. Blue shirt fell back heavily and glowered across the disturbed table. Bottle wiped his hands on a napkin.

'I need a fag. Putul, you coming?' The instigator of the outburst allowed himself to be dragged unprotesting from the room.

'What's the matter with that guy?' Putul had recovered

13

enough to complain. 'All I asked him was a simple question . . .'

'You thick or what?' Bottle practically threw his friend against a nearby pillar. 'Calling those guys salesmen! Man, you certainly know how to rub folks the wrong way!'

'What was wrong with it?' Putul protested. 'You said you were in sales and that those guys were your colleagues so I assumed . . .'

'I said I was in sales! You hearing things, man? Shit, am I fucking stupid or are you? Let me try to explain. I work for my father, remember?'

Putul did, sort of. 'And do you remember what my father's business is?' Alcohol-befuddled, Putul clutched the pillar and shook his head slowly.

'OK, he's in tea, like I thought you'd remember from school, *yaar*. But he doesn't own any gardens or touch the stuff, not the leaves, that is. He wouldn't know an orange pekoe or a Makaibari from a banana leaf! Doesn't even like drinking the stuff. Guess that runs in the family.' He grinned drunkenly. 'Anyway, that doesn't stop him from speculating in the stuff. Stocks, futures, anything to do with tea. Why tea? Why fucking not? You got better suggestions, *you* tell him!'

'So what d'you do?'

'I am the family apprentice,' Bottle drew himself up unsteadily. 'I am starting at the bottom, in the office, doing the accounts, checking the deals and payment – the dirty work. It pisses me off, man! My old man makes the bucks, I do the dirty work! It really fucking pisses me off! No commission for me, just my salary and my allowance. Whatever my dad wants to give me!'

'How about those guys? The ones you said were your colleagues?' Putul hugged the cool pillar closer.

'Those guys? Oh yeah, they're my colleagues. Sort of. They work for my dad. No fucking different, really. Only they get to keep a decent percentage of what they make. I don't. Thanks to my dad, that old bastard!' Bottle was almost purple now. 'Let's get out of here, leave those buggers to themselves. Let's go for a fucking drive. Hey, you! YOU!' A bearer approached.

'Get my fucking driver to bring the car round. And move it! *Jaldi!*' The bearer led the swaying pair into the sweeping entrance hall. A blue Ambassador pulled up. Bottle fell into the back face first. Then, just as his friend was climbing after him, Bottle changed his mind, pushed out again and clawed round to the front. A couple of club employees stopped to watch. Another drunk, their faces said, why can't the young babus learn to hold their drink? Shrugging their shoulders, they strolled off. The scene was too familiar. There was nothing for them to do.

Bottle pulled the driver's door open.

'Get out! OUT! Go home! *Jaldi!*' The driver looked at him just once and scrambled out. If the babu wanted to drive why should he object? No point inviting more abuse. From the back seat Putul watched him go. It crossed his mind that he should call him back, but what the hell. It wasn't worth the effort. After all, Bottle had been driving since he was ten (or so he claimed). The drunk in the front seat struggled with the key in the ignition. The engine coughed. Putul looked out. At the gate, an old *durwan* saluted and waved them through.

Bottle released the hand-brake and the car jerked forward. 'See that guard? He's a shit, a *banchod*, a real sisterfucker. Stands out there, salaams you when you're sober, then when you're slightly soft he demands his fucking pound of flesh. Tells you shit sob stories about how he needs the money to send his son to school, to get his daughter married. He's a

Bihari, they all say they're fucking Biharis! It makes your heart bleed – because they know every one of you Bangali babus thinks Bihar is one heck of a screwed up place, you'll believe anything about it! And you know what? All you Bangali fools fall for it! You're so fucking stupid!'

Putul did not reply. He had problems of his own, the world was spinning alarmingly.

'Tell you what, Putul – let's get the bugger! Fifinish him off! Don't look so scared, I'm only kidding, you stupid bastard!' But Putul wasn't scared. He was steadying himself against the door and trying to remember where he was. Bottle kicked a pedal, the car jumped towards the wall. The horn blared. The waiting *durwan* dropped his salute and ran towards them. One young Babu had collapsed over the wheel, forehead firmly pressing down on the horn. The other lay slumped over the back seat, snoring.

Putul woke at ten. Eyes firmly shut, he counted the strokes of the grandfather clock. As the last note died away, he opened his eyes carefully. Where was he? A framed photograph swam into focus in front of his nose. A familiar face stared out of it. His father. Younger, thinner than in other photos, with hair. And his mother, slim, svelte, dressed fashionably in an open necked shirt and what Swapna Kakima called 'slacks'. Putul's thoughts wandered. He couldn't imagine Swapna Kakima in anything like that, it wasn't her style at all, she wouldn't wear anything but a sari. Not that either he or his uncle would have dared suggest she did, it wouldn't have been her style at all . . .

He sat up, his head aching. As he waited for the room to settle, he tried to remember how he had got home that afternoon. Why had he been in a taxi? Bottle had a driver *and* he could drive. It came back in a rush. Crashing into the wall, the bearers pulling them out. Being bundled into a taxi. They threw the two in. Bottle had woken up and objected to the driver's choice of route. They drove round the block twice before the driver gave up and allowed Bottle to direct him. At that point Putul had fallen asleep again. The next thing he remembered was being helped out of the taxi by his uncle's *durwan*. He thought he recalled the sound of an altercation behind him as he staggered up the drive to the house. Had the *durwan* paid the driver? Or worse still, had Sailen Kaka? He groaned.

He staggered out of the room, pausing in the brightly lit corridor. Should he get some water or to just go back to his room? Neither option was particularly attractive. He stumbled down the stairs to the large, airy courtyard. Ah, there was a chair. He'd sit down for a bit and think about his next move. Moments after lowering himself into it, he passed out again.

CHAPTER TWO

The day after I arrived I slept late, incredibly late. Even though I had tried to ignore it, I *was* tired, jet-lagged. I needed time to adjust. Which was a pity – I had been so looking forward to this, to getting back home to talking to Ma, to telling her and my friends of what she would call 'my adventures'. But after that first evening and the brief visit to Dada's Rowing Club all I could do was sleep – I didn't wake until eleven.

In the bathroom, I splashed water over me, lathering myself with the glycerine soap I use every winter to soften my skin, relishing its smoothness. It was so pleasant, to be able to wash without freezing! I dressed in a cotton *salwar kameez*, glad too to be wearing loose garments again. How good it was to be free of heavy layers. I could hear Ma in the kitchen, telling

Durga how she wanted the vegetables sliced, how much turmeric to grind. Durga was, I knew, looking forward to this as much as Ma was. I was sure they were preparing a special meal, a treat to welcome me home. Ma would have asked Baba to pick up fresh fish from the market this morning. Still brushing my hair, I went out onto the balcony.

'Did you sleep well?' Ma came up behind me.

'Yes, Ma, like a baby,' I could have hugged her for the sheer joy of being home.

'I have some breakfast for you. *Luchi* and *tarkari*. Just as you always like.'

'Ma, you don't know how much I missed that!'

'Yes, I do. Meena without her *luchi* and *tarkari*, it, doesn't sound like a recipe for happiness. Come on in, the *luchis* are hot – you wouldn't want them to get cold, would you?' Naturally I wouldn't. Besides, it wasn't just the *luchis* I'd missed.

Ma and Durga stood by my side, watching me eat with vicarious pleasure. As so often since my childhood, my pleasure was theirs. After an age, I could eat no more and was evicted from the kitchen, my feeble attempts to be allowed to stay dismissed. I climbed the stairs to the roof. Out there in the warm January sun, I wove my way through the familiar lines of washing, cotton clothes bleaching in bright light. In spite of myself, my feelings were mixed. I was looking forward to the food and the company.

I could see the green expanse that borders the Lakes. A winter cricket match, boys (young men?) in shining and not-so-shining white, a once-red ball bouncing towards padded batsman. Sporadic cries of 'Howzzat?' and the defeated trudging back to the shade of the trees. In a corner, school-girls, smart in their white blouses and navy blue skirts, marching in formation. Kites in the sky wheeling hungrily overhead, hoping for a chance to drop down upon the tiffin boxes which they could see under a tree. But those had already attracted the attention of another feathered tribe, the blue-black crows. One of them, bolder than his fellows, was tugging hard at the string that bound one box, pausing after every tug to look around warily, just in case. But there was no immediate danger – the girls and their trainer were too engrossed in keeping in step. The string snapped and the box flew open, the contents instantly mobbed by the thief's squalling, quarrelling fellows. The girls marched on, oblivious. At last they wheeled and saw. One ran towards the boxes, arms flailing. But she was too late. The birds grabbed last morsels and scattered.

I could hear Ma and Durga in the kitchen. They were talking of the meal, of prices, of the crowds in the market, the state of the roads, the preparations for someone's marriage. For a while in my teens, the banality of their conversation had annoyed me daily. But with time I have grown used to it and, although I cannot join in, I love to hear it, the familiar background sound of home. I smiled.

Ma and I ate together, Durga serving us.

'Meena, did you meet Putul while you were in Scotland?'

'Yes, Ma. I went to his place for dinner. Believe it or not, he cooked.'

'He cooked? Well, well, well!'

'Yes, Ma. He was quite different there.'

'Different? How?'

'Well, besides cooking, he was quite different in other ways. Almost afraid of the world around him. Fortunately, he had some friends there.'

'Many?' Ma picked bones from her fish.

'One at least. He joined us for dinner. His name's John Stewart. His father's a business partner of Putul's uncle. Putul had spent some time in the summer with John's family. Apparently the Stewarts also have a family connection with India – John's grandfather used to work here.'

'Speaking of friends, Meena, Ratna rang. She wants you to call her.'

Ratna, my closest friend. I called her after lunch and arranged to meet.

When Putul awoke he was still in the chair. His watch told him it was already nine, and the sunshine that it was morning. His head felt heavy, his tongue furred. Swapna Kakima would not be pleased, he knew. She disapproved of his drinking, and of the company he kept. To mollify her he would have to promise to make the visits, he would have to visit Boro Dadu. He made his way back to his room and, as the sun grew warmer, he dozed.

By one o'clock he was feeling better. Not perfect, of course – that could hardly be expected – but certainly less hung-over. Finding his aunt, as he expected, in the kitchen, he announced his penance – the family visits – and she mellowed enough to inquire about the state of his head. Wary of a lecture, he was noncommittal and she did not press him. He looked like he had learned his lesson – at least until the next time. She joined him for lunch.

At around four, after a nap, he summoned the driver and set off for the old house. The afternoon traffic was light, they were there sooner than he expected. His heart sank as they pulled up outside the four-storey house – he reckoned it contained nearly seventy relatives of various ages and degrees of independence and senility. Of course, he didn't have to visit them all but there was absolutely no way he could complete more than a couple of visits that afternoon. If only he hadn't given his aunt his word. There was no turning back.

The first person to recognise him was not a relative but the *paanwallah* whose little shop adjoined the gate. He seemed to have aged greatly since Putul had last seen him five . . . no, six or seven years before. Now white-haired and stooped, he bore little resemblance to the rounded middle-aged man of the past. Reassuring, then, that this older man still sat cross-legged behind a clean marble board set with all the paraphernalia of *paan* making. There were subtle changes, though, the smart ranks of packaged cigarettes had shrunk to a few half-empty shelves, the glowing jute rope, the 'roadside Ronson', had vanished, replaced by a small oil lamp encased in tin and a box of card strips cut from cigarette packets.

'Putul Babu!' the *paanwallah*, almost a family retainer, greeted him. 'How are you? We have not seen you for so long!'

'Oh, I just got back,' Putul lied uncomfortably.

'From England, no? I heard you'd gone – but not that you had returned? *We* do not hear these things, it seems.'

'I've been very busy, and have come as soon as I could.'

'Ah, that's the way it is, isn't it? You have grown, Putul Babu, you have grown. And you working now, no?' He did not wait for an answer. 'It is good that you come . . . but I am keeping you, you must go and see your granduncle, he will be very happy to see you,' he beamed paternally.

'I will stop by later for a chat . . .' Putul promised.

'Please do that – please, do not forget . . .' Was there real emotion in his voice? Putul escaped hurriedly down the narrow passage to the second gate at the back. It was unlocked, as it always was, but closed, to keep out the stray dogs

and other animals. He lifted the latch and stepped through, carefully closing it behind him. Through a dark (once, now faded) green door he mounted stairs. On the first floor was the third gate. This too was unchanged, locked, the keys hanging on a hook inside, within view but out of reach. He knew the routine, he pressed the button beside it. Mercifully the electric bell still worked, he hated having to shout to draw attention. Priya Pishi's voice wafted down.

'Who is it?'

'I!'

'I who?'

'Putul, Priya Pishi.'

'Putul who? Aiii, *Putul*! Wait, wait, I am coming down! Here, are you listening? Baba, Raja – look who's here! Putul!' She materialsed to let him in. 'Come in, come in! Where have you been?'

Accustomed both to her effusiveness and to avoiding her, Putul sidled past, excusing himself. He would stop to talk to her after he had seen Boro Dadu, he said. She called after him that he was right, it was best of course that he visit his Boro Dadu first.

Boro Dadu, the patriarch, lived at the top of the house, three floors above street level. He was Putul's paternal grandfather's cousin, younger than Putul's own grandfather but, since the elder cousin had died many years ago, Boro Dadu had assumed the role of patriarch. He had been, it was widely rumoured, trained as a lawyer. In fact, some of the other older inhabitants of the block even referred to the house as 'The Lawyer's'. But Putul had never seen evidence of a legal practice and Boro Dadu had never referred to one so he suspected it was just a story born of the fact that Boro Dadu's father had been a lawyer of some sort in his day. All he knew was that the ol

man scrupulously avoided talking about his own past, preferring instead to discuss that of his many relatives and descendants.

By the time he reached the fourth floor Putul was quite out of breath, partly from lack of exercise and partly from the shouted conversations which he continued as he climbed. The old man was sitting with his back to the door, exactly as Putul remembered him – bald, thin as a rake, wreathed in pipe smoke and gently rocking in his huge Victorian rocking chair as he looked out across the city. Nothing had changed, even the tobacco smelled familiarly foul.

'Putul?!' the voice was querulous. 'Come here, boy, into the light so I can see you!' He beckoned the young man forward without turning round. 'So, you're back.' The watery eyes focused. 'Come closer, boy, my eyes are not as good as they used to be . . .' How much of the city could he see, Putul wondered as he approached, or did he face it only out of habit? Putul pronaamed his granduncle, touched his feet respectfully and then jerking upright just in time to avoid the chair catching him in the eye. Unconscious of Putul's narrow escape the old man regally acknowledged the respect.

'Pull up a chair, boy, and sit near me. I haven't seen you for so long.'

'I've been away, Boro Dadu.'

'Speak up, boy!'

'I said, I've been away!' Putul raised his voice. But the old man shook his head. Putul opened his mouth to repeat himself but was interrupted by a voice from the dimness of the room behind.

'HE SAID HE HAS BEEN AWAY. HE WAS IN ENGLAND – YOU REMEMBER, I TOLD YOU TEN MINUTES AGO!'

Putul turned round. It was Raja Kaku. Quiet, stay-at-home

Raja Kaku, youngest son of the patriarch. Now somewhere in his sixties, he had once been the sickly son, the one who never married, never left the house. Now he was the carer, patient-turned-interpreter beaming in the doorway, looking better than Putul recalled. It wasn't just the *paanwallah* who had changed.

Raja Kaku dropped his voice to normal volume. 'Hullo, Putul. Your Boro Dadu can't hear very well any more. First his eyes, now his ears. You have to shout at him. Only he doesn't like it, which makes talking to him difficult. But somehow he doesn't seem to mind if *I* shout. Maybe he doesn't associate a loud voice with me – there's no telling how youthful restraint can pay off,' he laughed cheerfully. Beside him the old man coughed. Putul turned back to the full glare of a benign smile. He responded cautiously.

'You've been in England, eh? What is it like? Full of Englishmen, no?' Boro Dadu weakly dusted ashes from his pipe. 'You know, you are not the first of the family to go abroad ...' He blew into the pipe, which stubbornly re-fused to rekindle. Disgusted, he coughed again and con-tinued, 'The first one to go was my cousin. You won't remember, you weren't born then. You are too young, far too young ... he went to England a long time ago, in the twenties ...'

'BABA, IT WAS THE THIRTIES. NINETEEN THIRTY-FIVE, TO BE PRECISE!' Raja Kaku's interruption though loud was res-igned. He had apparently heard the story so often he knew it better than the narrator. 'HE WENT IN NINETEEN THIRTY-FIVE.'

'That's what I was saying!' his father huffed. 'My cousin – your uncle ...'

'HIS GRANDUNCLE. LIKE YOU.'

'Like me? No, he was not like me. Not like me at all – quite different. He went to England – I didn't! He went in the twenties . . .'

'THE THIRTIES. NINETEEN THIRTY-FIVE, BABA.'

'That's what I was saying, before you interrupted me, Raja.' He addressed Putul again, 'My cousin went to study engineering . . .'

'MEDICINE. NOT ENGINEERING.

'What did you say? My cousin went to study in Oxford . . .'

'LONDON. NOT OXFORD. NO ONE WENT TO OXFORD, EXCEPT THE BHUTTOS AND THEY'RE FROM PAKISTAN AND ARE NO RELATIONS OF OURS.'

'The Bhuttos? I don't know any Bhuttos, except the ones in Pakistan. Who was that one, the prime minister? We aren't related to them – they're Pakistanis, aren't they?'

'NO, WE AREN'T. IT WAS A JOKE!' His son shook his head wearily.

'A joke? Why can't you be serious? I am talking about this young fellow's uncle . . .'

'NOT HIS UNCLE. HIS GRANDUNCLE. LIKE YOU.'

'Uncle, granduncle! What are you babbling about, boy? Don't interrupt. As I was saying, he went in the twenties to study engineering in Oxford . . .'

'IT WAS THE THIRTIES, MEDICINE AND LONDON!'

The old man glared angrily in the direction of the voice. 'Enough of these interruptions! I am trying to tell this young man about his own family and you keep interfering! You have no interest in the family history – why would you, you have no children! But it is important that I pass it on . . .' Raja Kaku, clearly used to this sort of abuse, smiled cheerfully and shrugged his shoulders. Boro Dadu snorted and spoke directly to Putul again.

'My cousin, your uncle went to Oxford to study engineering.' He stopped, his brow creasing, 'Of course he was no relation of the Bhuttos! Why did you bring them up?' He frowned accusingly at Putul.

'But I didn't say anything . . .'

'Speak up, boy!'

'HE SAID HE DIDN'T SAY ANYTHING. WHICH IS QUITE RIGHT – I SAID IT, AND IT WAS A JOKE.' There was amused despair in Raja Kaku's voice.

Boro Dadu nodded. 'My cousin was in Oxford, studied engineering . . .' He paused, frowned again. 'Where . . . what were we talking about?'

'YOUR COUSIN. BUT ENOUGH, BABA, I THINK IT'S TIME YOU HAD YOUR MEDICINE. He's on medication. Had a minor stroke while you were away.'

'Yes, I heard,' Putul replied, 'Swapna Kakima wrote me when it happened. She wrote me the day she heard.'

'Yes, that sounds like her. Very efficient, wastes no time. And now I must give Baba his medicine – why don't you go downstairs and meet your Priya Pishi? She will be pleased. Her nephews are away, they have their own jobs, their own lives and she feels left out these days. We all do.' He pursed his lips meditatively.

Putul rose. 'Oh I want to see her too – only I can't stay . . . not today, because it is getting late and I have to get home . . . to do some work I have promised my . . . my professor in Scotland.'

Raja Kaku measured dark liquid from a bottle, and counted some pills before replying.

'Well, you must come and see us all soon. Otherwise we

will be very disappointed, you know. We do look forward to you youngsters dropping in . . . Oh dear, I'm getting quite as old and sentimental as him . . .' he waved at his father who had returned his gaze to the window, and was now lost in memories, oblivious to the presence of his son and grandnephew.

That evening we took our cane chairs out on the balcony. All of us, Ma, Baba, Dada and myself. Since it was my first whole day back, Baba had come home early, leaving the shop under the supervision of Bablu, the young man who had risen from tea-boy to right hand man. Dada – that's my brother, Arun – had escaped his office early too. His boss is a very understanding man, one who appreciates him without taking advantage. A gem of a man is how Ma describes him. 'Bit of a rough gem to look at, Ma.' And she smacks me playfully on the arm.

We chatted under the darkening sky. The air was thick with mosquitoes which, in spite of the mosquito coils and incense, formed tall columns above each head. At last we turned to the topic Ma had raised in her last letter to me. A bride for Dada. Ma had been keen on it for a while, and Dada had finally agreed that the wheels be set in motion. I joined in eagerly. We discussed the possibilities, dividing the candidates into two groups. The first consisted of those whose families wanted my brother (or someone like him). These we called the Prospectives. The second, more interesting group, included those we considered reasonable candidates. These we called the Potentials. It was funny, now that I think of it, discussing people who were not present, people we hardly knew, and classifying them. And, not surprisingly, we dismissed most of the Prospectives as less than satisfactory. But there were still plenty of Potentials to consider, so we agreed some ground rules. No caste bar, no colour or religion bars (how easy it is to fall into the clichés!). What was definitely 'in' was education. A degree at least. Probably arts, though science would do. Not a stick-at-home. Someone who had a job or wanted to get one. Preferably not straight out of college, either. Tall, beautiful. Dada looked uncomfortable, but I couldn't help it. I've always teased him. When I was little I used to grab his hand and demand that he take me out to buy some sweetmeats. And he would, and then take the blame if we got told off. Now I wanted him to be happy.

Durga served us tea and sat with her own cup on the doorstep, listening to the conversation. Sometimes she would join in indirectly, making a face that only Dada and I could see as a comment on one candidate or the other. Baba said that his sister, our aunt, had told him – in her most mysterious tone – that she knew of a young 'girl' who would be 'ideal'. 'Convent-educated', doing a Master's in English at Jadavpur. She had refused to divulge the name over the phone so Baba was going to see her. He was just letting us know. It might turn out to be a red herring, he said, after all Pishi's tastes and opinions are rather different to ours. Still, we were intrigued. There was a good chance she would be unsuitable, but there was no harm checking up. Baba would go to see her.

Choto wasn't his real name. It was his *daaknaam*, his called or home name, the one everyone from his mother to Nawab, the *para mastaan* – the local heavy – called him. His official name, Kartick, had only ever been used by the police, and that mercifully only once, when he had been mistakenly arrested on suspicion of handling stolen goods. True, it wasn't a name he would have chosen for himself had he had the choice, but he hadn't so he was Choto, 'Small', at home and on the streets of the *para*. Actually, even though he didn't like it, it wasn't completely inappropriate. The young man sitting in the shade of an old knotty tree wasn't particularly big, he was rather small.

Choto was, in his own words, 'busy'. He was watching the world go by, critically examining passers-by as they paraded before him. Women hurrying to work in the markets and in the houses of the middle classes (reminding him of his mother, Durga), children on their way to school or to work in the tea-shops and garages as cheap labour, beasts of burden, men hurrying to and fro from shifts at workshops and factories. Choto's was a jaundiced vision. He was certain he was superior to the mass, that he was a young man of beauty and grand future, biding his time, waiting for the opportunity to prove himself. Reality, of course, was somewhat different. He was *bekaar*, unemployed, since he had dropped out of school several years earlier. His primary occupation, if one can call it that, was waiting for his friends Aziz and Chandu. And that was what he was doing right then. But they were still abed, sleeping late after the previous night's drinking. He had dropped out, claiming that he preferred the smoother trip of *ganja*. But the truth was he avoided alcohol because he found it difficult to sneak into the shack he shared with his mother without her smelling it on his breath.

The *bidi* spluttered. He stuck it back between his lips and dragged furiously. It was well and truly dead. He tried to relight it with a box of matches from his shiny-worn trousers, succeeding only after singeing his downy moustache. The hot smoke from the meagre centimetre left burned his throat. He coughed harshly and tried again. But it was no use. It was well and truly dead. He tossed the recalcitrant remains into the gutter where it fizzled briefly. Spitting tobacco-stained saliva, Choto cursed his two friends darkly and called to the tea stall for a cup. It was brought over almost immediately, steaming in its chipped glass. On principle, he clipped his supplier, a boy of eight, on the back of the head. Not too hard, just enough to remind him of his inferior status. The target ducked, dodged the blow. Choto did not try again, he was satisfied that he had made his point. He pulled his legs up under him and sipped.

The morning wore on, and the servant-women began returning from their morning shifts. There was still no sign of Chandu and Aziz. Choto wondered whether they had found somewhere else to go, something else to do . . . *Baanchhods*! They could have warned him! What a waste of time, sitting alone under a tree. He asked a passer-by the time. Nearly one o'clock. No wonder he was feeling hungry. He tapped another *bidi* from the packet, lit it and rose to leave.

'Ai, ChotoDa!' The voice wasn't Chandu's. Nor Aziz's. Too young, it must be . . . 'ChotoDa! Stop! Where are you going?' A small boy caught up. Kanchan, the factory *durwan's* son. Ten years old and already hanging around his elders, thought Choto disgustedly. He himself didn't care for the youngster but the idea of a mascot appealed to his two friends and the boy got to hang around. But Choto felt no need to humour the child. He turned away.

'ChotoDa! Didn't you hear me?' Kanchan was not so easily dissuaded. He caught up again and tugged Choto's sleeve, 'I shouted and I shouted,' he panted.

31

'What if I did? OK, I heard – now go away!' Choto snapped. Kanchan trailed behind. Like a stupid dog, Choto thought.

'Ai, ai! I thought you'd be glad to see me, ChotoDa!' he pleaded.

'Why should I be?' Without breaking his stride. 'Think I have nothing better to do than talk to *bachchas* like you?'

'Who's a *bachcha*? I'm not a child! ChotoDa, you can't call me that . . .'

The older youth spun round, fully intending to drive his tormentor away but relented when he saw the earnest, tearful glint in the boy's eyes. He cursed under his breath.

'All right, all right, you're not a *bachcha*. You're a big boy. Happy? Now go away – I've important things to do.'

'Can't I come? I'll help . . .' Eagerly.

'No you can't. It's men's . . . personal stuff.'

Kanchan's face fell briefly but then lit up again. 'Oooh, I nearly forgot – that's why I came to look for you, *personal* stuff!' He screwed his features into his version of a complicitious look.

'What do you mean "*personal stuff*"?' Choto demanded angrily. 'What do you know about "*personal stuff*"?'

'You know,' the boy produced a large wink that only annoyed the other further.

'No, you fool, I don't! Tell me or I'll . . . I'll hit you!' His brief patience exhausted, Choto snatched Kanchan's arm and raised his hand to strike.

'I'm going to tell you, I'm telling you!' Kanchan shrieked, wriggling violently. 'Ai, you're hurting me!' Tears welled.

'Tell me and I'll let you go. Not until then . . .' In spite of his words, Choto relaxed his grip. Too obviously. Sensing the change, the boy pulled free.

'Why do you want to hit me? I'm telling you, aren't I?'

32

Sniffing, he rubbed his hand vigorously across his nose, holding back the tears.

'You tell me or I'll really hit you this time . . .' Choto simulated a lunge. The boy jumped back, narrowly missing a lamp-post.

'Aiii! That hurt!' Choto made as if to lunge again. 'Wait, I'll tell you, ChotoDa. Wait!'

'Tell me quick – I told you I'm busy!'

'I was coming to tell you that . . . that *you-know-who* is back.' If Kanchan expected instant comprehension he was disappointed. Choto looked at him with a mixture of blankness and anger.

'Who is "*you-know-who*"?' Choto mimicked the boy's voice cruelly.

'You *know*!'

'No, I don't, you stupid little *bachcha*! Who?'

'Your girl . . .'

'*My* girl . . .?' Choto's voice trailed off. He realised which girl. Curse the child.

'*Your* girl, Gowri . . .'

Choto cut him short. 'Yes, yes, I know who you mean. Now you've told me, go away. Leave me alone. Here,' he tossed a *bidi* in the boy's direction, 'now disappear!' Kanchan retrieved his prize from the pavement, dusted it and stuck it in his pocket as Choto stalked off. Making no attempt to follow, the boy headed for the old tree to occupy the seat so recently vacated.

After a little thought, Choto decided not to go directly to see Gowri. He needed something in his belly first, he told himself, as he walked down the narrow alleys to the shack he and his mother called home. She was quite proud of it

33

because even though it leaked in the monsoon, it was a little more permanent than their neighbours', with brick walls and a corrugated tin roof. She had invested in it and kept it securely locked. At the door, Choto kicked off his *chappals*, unlocked the Godrej padlock and went in. Beside a small kerosene stove in the corner of the single room that served as their living space, was his midday meal. *Rutis* and *sabji*, unleavened bread and vegetables. He had expected no more, they could afford nothing else. He struck a match from the dwindling box on the shelf above and dropped it on the ring of wicks. One caught and spluttered, igniting its neighbour. He leaned over and blew gently, spreading the flames until all were alight, then put the blackened *sabji* pot on. While it warmed he rinsed out his battered *thala* and a stainless steel tumbler, filling the latter with water from the earthen *kolshi* in the corner.

A few minutes later, he ladled out the half-heated vegetables and, helping himself to a few *rutis*, sat on the low kitchen stool to eat. With his right hand he tore off small pieces of *ruti*, wrapped it round some of the *sabji* and stuffed it in his mouth, wolfing it down, unconscious, unappreciative of either taste or texture. He had eaten nothing since the night before and was hungry. If only he'd had the money to eat something earlier . . . but what was the point of wishing? He had no job, no money of his own. His mother did her best and made sure they never went without food, no matter how short she was of money, but there never was anything left over for him. That was just the way things were.

His hunger sated, Choto took a long draught of water. Stepping outside, he poured the remainder over the *thala*, sketchily cleaning it and the tumbler before stacking them in a corner, angled against a wall to drain. Having dried his hands on his shirt and smoothed down his hair, he was ready to go in search of his girl, his Gowri.

CHAPTER THREE

Gowri, though Kanchan thought of her as Choto's girl, wasn't really his girl. Not properly, at least. She was still young and even though she worked as a trainee blouse-maker, she went to night school in the *basti*. Choto had seen her almost every day of her fourteen years but when she was a child he had paid her no attention – then she was just another of the little girls who shrieked and giggled when they passed him and the other older boys. Then one day, without warning, things had changed. Last Puja, the day before it all ended, he had been standing on a corner with Chandu and Aziz. Nawab stopped by to talk and then she appeared. Dressed in festive finery, a purple *salwar kameez* with shimmering sequins, holding her father's hand. It was then that Choto noticed she had grown, blossomed. His eyes had followed her down the street and she had coloured in embarrassment. Fortunately her father saw neither his look nor her response. Fortunately. Otherwise there would have been trouble. A scene which her father would have got the worst of – Aziz and Chandu would not have been a problem, not really, they would have done no more than taunt the older man but Nawab was different. He might well have pushed him around a bit. Or touched the girl. Just for fun. Which would have ended Choto's chances even before they had begun – Gowri wasn't the sort of girl to be impressed by physical contact or attacks on her sole surviving parent. She was fond of her father and he doted on her, his beloved child. She was the apple of his eye and happy to be nothing but that until Choto had entered her life. Then, for the first time perhaps, she acted in her own interests, meeting the young man while knowing her father would not approve. Choto did not know how much it troubled her. He would never know.

En route to her house, Choto lit another *bidi* and stopped by the old tree to see if his friends had surfaced. But there was still no sign of them. Instead Kanchan was waiting for him, with another message. Nawab wanted to see him. Not immediately but soon, very soon. Why? The boy couldn't or wouldn't tell. Choto tried some persuasion. First a threat, promising to break Kanchan's arm. Kanchan informed Choto that he would have to catch him first. A couple of steps into the chase, Choto gave up. It was obvious that the younger, fitter Kanchan could easily outrun him. He tried another tack, bribery, offering *bidis* as payment. Still Kanchan refused to tell. Desperate, Choto resorted to pleading, reminding him of how he had always been a big brother to him, and how he would continue to protect him. Kanchan was doubtful. He could not recall Choto ever protecting him in any way, but Choto insisted. In the end, Kanchan gave in. The price was retraction of the threat to break his arm, two *bidis* and continued protection should it be needed. Choto insisted on throwing in the last. Kanchan accepted the bonus with a dismissive shrug.

'It's something to do with a car.' The young messenger offered mysteriously.

'A car? A *car*?' Choto was puzzled. It made no sense, 'But NawabDa doesn't have a car.'

'Maybe he does, maybe he doesn't,' Kanchan replied smugly, 'who knows? NawabDa has lots of things you don't know about.'

That was true. Choto sometimes worried about the Nawab's secrets. They made him uneasy – he felt that some knowledge of them would be useful, but wasn't too sure that he really wanted to know. He liked to be associated with the big man of the *para* but his own essentially honest, or was it cowardly, character balked at the side of him that was the talk of the streets and the basis of his status in the *basti* – his underworld contact and deals.

'Fine. So maybe he has a car, and maybe he doesn't. So why does he want to see me about something that he may or may not have?' No sooner were the words out of his mouth than Choto regretted them.

'Aha! So you don't know? Of course – who'd tell *you*?' Kanchan fled, clutching his payment. Choto cursed under his breath. He wasn't really any the wiser and he stood no chance of getting anything more out of the disappearing boy, curse him. He remembered he had been on his way to Gowri's.

He turned down an alley, stepping carefully over and around potholes and refuse. A half-grown cow blocked his path. He struck its side and it almost tripped over its own feet, flicking a soiled tail in his face. He dodged, barely managing to avoid being coated, and hit the beast again. This time it stumbled clumsily out of his way, allowing him to carry on past the closed *paan*-shops and shuttered windows. He crossed the deserted patch of bare land that served as football and cricket pitch for the local boys and, on the far side, he entered another narrow alley which led to a small temple. Directly opposite was Gowri's house, the door and window shuttered and sealed. But the absence of a padlock told him the occupants were home. What could he do now? A small girl stuck her head out from behind the shrine.

'Aii, ChotoDa!' A stage whisper, 'What took you so long?' She wore a passable imitation of an adult look of annoyance.

'None of your business!' he said crossly. 'Go tell Gowri to meet me behind the club-house.'

'But that's miles away . . .' she scowled.

'Just tell her! I didn't ask for your opinion!' The girl shook her head sullenly. Choto softened, realising he might need her services again some day. 'I'll bring you something next time, lozenges, a bangle . . .'

The small face brightened and she scuttled off around the back of the shacks. Choto sighed and turned away. He went back across the field, squeezing between two tin sheds to the crumbling *pukka* structure they called the club-house. Once there he heaved a sigh of relief to see the lock on the door. The last thing he wanted was for his friends to see him with Gowri. They would never let him hear the last of it.

He smoked to pass the time and was already half-way through his second *bidi* when Gowri appeared, slightly dishevelled from her afternoon nap.

'Choto!'

39

'Gowri!' He had an uncomfortable feeling that anyone watching would see parallels between their greeting and those in films. But there was no one. Besides, any resemblance their encounter had to screen romance ended with the repetition of each other's names – Gowri was too level-headed and demure to be a celluloid heroine, she allowed him no liberties like public embraces. Besides, she wasn't really quite as pretty. He banished the thought quickly.

'Choto, I'm so happy to see you! What took you so long? I told that boy, what's his name, Kanchan, to tell you . . . when, I can't remember. Hours ago, I'm sure.'

'You *told* him to tell me?! The little . . .' Choto bit his tongue in time. Gowri frowned. She didn't like him swearing, particularly in her presence. She was so, so *different* from the other girls in the *para*. A trait that both attracted him and also made it difficult to . . . he blushed.

'It doesn't matter,' she reassured him, mistaking his consternation for apology. 'You're here now. Any news?'

Choto winced. This he would have liked to avoid. He pulled hard on his *bidi* before replying. 'Well, you know what it is like, Gowri – a man tries . . .'

She shook her head fiercely. 'No, I don't. Choto, you have to do something about getting a job! How can we . . .' She broke off, her disappointment clear. Choto took a deep breath. It was not his day.

'Oh, Gowri, it's not that bad,' he began, 'I'll get work soon.' He remembered Kanchan's message. 'Actually, there's a chance of something coming up soon, very soon.'

'What?' she looked suspiciously at him. Might as well build it up, at least a little bit, he told himself. After all, it was what she wanted, it would impress her.

'Oh a job,' he said airily, 'a good job. With cars.'

'Cars? But what do you know about cars?'

Choto was hurt. 'I can drive, you know! Not like some of the fellows around here.'

'So it's a driving job?' She digested this. 'Where? When? With whom?'

'So many questions! Nothing's definite yet. I've got to see . . .' he stopped, '. . . someone about it tomorrow.'

'Someone? Who is *someone*?' She had seen the caution in his face before he averted it. 'Who is it?'

'Oh just someone I know,' he said, avoiding her questioning gaze.

'Do I know this *someone*? Choto, tell me!' She shook him.

'Not really.' He tried desperately to think of a way out.

'It's not . . .' She paused, and it dawned on her. 'It's not *Nawab*, is it? It is?' Choto's face confirmed her worst suspicions. 'Choto, how can you? Is it safe?'

'I don't know yet. Yes, it is! Of course it is! Would I be involved otherwise?! I'll tell you all about it when I find out tomorrow . . .'

'But *Nawab*! Choto, you know he's – not safe!' she repeated. 'Does your mother know?'

'No, she doesn't – you're the first person I've told!' He was irritated. Why couldn't she let him look after his own life?

'I don't believe you can be so stupid! To trust that Nawab!' She fled before he could defend himself.

After Gowri left, Choto lit another *bidi* to settle his nerves before going round to the front of the clubhouse. He unlocked the door with the second key on his neck-string and went in, tripping over a carom board someone had left in the darkened doorway. Kicking it out of the way, he opened the window. Light flooded into the dusty room. The furnishings were basic, a frame for the carom board, four collapsible wood-and-hardboard chairs (one very rickety, the others less so), an old table, and a steel almirah with a dented door. Inside this last, Choto knew, were a kerosene stove, a beer bottle (its neck stuffed with a rag) half-full of kerosene, a battered saucepan (for tea), a collection of grimy, chipped tumblers (which served for whatever beverage was on offer), and a pile of old magazines, mainly 'filmi' ones. He selected one of the last, unfolded a chair and sat by the window to 'read' (his word for leafing through the pages and looking at pictures and their captions).

He had been thus occupied for nearly an hour when Aziz appeared.

'Ai, Choto! Here you are! Where have you been all day, *bokachoda*?'

'Stupid fucker yourself!' Choto spat back. 'Where have *you* been? I waited for you two for hours – all morning, while I could have been doing other things!'

'Other things?' Aziz was unfazed. 'Like what? A *bekaar* like you has other things to do? With whom?' Aziz winked suggestively.

Annoyed, Choto returned to flicking through the pages of the magazine, ostentatiously studying the photographs of his favourite Marathi actress.

'Hey, idiot, what do you have to do?' Aziz snorted. 'And don't pretend to read, I know you're too stupid for that!' Choto lowered the magazine deliberately.

'Aziz, why didn't you show up this morning?' he demanded. 'You knew I was waiting for you.'

'Listen, fellow – we had a good time last night.' Aziz was enthusiastic. 'That booze, wow! It was great stuff, you should have seen Chandu fall over – that *mathal* couldn't stand, I'm telling you! Every time he tried to get out of his chair, he just fell back again. He wanted to go and get some girls – in his state, can you imagine? No danger he'd have been to them, I can tell you!' He chortled at the memory.

'And what about you? I suppose you were sober?'

'Me? I know how to hold my alcohol,' Choto's sarcasm was lost on Aziz. He pulled up a chair, 'I'm not an amateur like Chandu. What would you know, anyway, *smoker*?' He pushed his face into his friend's. Choto drew back.

'Nothing, I suppose. I *smoke* because I'm too smart to let booze ruin my constitution.' He stopped. '*Arré*, Aziz, something else – have you seen NawabDa today?'

'NawabDa?' Aziz frowned. 'No, why?'

'Nothing, just asking.'

'Just asking?' Aziz was suspicious. 'You'd better not let him hear you were "just asking". He doesn't like people who "just ask".' He mimicked Choto. 'No, I haven't seen him –what do you want with him?'

'Nothing,' Choto said.

'Nothing, nothing.' Aziz twisted Choto's arm playfully. 'Are you going to tell your AzizDa or am I going to have to get it out of you?'

'Hey, let go, Aziz!' Choto nursed an imaginary bruise. 'I just heard there was something he wanted to see me about, something about a car.'

'A car? No, I haven't heard anything.' Aziz lost interest in the interrogation. 'How about a game of cards? I've got my pack here.' He produced a well-worn deck.

'No. I want to read,' Choto put up his magazine. Aziz stopped collecting the *bidis* that had spilled out with the cards and snatched it away.

'Read? You? You just want to look at the pictures of the

43

women, no? Come on, let's have a game. For cash – look I've got some!' He shoved a wad of notes under Choto's nose.

'Where did you get that?' It looked like a lot.

'None of your business!' Aziz replied. 'Come on, let's play!'

The game began. Choto played as well as he could but was no match for the practised Aziz and, before long, found he owed fifty rupees, more money than he had seen in a long, long while. Aziz showed no signs of losing. Worried, Choto tried to end the contest.

'How about some tea?'

'Tea?' Aziz saw through the ruse immediately. 'Why? Because you're losing? That's it, isn't it? Afraid you'll lose your clothes, Draupadi?'

'No, it's just that I'm thirsty,' Choto lied, 'I need a drink.'

'If you need a drink, why don't you say so?' Aziz rose. 'There's a bottle behind the carom board. Here, I'll get the glasses.' He crossed to the almirah. Choto considered his options. He could fall back on his *ganja* excuse, but no, he couldn't be bothered. One drink wouldn't do him any harm, he'd have plenty of time to wash his mouth out before going home. He accepted the rather large measure Aziz poured. The first sip burned his throat. He choked and spluttered. Aziz, who had been watching with interest, grinned broadly, even though his own eyes looked suspiciously watery. The second sip seared its way down Choto's throat and slopped uneasily around in his stomach. He took another. By the fourth draught he felt pain no longer. The alcohol now slid down with no appreciable effect, except for the tears that stayed, permanently sprung, in his eyes. An hour – or was it two – passed? Choto's losses mounted, seventy-five rupees, one hundred, one hundred and fifty, two hundred . . . he lost count. So apparently did Aziz. He quoted figures at random, slammed his cards down. Choto lost all sense of proportion and began to wager sums he had never dreamed of. Five hundred rupees. He lost. He was a thousand in debt if Aziz was right. What of it? He would win it back. Another thousand. Another loss. Aziz claimed two thousand rupees. Choto swore and wagered his losings. Aziz, no soberer than his companion, accepted this unusual bet. Choto lost again. Aziz claimed three thousand. The sums did not seem right to Choto but he was in no state to complain. He wagered his losings again, throwing in another two thousand for good measure . . .

Darkness fell and Aziz stumbled over to light the hurricane lamp. As he struck the match the third member of their little group walked in. Chandu, apparently sober. He swore greeting at his friends, then swore at them again for finishing the bottle. They blustered excuses, he waved them away and, beaming broadly, produced a replacement from a bag. He had not been alcohol-free himself that evening! No, he explained, Nawab had been in a good mood and had supplied his *chelas* with alcohol. And he, Chandu, always one of the circle (or so he claimed), had been there. Being a generous soul himself, he had decided to share his windfall with his less-fortunate friends so he had – with Nawab's permission – brought them some. 'NawabDa said I could take it,' he told his friends. Both Choto and Aziz were too drunk to worry about the unlikelihood of Nawab *sending* them alcohol. Chandu found a glass in the almirah and the threesome settled down to another game.

It was half an hour before it dawned on the befuddled Choto what Chandu had said about Nawab. He tried to marshal his thoughts.

'Chandu, you were with NawabDa?'

'That's what I said, sisterfucker!' Chandu played the five of clubs. 'You deaf? Where do you think this bottle came from? Your father?'

'I'm not deaf, pig! I heard you.' Choto peered at his hand, unsure what to play next. 'You said you were with NawabDa . . .'

'What if I did, sisterfucker? What's it to you?' Chandu leaned towards him.

'Shut up, *shala*! I'm talking!' Choto pulled back and played the two of clubs. Aziz sniggered.

'Yeah?' Chandu growled. 'So what have you got to say, sisterfucker?'

'You were with NawabDa?' Choto was having a hard time remembering.

'How many times have I got to tell you that, sisterfucker?' Chandu snorted. 'I told you when I came in and have repeated it a thousand times since . . .'

'*Arré*, give me a chance, Chandu,' Choto said placatingly. 'Did NawabDa mention me?'

'You? You? Come on, sisterfucker, why should he talk about you?' Chandu nearly toppled off his chair in disbelief.

'No reason. I just wondered . . .' Choto grinned foolishly.

'He "just wondered"!' Aziz broke in. 'That sisterfucker hasn't been doing anything else all evening! I think he fancies NawabDa – do you think NawabDa fancies him?' His laughter stopped abruptly when he saw the gleam in Chandu's eye. It didn't pay to take Nawab's name in vain, it said. Chandu swallowed nervously and turned back to Choto.

'So why do you think NawabDa might be talking about you?' he demanded.

'I just heard . . .' Choto blustered.

'Heard what?' Fear that something was wrong sobered Chandu.

'That he wanted to see me.'

'You?' Chandu was relieved. 'Why?'

'Something about a car.' The alcohol had loosed Choto's tongue and the words slipped out unbidden for the second time.

'A car?' Chandu scowled, puzzled. 'What about a car?'

'Nothing, nothing,' Choto mumbled. 'Someone told me NawabDa wanted to see me about a car, that's all . . .'

'Someone? Like who? Gora?' Nawab's right hand, his second in command, a man of evil coutenance and viler temper. Long whispered to be Nawab's successor, if not his usurper. One false step on Nawab's part and the territory would be Gora's.

'No, no! Not Gora – Kanchan . . .' He bit his tongue in shame. It was too late, the truth was out. His companions slapped their thighs and guffawed noisily.

'So you rely on children for your information?' Chandu gasped, tears streaming from his eyes. 'Sisterfucker, you are pathetic! Pathetic!' He fell off his chair. Aziz tried to help him up but failed, succeeding only in joining him on the floor. The two rolled around, laughing and choking. Choto sat above them, swaying, trying to maintain a semblance of dignity. After a while, Aziz recovered enough to ask the question that brought the conversation to an end:

'So you are *playing with* children now?' The innuendo was too much for Choto. He glared unfocusedly at his – erstwhile, he told himself – friends and rose, his dignity and self-esteem in tatters. In the doorway, instead of a word of farewell, he swayed and belched, tasting alcohol in his mouth. They deserved no more, he said to himself.

Outside the air was warm and humid. He fumbled in his pocket for his *bidis* and, with great difficulty, lit one, dropping both the box of matches and the half empty packet as he did so. He had to sober up. Otherwise he would wake his mother, and she would know that he had been drinking. The last time she had thrown him out of the shack. He cursed himself for not having had the sense to refuse. Something else came back to him. How much had he lost? The figure was astronomical. Perhaps he had not lost at all, he consoled himself weakly, perhaps he had just assumed he was losing after the first few games. But surely he would have been able to tell if he was winning. No, Aziz's confidence had been overpowering, his own underwhelming. He stopped – wasn't that his own doorstep? He stumbled and fell. There wasn't any point going inside, his mother would throw him out again, so he might as well . . . he passed out under the stars.

CHAPTER FOUR

❖ ❖ ❖ ❖

D hiren Ghosh, senior police officer of Sonapukur Thana was at home. In Calcutta, of course. He spent as much time as he could in the city – it was more interesting and allowed him to meet his friends. Tonight his guest was his old school friend, Putul. They were drinking whisky.

Dhiren stretched out on the divan and sipped his drink.

'Putul my boy, you realise that we mean nothing?'

'We? Who is we?' Putul rattled the ice in his drink. He had already forgotten his hangover.

'We?!' Dhiren raised his eyes heavenward. 'The missionary school-educated sons of the middle classes, who else? The Bhutanese royal family? Don't be dense!'

'Oh, *that* we,' Putul shrugged.

'Yes, that *we*. We add up to a big fat zero, you understand?' His friend glared at him. 'No, you probably don't!'

'I guess you're right.'

Dhiren revived at Putul's response. 'Let me put it this way: we, as a class, own the means of production, right?'

Putul nodded. He still wasn't really interested. A couple of drinks, that was all Dhiren needed to get him started.

'And we make the most of every opportunity that comes our way, right?' Undaunted, his host continued.

'Uhuh . . .' Putul's tone was noncommittal.

'Wrong! We merely fit in, adapt to the rules of the society we live in, the economy that governs our lives. Do we make the rules?'

'I don't know. Don't we?' Putul frowned at his reflection in his glass.

'No, we don't, you fool,' Dhiren retorted. 'Never have. The rules are made by someone else. And do you know who that is, pray?'

'No, I don't . . .' If he was initially uninterested, he was positively bored now.

'You do but you don't want to! That's precisely the problem, none of us does. There they are, telling us how to run our lives and we don't want to know!' Dhiren leaned conspiratorially towards his friend. 'I'll tell you who they are – they're the people who bear a superficial resemblance to ourselves, being sometimes similarly educated, but are not us. Not by a long chalk. But who are they?'

'You tell me.' Putul yawned.

'I am going to. They are our rulers, our democratically elected representatives, the politicians. The people that I, an official of the government, a servant of the nation, deal with every day of my life.'

'Every day?' Putul absently spilled some whisky on his trousers. 'Damn.' Apropos of the whisky. Dhiren, however, took it for a contribution.

'Damn them if you will! Yes, every day, I deal with them every day! Who else do you think a police official deals with, day in, day out? Criminals? Not a chance. It's politicians, politicians, politicians. Big, small, ugly. Everything I do is ordered by, scrutinised by, and reversible by, politicians – men who have no allegiance to anything but themselves.'

'So?' What Putul wanted was the bottle.

'So, we live an illusion. Every single one of us, victims of the drug of self-delusion. Every one a pawn in the hands of the politicos who manipulate the system to their own ends . . .'

'And you know this and do nothing?' Putul asked the question he knew his friend wanted of him with little enthusiasm. *He* was more interested in figuring out how long it would take him to complete the rounds of the family house. If only there was some way of getting out of it.

'Yes, I do nothing.' Blind to Putul's indifference, Dhiren was getting into his stride. 'Nothing at all. What do you expect me to do? I am merely a functionary – one with a form of a brain but still no more than a functionary. I am, like every one around me, looking after my own interests, nothing more. Are you asking for more? Is *anyone* asking for more? No. Why not? It surprises, nay, *shocks*, me that so few of us demand change! Why do we prefer to accept the illusion that things are getting better when they aren't? It's incredible, isn't it?'

There was no response from Putul who was fending off a mosquito that had somehow slipped through the wire mesh on the window.

51

'Has this always been the case, I ask myself?' Dhiren rattled on. 'Am I indulging in nostalgia for an era that never was? But then I think again and know that I am not. Remember "*Garibi hatao*"? Of course you do. Not that we understood a word of it. Not really, that is. We just took the word of all those around us. "Banish poverty". But what did we do? We got rid of the poor by clearing the slums. Then, two years later we rejoiced when the Emergency ended, again behaving as we were told by the leaders of the time. "What sheep could have followed so blindly?" we demanded of those leaders, joining them in calling for change. But they were tricking us again. *We* were the sheep, the ones that followed blindly. And, as soon as someone told us to, we wrote off the whole period as an aberration, and followed the new leaders as blindly as we had the ones before!' He smiled triumphantly. Putul nodded vaguely and raised his empty glass.

'Get your own – I can't move. You know where it is.' Dhiren had abandoned his role as host. Putul hauled himself out of his seat and made his way unsteadily to the cabinet from which he gingerly extracted another bottle of Director's.

'That's right, help yourself. Just like old times!' Dhiren gestured expansively before returning to his theme. 'When I was in police school we sometimes discussed politics. And, you know, it was simply amazing how many of my fellows – and these, mind you, are the cream of the cream, police officers in training – were willing to accept that those in power now are better than those we had during the Emergency! As if they were. The fools couldn't see that it was the same lot, new name. Politicos absolved of the sins the *ancien régime* committed because they marched under a new flag, asking voters to stamp on another symbol.'

'Uhuh.' Politics. Putul slumped lower. His companion took no notice.

'Of course, we all want to believe that our votes do something, that we change things in our own country but the reality is nothing could be further from the truth. We are just easily hoodwinked, there's no two ways about that! We have neither the intelligence nor the wherewithal to choose our own rulers. Believe me, I deal with those elected representatives on a daily basis so I know. Let me tell you, it is easy to tell what they want. It is crystal clear and there is no telling them apart, Communists, socialists, Gandhian socialists, Nehru socialists, poof! Every single one of them wants the same thing when they see me. We, the civil servants, are their women: we know what they want, we play hard to get, then we deliver. Every time. Why do we bother to play at all, huh?' He glared belligerently at Putul. Putul ignored him.

'We play because we are stupid! Because we lack the intelligence to do otherwise! We forget that *they* are the whores of our society, not us! They get paid for telling the electorate that they love it, that they will be faithful to it and, when the voters have paid for their beautiful words, they know they can turn their backs and line their pockets. And, guess what? Every single one of them does. That's why nothing in this country works.'

'That's a bit sweeping.' Putul felt obliged to provide at least token argument.

'Sweeping? Not in the least!' Dhiren brushed him aside. 'What works, huh? You tell me. The streets have more holes than tar, the telephones don't work, the water is undrinkable, the electricity comes and goes at will . . .' As he said this, the lights flickered and went out. Dhiren waited till the generator roared into life and the power came back on before resuming his tirade.

'OK, you tell me – what can we expect in a state, in a country where even the electricity company – owned and operated by the state in the name of the consumers, the people – cannot provide those same owner-consumers with a regular supply of power? It is not as if the plants are over-stretched, no. They have the capacity but have never functioned at more than one-third of it! Why? Because they lack coal? We have coal aplenty. Great bloody seams of it. So it can't be that. So, do we lack skilled operators?' Dhiren paused rhetorically, a habit from college debating days.

'Of course not!' he answered himself. 'We have all the operators we could want. In fact, we have, we are told, the second largest skilled work force in the world. So if it is neither the resources, nor the skills that we lack, what is the problem? Let me tell you – politicians! The politicians who control the unions are the stumbling block in the path of the people's own company, the electricity generators! During the Emergency we had none of this nonsense. It was, literally, for once, for the only time, a case of power to the people! And why? Because our politicians, and their front organisations, the unions, were held in check, for the greater good of the nation. But we turned our backs on that, yapping on instead about how effective we are as a democracy, denying every single achievement of the Emergency. What use is this democracy? None, let me tell you, none! We are now at the mercy of a bunch of thieves and charlatans!'

Putul was asleep. Dhiren sighed. He was used to his audience dropping off. He poured himself another drink.

I stood by the familiar entrance to the New Empire. Ever since the first time I was allowed to go out on my own, it has been one of the regular meeting points for Ratna and myself. Ratna and I had been to many a film here, more often than not crossing the road before the show for a plate of *bhelpuri*, *chaat* or, if we had the courage, *puchkas*, each light puffed pastry dripping the sauce my mother so vehemently denounced as disease-ridden. Watching a young man eat at the stall I could still almost see the germs swimming in it.

I looked at my watch. Ten minutes past the hour, ten minutes later than we had agreed. Ratna and Rasheed had not yet mastered time, I thought, smiling to myself. And then they were there, half-walking, half-running, the wings of Ratna's *dupatta* billowing out behind her, Rasheed's *chappals* flapping about his feet.

'Oh, Meena, are we late again?' Ratna was breathless when she reached me. Rasheed's face glowed in a smile of welcome and apology.

'I beg your forgiveness!' Rasheed laughed, hands folded in friendly greeting.

'I've been here for hours and hours,' I said and they did not know whether to believe or disbelieve. 'Of course not! I'm just joking! Come on, let's get something to eat.'

'Where?' Rasheed put on his most innocent expression.

'Where? Nizam's, naturally!' Ratna spoke, not I. 'Where else . . . you're pulling our legs!' And of course he was teasing, he knew as well as we did there was nowhere else we would go.

We crossed the road and headed, almost single file, along the street that is impossible to negotiate side-by-side. The crush of people – shoppers, traders, coolies – flowed around us, against us. First one, then the other, pushed ahead or fell behind. But it isn't far and we were at our destination in fifteen minutes. A table was free and Rasheed, moving swiftly, secured it for us. The waiter cleared away the dirty plates and we ordered beef and chicken rolls – spicy meat and onions wrapped in *parathas* – and cooling, yoghurt *lassi*.

I wasted no time. 'So, Rasheed, what are you doing these days?'

He grinned. 'Haven't you heard? I'm no longer *bekaar*. I have a job – you see before you a man with his foot on the first rung of the ladder.' Ratna spluttered, nearly choking on food and laughter.

'A job? Where? Doing what?'

'In an advertising company called Swaraj. What a name! An advertising agency called "self-rule"!'

'That's wonderful! What do *you* do? Make the tea?' I raised a mocking eyebrow.

'Make the tea? No way! I'm part of the creative team, a copywriter, no less. My task is to produce those slogans you see emblazoned on the hoardings all around this great metropolis of ours.'

'Really? You're making slogans? Which ones?'

'Well,' he amended, 'actually, my slogans have yet to be unleashed on the unsuspecting public. However, the extent of my talent, of my way with words, will soon be revealed.'

'And what are you going to be selling?' I interrupted. 'Toothpaste?'

'Toothpaste? What do you take me for? A hack? No, I'm in technology. We have a big contract in hand,' he smiled proudly.

'A big contract? Any chance of free samples?'

'Don't get your hopes up, Meena,' Ratna butted in. 'It's not exactly something you'll be going out to buy every day

– or ever, possibly. I won't, that's for certain!' Her eyes twinkled.

Rasheed pretended offence. 'Daily use, no – but it is of major significance in the march towards modernity, towards self-sufficiency . . .'

'What utter nonsense!' Ratna could not contain herself. 'It's selling car bits, not building satellites!'

'Car *bits*? *You* may call them that, but in the industry we call them "Autospares", or is it "Automotive parts"?' Rasheed scratched his head. 'Doesn't matter. The point is, we have the contract to launch India's latest, most modern autospares – or whatever they are called.'

It reminded me of something. But I wasn't too sure what. 'Who's the contractor?'

'They will hit the streets – not literally, I hope – soon, under the banner of Anglo-India. The irony of it – "Self-rule" advertising British techology,' Rasheed laughed.

'I don't think I have ever heard of them – are they new?'

'Yes, they are. It's a joint-venture enterprise involving a British company and an Indian one. The Indian one is, if I remember correctly, Shiva Enterprises.'

'Shiva Enterprises? Now, that's familiar . . .' I racked my brains.

'It's owned by a namesake of yours, Sailen Sen. Know him?' Rasheed looked at me expectantly.

Of course I did. It all came back to me now. Putul's uncle.

Rasheed was waiting. 'Yes, he's a distant relation,' I said. 'In fact, I met his heir-apparent while I was in Britain. He was doing a doctorate in economics or something in Glasgow. He's back in Calcutta now.'

Rasheed loves that sort of thing and could not let it pass.

He grinned. 'Aha! So your family is now firmly entrenched in the capitalist class . . .'

'Certainly not!' I retorted. 'Anyway, that's hardly fair coming from you.'

'Stop that, you two.' Ratna wasn't interested in playing. 'Rasheed, tell her what this really means. To us, I mean.' Her tone was impatient.

'It means you are now both parasites!' I couldn't resist a final dig. 'OK, what *does* it mean? Besides meaning that Rasheed can afford to pay for the food now . . .'

'No, that I can't,' he replied. 'Haven't been paid yet. Ratna is referring to our long term plans.' I held my breath as he munched his roll.

'Ratna,' he looked at her, '*you* explain.' He could see as well as I that she was bursting to tell.

'Well, it's like this: since Rasheed has a job, he can afford to support a family . . .' she began.

'Only, I don't intend to have any children yet . . .' Rasheed interjected mischievously.

'Shut up, you! He can now present himself as a responsible man.' She gulped some *lassi*. I was fairly sure I knew what she was getting at but wanted to hear it spelled out.

'He can now present himself as a man with an income, thus becoming, shall we say, an eligible bachelor,' Ratna continued.

'Oh, I always considered him very eligible,' I wagged my head at him. He grinned broadly.

'Find yourself another man – he's taken!' Ratna placed a proprietorial hand on his arm. 'I'm sure you know what I mean – we think we may soon be able to tell our families that we want to get married.'

'That is wonderful news! Do you have an idea when?' I was almost beside myself with joy.

'Not immediately, of course. We are going to wait for a bit . . .' I hardly heard her. I had already heard the most important bit, the news I had been hoping to hear.

CHAPTER FIVE

The day after his visit to Dhiren, it was time for Putul's second visit to the family. As Swapna Kakima put it, 'Better get it over with.' For once, Putul agreed with her. She also reminded him, as if he didn't know, that it was best not to leave the visits till too late in the day, because if he did, he'd just have to keep going back. An early start, she told him, would make for fewer trips. Thus it was that once again Putul found himself closing the gate that kept stray animals out, mounting the stairs and ringing the bell. The same pause, the same voice:

'Who is it?' The same question.

'I, Priya Pishi.'

'I who?' But this time she recognised his voice. 'Oh, Putul!' And she was on her way down before he had even begun to answer.

'Aii, Putul! You've finally come to see us?' She ushered him in. 'Why did you rush off like that last time? Come in, come in! This time we are not going to let you leave without having something with us. Raja, RAJA! Come down, Putul's here. So soon, too . . . less than a week since he was here last! And we all thought you'd forgotten all about us once you'd seen the old man. We were saying "at least he came to see his Boro Dadu". He's not well, you know,' she led the way inside, 'so company is good for him, even if he is very forgetful these days. Always forgetting this and that, forgetting who is who, what is what, where is where, when is when. Even his own grandchildren – I mean no offence, you are just a grand*nephew* – but his own grandsons! It's terrible! And he forgets to have his medicines and thinks he has had them and argues about it. I don't know how we manage, but we do, you know. We do, but it is nice to see some of you, the younger generation, coming to see us. But you are not the youngest generation, you know, not anymore. You have nieces and nephews and they are growing up so fast I can barely keep up with them! Soon they'll be getting married too – and you're still single! You should get married soon, you're old enough. And handsome, too – and well-qualified. Don't get big-headed when I tell you but I'm sure there are lots of girls who'd want to marry you. You be careful, though – families these days are quite capable of telling lies just to catch the right groom for their daughters . . . Oh, I'm so glad you didn't come back like some of the others, with a foreign girl! It's difficult, you know, not all of them are like your cousin's wife, Anne. She's very good, always comes to stay with us for a couple of days – though they do stay in a hotel most of the time – and she wears saris and *sindoor* . . .'

They were in Priya Pishi's entertaining room. She

61

smoothed the cover on the huge double bed and motioned Putul to take a seat on it. Two small children, a boy and a girl, peeped round the door.

'There you two are!' she spotted them. 'Come in, come in and say hullo to this Dada . . . no, he is your Kaka, isn't he?' The two allowed themselves to be dragged into the room and stood shyly in the corner, alternately staring at their feet and peeping up at Putul.

'These are your cousin's children. You know them, don't you? Of course you do! You saw them before you left – you were at her birthday party. Her first! Of course she won't remember that but how she's grown, hasn't she? You'd never imagine that she's the little girl in those pictures we have of her first birthday, would you? And her brother, too. He was just three then. How they've grown, how they've grown! Putul, you've grown too. You look like a man now, not the boy who left us. What is it that these travels do to all of you? You go away and then you change – not all for the worse, thank the gods. *You* haven't changed that way – you still remember to visit your Boro Dadu, your Raja Kaku, Priya Pishi, your family. We aren't getting younger, you know. We grow old in this very house while you young people just move out and away. Not you, of course, you weren't born here. Your parents left . . . would you like some tea? And some sweets? Of course you would! As a child, I remember, you always liked sweets. My, my – how you liked sweets! Not as much as those two over there – but you were one for sweets. A family trait – your Thakurda, your paternal grandfather, he had blood-sugar, you know. Died of it. But you wouldn't remember, it's too long ago for you. How young you are and yet you are grown up already! How are we supposed to keep up with you? First we hear you are going to college, next thing we know you've got another

62

degree from abroad and now here you are, qualified and done! You don't visit us enough . . . but at least you *do* come sometimes!'

She bustled around, placing a small carved table beside the bed and, on it, a glass of water, a once-white china plate, now veined with age, full of sweet *sandesh*, and a cup of milky tea. On the edge of the bed, his feet dangling a couple of inches off the floor, Putul sipped gingerly and wondered where to put the cup.

'So what are your plans now, Putul? No doubt your uncle will want you to join him in his business, no? Oh, your Raja Kaku was telling me, your Sailen Kaka is into something new. Not that I understand anything about business. Me, I live my life in the house, let people like your Sailen Kaka worry about running businesses. I have quite enough to do without this sort of thing. Children, that's my life! There are always children around, first I am an aunt, then I'm a grandaunt. What would they do without me?' She laughed. 'And I mustn't forget your Boro Dadu. He gets feebler every day. No longer waits for grandchildren, can't even recognise them any more. And they're all growing up so quickly. You'll be the next one married, you know. It's about time – all this studying is enough now, you need to find yourself a nice girl and settle down. But your uncle is quite right to be careful, people are so dishonest these days, always making out that they – and their daughters, of course – are better than they really are. So that they can get the son-in-law they want, not the one they really deserve . . .'

'Leave the boy alone, woman,' Raja Kaku ambled in, smiling genially. 'How are you, Putul? Found time to visit the rest of us, eh? Good, good. How does it feel to be back home? Are you settling in well?' He asked the questions without expect-

63

ing answers. 'You know, I've been wanting to ask you about some things – you are the educated one, you see. The one who understands the changes being made. Liberalising the economy or whatever they call it. But first, drink your tea. We can talk later.' He sat down in the easy chair opposite and waved Putul to the food. Putul helped himself to a couple of sweets and moved further up the bed. Oh no, it wasn't any more comfortable, his feet were now further from the floor. He should've taken his shoes off, he realised.

Raja Kaku waited for him to settle before continuing. 'Well, Putul, explain to your ageing uncle about how this "liberalisation" or whatever it is the government is doing works. I am a layman, I know nothing about that sort of thing, only that things are changing and I don't understand what's happening or why. You can tell me, no? You're our family economist, after all.'

Putul shifted uneasily on the bed. 'I'm not sure I can. You see it isn't really my field . . .' He shrugged his shoulders helplessly.

'That is the problem, isn't it?' Raja Kaku said wistfully. 'It's not anyone's field, but it happens. How are we to find out whether something is right or wrong? We rely on you, the rising generation, to help us, to lead your ageing relatives to comprehension . . .' he shook his head. 'Never mind, have some more tea and sweets. I must go and see to your Boro Dadu, it's time for his medicine.' Putul was left alone with his tea and the two children in the corner.

I bumped into Rasheed unexpectedly. Most unexpectedly. I was well off my track, walking down Park Street. I'd just been to a shop to see if a book I had ordered had arrived. Of course, they couldn't tell, they didn't think so, but they couldn't be sure one way or the other so could I return in an hour when the person who might know would be back and would be able to check it for me? The choice was between wandering around for an hour and possibly getting the book, or going away in the certainty I would have to come back to Park Street another day. The latter I did not much care for because, even with the convenience of the Metro, I do not like having to travel so far. I said I would come back – it was the easier. And so, there I was, walking down Park Street, wondering what to do with myself when Rasheed called my name.

'Meena! This is a surprise – I didn't expect to see you around here.' He was out of breath. Just like when he was late.

'Nor I you,' I said, equally surprised. 'What are *you* doing here?'

'I asked first,' he laughed. 'OK, OK, I'll answer first. I work round the corner from here and have come out to get some pencils. What's your excuse, what're *you* doing here?'

'I came to get some books from the bookshop over there, but the person I need to see is not around, won't be for an hour, or so they say. Probably two or even three. You know how it is. So I'm taking a walk, killing time.'

'Killing time? What has it done to deserve such a fate? Why not join me for a pot of tea?'

'A *pot* of tea?' You don't often hear anyone say that. 'Surely you mean a cup – or a *bhaar*?'

'No, I mean a pot,' he said firmly. 'At Flury's, just across there. I'll happily treat, if you care for it.'

'I don't know . . .' I dithered. 'Oh, why not! I haven't been in there for ages.'

'Nor I, I hasten to add,' he grinned, 'but their cakes do look tempting . . .'

I shook my head. 'Not for me, I can't stand icing sugar.'

'Who said anything about you?' he retorted. 'I offered to treat you to tea, not cake.' We dodged our way through the traffic into the air-conditioned clamminess of the cake shop. Only two tables were occupied, one by two young Europeans (or Australians? Westerners at any rate) in uniform shorts, faded T-shirts and rucksacks. I wondered what had brought them to Calcutta – *en route* to Nepal or somewhere perhaps, few others come this way. At the other table was an elderly Anglo-Indian couple, a balding man in a suit, and a snowy haired woman, fake pearls and pink lipstick.

Rasheed led the way to a table between two windows. Outside, silent behind the panes of glass, the traffic crawled past. 'Now, do you want a cake?' Rasheed asked. I shook my head. I wasn't hungry.

The tea and Rasheed's cake, fluorescent with icing, arrived. Rasheed ceremoniously filled our cups, putting two teaspoons of sugar in his.

'All right, Rasheed, tell me more about this job of yours.' I didn't want to pry. After all, I told myself, they'll tell me if they want to. Who else could they confide in? But I desperately wanted to ask.

'There's not that much to tell,' Rasheed said, 'I started less than a month ago, hence my continuing state of penury. The salary – which shall remain my secret – is not fantastic but there is the possibility of it increasing as the agency grows. It's all very small still. They needed someone for the Anglo-India contract, and I got the job.'

'So you're employed now,' I faltered. Might as well take the plunge, I decided. 'Ratna and you seem to be counting on this to make things . . . happen . . .' I fumbled for words.

' . . . To make marriage, for example, possible?' He finished my question for me. I blushed.

'Well, the idea is this,' he explained, 'I get settled into the job, get paid – hopefully – and then I look around for somewhere for us to stay.'

'But have you discussed this with... you know, your families?' I had to ask. It couldn't be that easy!

'So Ratna hasn't told you, eh?' I shook my head and he continued, 'Arrangements are well under away. I've met her mother and have mentioned her to my parents. The surprising thing is my father took it easily. He only said an old man – that's himself – can't support another family for the rest of his life. He'd forgotten I had a job already!' He grinned broadly, then saw the clock on the wall and started up.

'Oh dear, I've been away too long! I'd better get back otherwise it'll be no job for me again!' He paid the bill and we left, he for his office, I for the book shop. I wasn't surprised to find that I'd have to return, the book hadn't arrived.

The family was on the verandah again, chatting about the day that had passed. Durga appeared, a shadow in a doorway.

'Durga?' Ma noticed her first. 'You still here?'

'Yes, Mashima. I've finished.'

'So, are you leaving now?'

'Yes, Mashima,' but she made no move to go.

'What is it, Durga?' Sensing her unease, Baba spoke gently.

'I have a request, Babu . . .'

'Of course . . .' We waited. In all the time I have known her she has asked for very little for herself. A small advance on her salary for a journey or her son's expenses (we have always tried to get her to consider them an extra payment but she has always repaid), a couple of days off now and then, no more. We wondered what it was this time.

Durga shrank, her already slight frame slimming into near-nothingness. 'It's not for myself, Babu . . .'

'Of course, Durga. But even if it were, we would not mind,' my father smiled reassuringly.

'It is for my son,' she blurted out.

'What is it Durga?' Baba sounded worried. 'What about your son? Is he in trouble?'

'No!' She bristled slightly. 'No, it is nothing like that. It is just . . .' she fumbled for words, 'it is just that he needs to find work . . .'

'To find work? Can we help in any way?' Baba knew what was being asked and was already formulating his response. He wasn't enthusiastic about Durga's son, Choto/Kartick. In his opinion he had grown from a likeable child into a spineless, good-for-nothing, although not really bad, adult.

'If you can, I would be grateful, very grateful. In any way . . .'

'Let me think about it, Durga,' Baba said thoughtfully, 'he is your son, he deserves a chance.'

'For his own sake, not mine,' she said sadly. It was too dark to see her face. The cost to her pride must have been great, greater than anything she had ever tried before.

'I will try, Durga . . . we will try.' He turned to us and, though it was too dark to see, he could feel our embarrassed agreement. Embarrassed for Durga, not for ourselves. Embarrassed that she should have to ask, embarrassed that none of us had considered this before. Why hadn't we?

'Thank you. I will go now.' Before he could protest, she touched my father's feet and was gone. A shade flitting through the room. We heard the door close quietly behind her. And we waited for each other to break the silence. Finally, Baba spoke.

'It's late. Shall we eat?'

68

'Yes.' Ma rose first. As we followed, Baba touched my arm and said, almost in my ear, 'Meena, don't worry, I'll find him something.' Why did he say that to me? I didn't need to ask. He knew that more than anyone else in the family I consider Durga one of us.

Feeling the need to make amends for his drunken stupor, Choto came home earlier than usual. But, as luck would have it, that night his mother was late. So he sat in the dark, alone and unhappy. It had not been a successful day. Nawab had remained elusive and Kanchan had been unable to convince Gowri to meet him. Besides, the boy had relieved him of half his remaining stock of *bidis* in payment. Hungry, he had considered trying to find some snacks to keep him going but knew that, as usual, he had no money. He could have raided his mother's savings which were hidden behind a brick in the wall but he did not dare, not after the night outside. He waited patiently.

When Durga returned she knew immediately, by the open door, that her son was home. The lack of light, past experience told her, was his way of making amends by not 'wasting' precious kerosene. It was his way of apologising. He was not normally so careful. She entered.

'Choto?' she said softly.

'Ma?' he replied humbly.

'You are home. Are you hungry?'

'Yes, Ma.'

'I will make us some food. But it will take a little while. Would you like some *moori* for now?'

'Yes, Ma.' Durga lit the hurricane lamp, flooding the room with flickering yellow light, and measured a bowl of puffed rice from an old Dalda tin. Her son ate silently while she chopped cauliflower leaves. When he had finished she was still preparing so he lit the stove, and waited. The preparations and cooking took a good hour, an hour during which neither spoke to the other. The meal was simple, rice, dal, the leaves and some chillies. Choto washed his hands. His mother served, watching while he ate. When his plate was clean she offered him more but he declined. He did not, however, rise. He had something to say.

'Ma?'

'Yes, my son?'

'Ma, I . . . I am looking for work.' She understood him and, though she had no faith in his enterprise, accepted his words as another form of apology. After all, was he not her son, her reason for being alive?

'That is good, Choto,' she replied, 'very good, and I have asked for you too . . .'

Choto stiffened. 'Asked who, Ma?' He had not expected this.

'People. People I know, people who might help.'

'People? Like who, Ma?' he asked, slowly.

'Like – never mind, Choto,' she sounded tired.

'Ma, it is my life!' His voice rose.

His mother answered without heat, 'My employers, the Sens.'

'The Sens?' Choto was outraged. 'Are you not ashamed to ask for charity?'

'Charity? Charity?' Durga's annoyance deepened. 'And who are you to talk of charity? When have you done anything that brought money to this house?'

'That is not the point, Ma . . .' Choto tried to intervene but his mother was in no mood for discussion.

'That is! That is exactly it!' She was now angry. 'When will you begin to earn your own living?!' As soon as she said it she was sorry. But it was too late, before she could take it back Choto stormed out. She wondered whether to call him back. No, it would be futile. She ate her share of the food, blew out the lamp and lay down.

Choto returned late. His mother heard him come in and lie down on his *charpoy*. She could smell alcohol. Soon he was snoring, louder than usual. The mother turned on her side, silent tears coursing down her cheeks.

CHAPTER SIX

Evening again. A beautiful evening, the heat of the day tempered by a breeze from the not-too-distant Dhakuria Lakes. It was hard to believe that in a few month's time it would be impossible to sit out like this while the sky was still light. But for now it was pleasant, there was even a hint that a *kaal-baisakhi*, a spring thundershower, might spring up. We hoped, knowing it was too early for that blessed relief.

We were all out again, in our cane chairs, the incense and mosquito coil smoke curling around. The conversation rolled round to the topic of several evenings ago: potential brides. Dada fidgeted and tried to look uninterested while Baba, Ma and I discussed, nay debated, the candidates. Baba had been to see his sister, our Pishi. She had welcomed him, almost beside herself with happiness (Dada and I exchanged meaningful glances). Pishi is not one for getting straight to the point, she drops hints, skirts around the subject, circles the topic, eventually getting close enough for the listener to complete the jigsaw – and then she hurries off to get another cup of tea while the victim ponders a response. And that's how it had been when Baba visited. She had asked about me, about my trip. Baba had patiently repeated the news we knew she would demand again when I went to see her. She had expressed her joy, her pride, in my success (at this point in the narrative I tried not to blush, and Dada poked me in the ribs). Then she had wanted to know how it felt to have me home, expressed the opinion that it must be wonderful to have the whole family together again. Baba assured her it was and she sighed and said how nice it would be to have her whole family together. Baba took his cue and asked after her son who lives in Texas. She had new photographs of him, and of her daughter-in-law and the one-year-old grandson. Baba obligingly expressed an interest in seeing them and made appropriate noises of approval on being shown them. Pishi was very fond of her grandson, wished she could see him more often. Hoped he would grow up a proper Indian, not too American. It was a good thing that her son had had an arranged marriage, wasn't it? Such a nice girl too, able to adapt to America but a real Bengali wife still. Pishi's only regret was that they lived so far away. But she was going to visit them soon. Baba paused in his story to allow us to speculate on Pishi in America. The thought amused us in a gentle sort of way, we are very fond of her.

Pishi elaborated on the virtues of her daughter-in-law. She wished such a daughter-in-law for her brother and his wife, our parents. She, Pishi, had had such a hard time finding one.

73

Not that it was entirely her doing (or finding), Baba had played his part too and she was grateful. And had Baba found any suitable girls? Baba coughed and said we were still looking for a bride for Dada. Of course, how could she have forgotten? she exclaimed. She reminded Baba that we should be careful. There were people around who would go to any lengths to get a son-in-law. She knew of some, she said darkly. She did? Oh yes, she assured Baba, lots. The families were not suitable, not one bit! He was her nephew, which meant that she, as much as any mother, wanted only the best for him. Baba, unable to resist it, asked whether she had not chosen the best for her own son? It wasn't like that, she sniffed, it was like having two sons. Baba said he hadn't meant to hurt her feelings. She forgave him, her younger brother, and told him of a family, a Calcutta family, who had a daughter. A very nice girl, well-educated. That sounded like a recommendation. But it wasn't, the girl wasn't ready for marriage, wanted to do higher studies. She was a popular girl and had finished her degree from a reputable college. A college where one of Pishi's husband's cousins taught. A nice man, a very nice man. Good family. She paused. And did he have any children? Two sons, and a daughter. Pleasant girl. Might make someone a good daughter-in-law some day. Some day? No plans for her marriage yet? No, no, not yet! She was still at college. Wouldn't finish for another year. Maybe then. And Pishi went to get another cup of tea. When she returned she suggested the daughter of one of the cousin's colleagues. She brought out a picture of the girl.

Here Baba paused. Ma and I demanded to know more but he had changed his mind. First, he said, we had to ask proper questions. Dada wasn't talking so it was up to the two of us,

74

my mother and myself. Her age? That too would have to wait. We threw our hands up in disgust.

'Come on, Baba, what can we ask?' I demanded.

'I don't know – where she lives, what she studies, something like that!'

'So, where does she live?'

'North Calcutta, Shyambazar.'

'An old family then?'

'They've been there for a few generations,' Baba confirmed.

'Landed family?' I hazarded.

'No, business, I think. Ask me about her, not her family!'

'What's she studying?' Ma joined in.

'History.'

'Degree? Honours?' Myself.

'Yes, Honours.'

'Can she cook?' Ma.

'Cook? How should I know?'

'Show us the picture, then!' I demanded. He shook his head. I tried again. 'Tell us something about her.'

'Well . . .' He scratched his head.

'Show us the picture, Baba,' I took advantage of his hesitation.

'I can't. I don't have it,' he recovered quickly.

'How old is she?' Ma asked.

'Eighteen.'

'Eighteen?' I couldn't believe my ears. Baba chuckled. Dada tried to look inscrutable but his dismay was palpable. Ma shook her head.

'Too young, far too young.'

'Of course. That's why I didn't bring the photo.'

That was that then. We were no further in our search.

*

The next relative on Putul's list was a retired doctor, a cousin of Boro Dadu. Instead of living in the family house, he lived in a newer part of the city, an area that had been wetlands until not so long ago, but then had been reclaimed and sold off as plots of prime, or near prime, real-estate to affluent middle-class folk. On his personal plot the old doctor (this one really practised his profession) had built a strange edifice. Intended to be a dream house, money had limited it and it was but a scaled-down bungalow with some of the trappings of a mansion. Like a mansion with a truncated driveway lined with miniature ferns.

Putul pressed the button by the door. Electric chimes mimicked a grander bell. On the second floor a window flew open and a woman's voice demanded his name and business. Putul stepped back from the porch so he might be seen and called his name. The window slammed shut and, a few minutes later, huge bolts were drawn back and a young woman opened the door. She scowled at him almost angrily and drew her sari over her head before ushering him into the large, cool hallway and directing him to a chair in the sparsely furnished room at the end. He waited, wondering what to expect next. The maid came back. The *daktarbabu*, she informed him distantly, would be with him soon. She stomped out of the room.

Half an hour later his host appeared, looking as if he had just woken up. Putul rose to welcome him but found himself ignored while the old man prowled round the room, opening windows, coughing and clearing his throat noisily. Putul cleared his own throat politely. The doctor fixed a beady eye on him.

'So, Putul, you've made it back in one piece? Good, good! You have been looked after by that girl? Water? You should have some already . . . sweets? Of course, you will have some. Young people like sweets.' He rang a bell and the surly maid appeared and was despatched to buy a mixture of savouries and sweets from a nearby shop. The doctor sat down in a comfortable cane chair.

'How did you like Scotland? Was it as grand as they say?'

Putul blinked. 'I'm not sure what you mean by "grand" but I think it was very nice,' he hazarded.

'Grand? Oh, you know what I mean: it is, I am told and have read, a land of rolling highlands, of mist, shaggy Highland cattle, of lochs,' he pronounced this 'locks', 'glens, romance and castles . . .' He paused expectantly. Putul squirmed uncomfortably in his chair.

'I lived in a city, Glasgow – it was wet,' he offered.

The doctor dismissed the city with a gesture. 'Did you not venture out of the city, into the wilds of Scotland?'

'Well, I did make it to Loch Lomond, the Highlands, that sort of thing,' Putul said.

'And were they not magnificent?' the old man snapped.

'Oh yes, they were!' Putul was taken aback. 'But the rest was pretty normal.'

'Normal? What do you mean by that? Like here?'

'Yes . . . no, not like here,' Putul corrected himself hastily. 'Different but not, not any of those things you seem to be suggesting!'

The old man's eyes flashed. 'And how do you know what I am suggesting, boy? Are you telepathic? Can you see inside my head, trace my thoughts?!'

'No . . .' Putul mumbled.

'Then, if you cannot see my thoughts, how can you know what I am "suggesting"? And what gives you the idea that I "suggest" without knowing? That my impressions of any place, of any space and of the things that occupy and inhabit that space, are purely imaginary?'

'I, I didn't mean that, sir . . .' Putul gabbled helplessly.

' "Suggesting"!' the doctor roared. 'So my impressions of space and time are deemed fantastical? The long hours I have spent reading, learning, improving my mind, widening my horizons are to be dismissed in a single phrase?'

'I . . .' Putul choked.

'I have read Scott, Buchan, even Burns and I know nothing of Scotland! Do you know how much time I have spent studying these? How many years of my life have been spent reading precisely that which you dismiss?'

'No, sir,' Putul said meekly.

'Years! Years and years! More years than you have been in this world! And you, after a span of what is barely days when compared to the time I have spent poring over pages, reject all I have learned? You know how that makes me feel?'

'I don't, sir but I am sorry. I didn't mean to . . .' Putul broke off before the word 'suggest', afraid that its repetition might provoke another outburst.

'Not too good.' The doctor was suddenly calm and friendly. Putul stared at him, stunned. The storm had passed as quickly as it had arisen.

'Ai, we are talking about *you*, not *me*,' his host apologised urbanely. 'Tell me, did you enjoy Scotland?'

'Yes, I did,' said Putul, warily.

'It is, of course, the land that has inspired many great minds, is it not?'

'So I have been told, sir, but I am not a great reader . . .' Putul regretted his words as soon as he said them. But the doctor did not seem to mind.

'Pity, pity. You should read more, Scott, Buchan, Burns,

some of the greatest writers in the English language. What did you see there? Anything that excited you, that brought great revelation?'

'Revelation?' Putul was genuinely puzzled.

The doctor's face took on a look of cunning as he leaned forward. 'Listen!' He cupped his hand to his ear.

Putul was baffled. There was nothing out of the ordinary to hear. Distant cars and buses, the clink and rattle of rickshaws. Crows, the cries of itinerant salesmen, the occasional aircraft. His granduncle sat still, his finger on his lips, gazing into the middle distance, listening attentively. Five minutes passed, Putul waited. The silence was broken by the entrance of the maid.

'Shall I bring tea?'

'What?' The doctor glared at her, 'Yes, yes!' He turned to look at his guest again.

'These interruptions! Disturbances! But, tell me – did you hear them?' His tone was eager.

'I think I did, sir,' said Putul, cautiously.

'It is amazing, isn't it? You must have heard much of them in Scotland too?'

'Yes, sir.'

'Tell me, my boy, were they very different? Did they sound, oh I don't know, Scottish?'

'They did, sir,' Putul, completely out of his depth now, gave the vaguest answer he could think of. It worked.

'Ah, interesting, interesting. And did you see them?'

Putul stared. This was one he could not answer. What if he were asked to describe 'them', whatever they were? Fortunately for him, the doctor had more to say. 'I never saw one until I was forty, you know. You have to concentrate very hard to see them,' he nodded knowingly.

Putul copied the movement slowly, bemused.

'It is nice to know that they are everywhere, isn't it?' The old man stroked is moustache.

'I . . . yes, sir . . .' Putul faltered.

'When you see them, for the first time, or anytime, they are so beautiful! Such light frames, such gossamer wings. No silk is so fine, no mosquito net so delicate. What an honour it is that we are allowed to share this world with them. And what an honour that they should manifest themselves to us.'

Putul decided to risk the old man's wrath. 'Who, sir?'

The doctor drew back and frowned. 'Why, fairies, of course.'

'Fairies?' Putul could not believe his ears. '*Fairies*?'

'Yes, fairies. What did you think I was talking about?'

'Oh, I knew it was fairies, sir . . .' Putul blustered. The tea arrived and an uneasy silence reigned while it was poured. The doctor took one sip from his cup and abruptly stood up and walked out of the room. Without so much as a word or a backward glance. Putul waited for ten minutes, then, when the maid appeared to clear the plates, he asked after his host. She informed him that he had retired, as was his custom, for his mid-day rest. Putul had to let himself out. At least, he reasoned, one more visit was over.

Durga hoped that her son would be home, that he wouldn't be out with his good-for-nothing friends and, for once, he didn't disappoint her. They performed their ritual, she served him a bowl of dry puffed rice, *moori*, lit the lamps, prepared the meal. He ate the *moori*, lit the stove, and ate his meal while his mother waited on him. He did not speak, he had no news – he had met Nawab but the meeting had been inconclusive. Nawab had asked if he could drive and he had said he could but then the *mastaan* had lost interest. A fight had broken out amongst neighbours and he was needed. Choto had been forgotten immediately. He had nothing to report.

His mother, however, had news for him. She waited, as she always did, for him to finish his meal. She would eat later.

'Choto, I have some news for you.'

'Yes, Ma?'

'It is about work for you . . .'

'Yes, Ma?' He had been afraid of this. Why couldn't she wait?

'The Sens have a friend . . .'

'The Sens, Ma?' Choto did not like the sound of it. 'The Sens?'

'Hear me out, Choto, hear me out,' Durga's tone was uncharacteristically sharp.

'All right, Ma, I am listening.'

'A friend of the Sens needs an office assistant and is willing to try you out.'

'An office-boy? A *clerk*!' Choto was horrified. 'Ma, I can't possibly work in an office as an assistant!' An excuse suggested itself, 'I can't read – it gives me a headache!' If he took the job, he would never be able to face his friends – the entire *para* would laugh at him, a *peon*.

'Not a clerk, just a helper. To take messages, fetch parcels, arrange things.'

'How can I, Ma? I know nothing of these things!' he exclaimed.

'You can learn, can't you?' his mother retorted.

'Yes, Ma – but . . .'

'Why but?' she interrupted. 'Why not try it? Have you something better?'

'Not yet, Ma . . .' he pleaded.

'So when? If you have something else, tell me. Otherwise do

81

as I say, or leave my house!' She began serving herself. The discussion was closed. Choto knew this time he could not walk out, he had no choice but to obey.

CHAPTER SEVEN

C hoto's mother had given him the bus fare but Choto decided to walk, saving the money for *bidis* and tea. He trudged the length of the busy Gariahat Road, almost all the way to Park Circus, before he reached the street opposite the Electricity Supply complex. As instructed, he climbed the stairs to the second floor and knocked. The door was opened by a boy not much older than Kanchan, dressed in a similar fashion, ragged *ganji*, grubby shorts and rubber *chappals*. He scanned Choto from head to foot, his lip curling ever so slightly at the corner. He showed no signs of being impressed.

'Yes?' he growled.

Choto drew himself up to his full height. He was not going to be intimidated by one so small. 'The sahib is expecting me,' he declared.

'The sahib is expecting you?' the boy snorted derisively. 'That's what everyone says. Prove it!'

Choto was taken aback. 'What do you mean, "prove it"?' He frowned. 'Get in there and tell him I'm here!'

'Why? Prove that he is expecting you, first.' An idea struck him, 'Tell me, for instance, which sahib?'

'The burra sahib, of course!' Choto blustered in a mixture of confusion and annoyance.

'The burra sahib?' the boy pooh-poohed his answer. 'That's not even a guess. Every office has a "burra sahib". What's his name?'

'What? Get out of my way!' As Choto tried to push past, his interrogator shoved back with surprising strength. Choto staggered, teetering briefly at the top of the stairs. Regaining his balance, he paused but decided against another attempt at physical entry when he saw the gleam in his opponent's eye. All things considered, a brawl was not worth it, he told himself. It would not create a good impression. He therefore stepped back dignifiedly, flicking imaginary dirt off his shirt before answering in an injured tone.

'Tell Biswas Babu Kartick is here.'

'Biswas Babu? That's better. But Kartick who? And on what business?' Was there no end to the boy's insolence? But maybe, just maybe, Biswas Babu had vested some authority in the kid . . . right now Choto needed to get in.

'Just tell him Kartick, sent by Mr Sen . . .'

'Tell him yourself!' The boy laughed as he forced his way past and fled down the stairs, leaving an astonished Choto to watch open-mouthed as he scrambled past a burly guard who was ascending at that very moment. This newcomer sped the boy on his way with a blow and a curse before addressing Choto.

'And who may you be?' The *durwan* asked, twirling his moustache speculatively.

Choto sighed, 'Does everyone here ask the same question?' The *durwan*'s face darkened, and Choto hurriedly continued, 'I've come to see Biswas Babu.'

'I asked who you are, not whom you want to see, fellow!'

'Kartick. Mr Sen sent me,' Choto stammered.

'Mr Sen?' The man's tone became welcoming, 'Why didn't you say so before? Wait here, I'll tell Biswas Babu you are here.' He stepped through the door, closing it firmly behind him. Choto shrugged and sat down on the top stair. This was not the start he had been hoping for. In his dream world, he had been ushered into a modern Bombay-style office, into the presence of someone who instantly recognised his talent and begged him to take over the running of the entire business. He, Kartick – for he went by his 'real' name – then took on the world, impressing them with his knowledge and . . .

'You can come in now. Biswas Babu will see you.'

Choto smoothed his shirt and hair and followed the moustaches through the offices. The first was shared, three or four desks, the spaces between them occupied by piles of paper and boxes. Beyond this was a corridor which led to a smaller room with a single desk. To his disappointment neither the setting nor Mr Biswas – a small, rather dark, balding man in a shabby shirt – resembled Bombay. Not even remotely.

'Kartick?' No effusive greeting either. Choto came back to earth.

'Yes, sahib,' he folded his hands respectfully.

'Mr Sen told me you were coming,' Biswas Babu looked at him critically, 'Tell me, can you read?'

'A little, sahib.'

'A little? Here, read this,' he pushed a sheet of paper across the desk. Choto recognised Bengali. Aii, he was lucky – he might have been asked to read Hindi, or even English . . .

'Come on, read it out!' Mr Biswas was impatient.

'Yes, sir . . . I'm just reading it through first . . . "There is . . ."' Choto struggled. He couldn't be expected to read so fast!

'That's enough!' Mr Biswas took the paper back. 'When did you leave school?'

'After class six . . .'

'And that's how you read? No, no, tell me the truth now, I don't have all day.'

'Class four, sahib,' Choto said miserably.

'Sounds more like it,' Mr Biswas considered this. 'Never mind. Maybe I can still use you. How well do you know this area?'

'Not very well, sahib. But I can learn,' Choto tried to sound more enthusiastic than he felt.

'I suppose a willingness to learn is better than nothing,' Mr Biswas almost smiled. 'Tell me, do you know what we do?'

'No, Mr Sen never told me.' What did it matter what they did?

'And you never thought to ask?'

'No, sahib . . .'

'We deal in utensils, stainless steel utensils. Tell me, have you ever worked in an office before?'

'No, sahib . . .'

'Well, you'll have to learn fast. Your job will not be to sell utensils, it will be to keep the office supplied with whatever it needs. You just make sure that if we need tea, you know where to get tea, if we need to get railway tickets, you know where to get railway tickets, if we need pencils, you know where to get pencils. You understand?'

'Yes, sahib.'

'No, you don't. I can hear that in your voice. Let me explain simply. You must find out where to get anything and everything around here, and learn it fast, OK?'

'Yes, sahib!'

'If you do it well, maybe we will find other work for you. In time. Right now, wait in the front office. And watch. That's all. You are dismissed. Go!' Choto folded his hands in farewell and backed out.

The *durwan* was waiting for him in the main office.

'So, how did your meeting with Biswas Babu go?'

'Fine. I think,' said Choto wearily.

'What's your job?' He pulled a face. 'Don't tell me: to help around the office. Get the tickets, the pencils, that sort of thing?'

'Yes,' Choto was astonished, 'how did you know?'

'How did I know? Easy, your type comes and goes. Don't last, your kind,' the *durwan* twirled his moustaches again and went outside to sit on his bench, leaving Choto in the room of empty desks. Unsure of what to do, he walked over to the window and looked out. A small figure on the street below caught his eye – the boy, serving tea at a stall on the other side of the road! How dare he! That decided it. *He*, Choto, could not work here! He stormed out, past the *durwan* who looked up at him in surprise.

'Where you off to? I thought Biswas Babu told you to wait?'

'I've changed my mind! Tell him to find someone else!' In a flash, Choto was down the stairs, out of the door and on a passing bus. The *durwan* shook his head and rolled himself some chewing tobacco. No sense of responsibility, the youth of today. Loafers, the lot of them. Biswas Babu should've expected this.

*

He did not go directly home. It was too early for his mother to be back, even though it was one of her half days. She had arranged with the Sens to leave their house early two days a week (or rather, they had insisted that she shorten her working week by at least two half days). Initially Choto thought that it was a ruse to cut her pay or, worse still, to get rid of her completely but he had been wrong. Not only had they not cut her pay, they had continued to increase it occasionally, just as they had done before. Choto had to admit that they had been fair to her. Though once, in a moment of anger, he had pointed out that every working member of that household had at least a day and a half off every week, if not two. And several other days if one counted national holidays. So she was not really getting such a good deal. Relatively speaking, of course. The argument had been inconclusive, his mother had countered that for him every day seemed a holiday. He'd had no reply.

Disembarking from the bus he had felt a twinge of regret that he had left Biswas Babu's office so hurriedly but the sight of Kanchan crossing a road some hundred yards ahead reminded him of the obnoxious boy who had prompted his decision, and he was happy again as he sat down to wait under his favourite tree. He had a feeling it would be worth his while. He had this feeling often – of course, when the day turned out to be as barren, as it usually did, he conveniently forgot about it. Today something *would* happen, he was sure of it. And, for once, he was right, after a fashion – he had been there but a short while when Chandu appeared.

'*Arré*, Choto!' Chandu greeted him cheerfully. 'Where have you been? I have been looking for you all morning, *banchod*!'

'Hullo, Chandu,' said Choto resignedly. He did not want to go into the events of the morning. Not with Chandu, or anyone else. 'And don't you call me a sisterfucker – I don't have a sister, *shala*!'

'I don't either so I can't be your brother-in-law,' said Chandu logically. 'Anyway, where have you been?'

'Oh here and there, you know,' Choto tried to be vague.

'Here and there? What use is that?' Chandu demanded. 'NawabDa has been looking for you for hours.'

Choto pricked up his ears. 'NawabDa?'

'You deaf or something? NawabDa! You know NawabDa, don't you?'

'Of course I know who NawabDa is! When was he looking for me?'

'Since nine. But no one could find you. We even sent your *chela*, Kanchan,' Chandu smirked, 'to find you. But you were nowhere to be found. Nawab isn't happy about it, that's for sure.'

'*Jaa shala*! Where is he now?'

'Down by the club. If I were you I'd get down there fast, very, very fast!'

'I'm on my way!' Choto leapt to his feet. 'You coming?'

'To watch the fireworks? Of course – but from a distance. You're in for it . . .'

'No, *bhaai*, no!' Choto wished he could be as sure as he pretended. 'Come on, let's get moving.'

The two broke into a run, Kanchan following at a discreet distance. Down the narrow streets, over the piles of refuse and puddles of stagnating green water from the overflowing gutter and standpipes, they ran. Their tail, confident he could overtake the slower older youths at any time – and often in danger of doing so – amused himself by pausing to kick empty coconut shells and throw stones at passing dogs. He hit one which yelped loudly, attracting the attention of some small boys playing nearby. They abandoned their game to join him in speeding it along with more missiles.

Chandu and Choto stopped a few yards short of the club-house, waiting to regain their breath before they entered the presence of the *mastaan*. Unnoticed behind them, Kanchan made his way quietly to the back of the building.

Nawab sat at the table, back to the door, casually turning cards from Aziz's deck and tossing them into a corner. His bulk filled and overflowed the rickety chair, a cigarette – for Nawab could afford such luxuries – dangling from the corner of his thickly moustachioed mouth. He turned as they entered. And smiled the practised smile of one who models his every action on screen idols.

'Aha, look who's here,' Nawab flicked ash into a glass. 'Tomorrow's leaders, who arrive tomorrow instead of today! You took your time, didn't you?'

'He just got back,' Chandu replied, forgetting he had intended to be merely a spectator. Nawab ignored him, instead narrowing his eyes to look over Choto and his 'interview' clothes.

'Where have you been, *bachcha*?' Nawab asked. 'Why the clothes?'

'I had to see someone . . .' Choto bit his tongue '. . . for my mother.'

'For your mother?' Nawab responded. 'Mother's boy, are you? Ma more important than your Dada?'

'No, it's not like that, NawabDa,' Choto began ingratiatingly. The older man cut him short with a gesture.

'I'm not interested in your domestic life – though you will have to get your priorities right if you are going to work for me, won't you?'

'Oh yes, NawabDa, of course, NawabDa. It's only that . . . you know mothers?' Choto pleaded.

'No, I don't,' Nawab contemptuously dismissed the excuse, 'I have no time for mothers, not yours, not mine, not Chandu's, not anyone's! All I know is I have work and if I can't get one of you to do it there are plenty of others around.'

'It won't happen again, NawabDa.'

'It had better not. But I haven't come here to talk about your mother.' He paused and looked around. 'Nice place you boys have here, no?'

'Yes, Dada . . .' Chandu answered reflexively.

'Yes, very nice,' Nawab's eyes narrowed again. 'Lots of people would like to have something like this, wouldn't they?'

'Dada, everything that is ours is yours,' Chandu mumbled.

'So you tell me, so you tell me. So *everyone* tells me. But then they keep some things secret from me, no?'

'NawabDa, we did not keep this secret, everyone knows it is ours . . .' Choto intervened, trying to defuse the situation.

Nawab considered the reply. 'But you never told *me*, did you?' he drawled.

'Dada, we apologise for forgetting – we did not think of it. Please treat it as your own!' Chandu squirmed like an errant schoolboy in the presence of his headmaster.

'I will, I will. In fact, I am – or haven't you noticed?' Nawab guffawed, threw the remaining cards to the floor, and stood up, kicking the chair away. The two youths shrank into the doorway. Outside Kanchan pressed his ear closer to the wall.

'So. Choto, you have a girl now, don't you?' Choto's jaw dropped. Nawab knew!

'Sort of, NawabDa,' he struggled with his reply, 'You know what girls are like – they like you and . . .'

'That's not what I heard. Good in bed, is she?' Choto's

stomach churned. Should he defend Gowri? Dare he risk offending Nawab? Outside, Kanchan held his breath. The *mastaan* smiled at Choto's discomfiture. Then he continued.

'Ai, no offence, Choto! I was just asking. What you do – or don't do – with your girl is your business, I won't interfere. You like her, no? And you are loyal – you want to answer me but chose not to – that is good. Now, never let your loyalty to a woman get in the way of your work for me, OK?'

'Of course not, NawabDa!' Choto breathed more easily. The test was over, the danger past – for now at least. Nawab moved away from the chair.

'Come closer, boys. Make yourself at home!' His 'guests' smiled weakly, stepped past him and unfolded chairs for themselves. Nawab drew his own closer and sat down again. He eyed them carefully, first one, then the other. The two youths waited nervously.

'Chandu, I need some tea,' Nawab suddenly spoke and, as Chandu hesitated, he snapped, 'get me some – now!' Chandu bolted out of the door. Alone with the *mastaan*, Choto shifted uneasily in his seat. Nawab reached out and patted his shoulder reassuringly.

'Take it easy, Choto. I won't bite you – I'm your big brother, your Dada, no?'

'Yes, NawabDa!'

'And I always look after my younger brothers, don't I?'

'Yes, NawabDa!' Try as he might, the young man could detect no menace in the words but was still cautious.

'Relax, *bhaai*, relax.' Why was Nawab calling him *bhaai*? A shiver ran up Choto's spine. He prayed it was without cause. Nawab drew another cigarette out from his packet and tapped it on the glass of his watch, before lighting it with a large steel lighter.

'Choto, *bhaai*, I think it's time you showed your NawabDa what you can do. What do you say?'

'Yes, NawabDa,' Choto shivered. 'If you need me to do something, I am ready.'

'Choto, Choto!' Nawab patted him again. 'Don't be afraid. I am your elder brother, am I not?' There was a shriek outside the door. 'What is that?' Chandu burst in, dragging Kanchan by the ear.

'Look what I found in the gutter – a little pig!' He twisted the boy's ear hard and Kanchan yelped again, louder than before.

'Let him go!' the *mastaan* ordered.

'Let him go? Yes, Dada!' Chandu released Kanchan, who fell back into the corner, nursing his ear, tears of pain trickling down his cheeks. Nawab looked at Choto.

'Choto, you have friends, no?' He jerked his head towards the boy. 'Like Kanchan here?'

'Yes, NawabDa . . .' Choto and Chandu were confused. They had expected swift punishment.

'Kanchan is a good boy,' Nawab drew deep on his cigarette. The two youths held their breath. 'He tells me lots of things. About a girl called Gowri, for instance . . .' He paused to see the effect. Choto's eyes widened and he exhaled sharply.

'Yes, Choto, Kanchan tells me things you do not.' Nawab smiled. 'But I don't hold that against you, it is your private life, isn't it?'

'Yes, NawabDa . . .' Choto shot the treacherous boy a murderous look.

'Right, Kanchan, piss off!' Nawab did not turn his head. Kanchan scrambled out of the door and vanished. 'Now, Choto, let's talk. Kanchan gave you my message?'

'Yes, NawabDa . . .'

Nawab raised his eyes heavenward. 'You've said "Yes, NawabDa!" a thousand times already. Just listen for a change. I have a proposal for you, a business proposition. One that will profit you. Are you interested? No, don't say "Yes, NawabDa". I know your answer so let's say you've said it. Now I will tell you what it is – you want to know, don't you?' He turned to Chandu, who was still standing by the door. 'You, get out!' Chandu went unwillingly. Nawab drew on his cigarette and addressed Choto again. 'I'm going into business, I have a car for it. All I need is a driver. And you can drive, so I call on you. It's very simple. You run it like a taxi, but one without a meter. When you find a customer, you fix the price and you drive. We split the profits like this – twenty per cent is yours, the rest mine,' he blew a smoke ring. 'Naturally, you will pay the petrol and rent for the vehicle – a nominal sum we will discuss later. Does that sound good to you?'

'NawabDa, how can I thank you?' Choto's joy was real. Here was the chance he had been waiting for, and Nawab was providing! How wrong his mother and Gowri had been to doubt him.

'Never mind the thanks, *bhaai*,' Nawab said distantly, 'Just look after the car.'

Putul was in the living room reading *Sportsweek* when the telephone rang. Someone answered on the floor below.

A servant appeared in the room. 'Babu, it's for you.'

'For me?' Putul was surprised. 'Who is it?'

'I don't know, Babu,' the servant shuffled his feet.

'Ask, then. And say I'm not in,' Putul was in no mood for conversation.

'I can't, Babu.'

'Why not?' Putul said sharply. 'You can talk, can't you?'

'The man doesn't understand me, Babu – he only speaks English, Babu.'

'So how do you know it's for me?' Putul said wearily. 'It could be for my uncle, no?'

'But he spoke no Bengali, Babu, I couldn't ask him. He said Sen, Babu!' The servant wasn't going to leave him alone.

'All my uncle's callers ask for Sen. Oh, never mind, I'll come.' In the next room he picked up the receiver and waited for the click that told him the phone on the floor below had been replaced. Then he spoke.

'Hullo? Putul Sen here.'

'Hullo?' The voice crackled from very far away. 'Hullo? May I speak to Putul Sen?' 'Putul' mispronounced as in Britain. The voice, the mispronunciation of his name was familiar. Very familiar.

'Speaking. Who is this?'

'John. John Stewart, Putul. Don't tell me you've forgotten me already?'

'John! Of course not!' Putul mentally kicked himself. 'This is a surprise! How *are* you?'

'Fine, fine, thanks.' There was a pause.

'And your parents?'

'Oh, they're fine too. My father sends his regards – to you and your uncle.'

'That's very nice of him. I'm sorry I never sent the card I promised.'

'The card?' John was puzzled.

'You know – I promised to send them a card from here.'

'Oh, that card!' John laughed. 'Don't worry about it. I think my father gets enough letters from your uncle.'

'Business, eh?'

'Yes, business. They seem to get on quite well.'

95

'They do. In fact Sailen Kaka was wondering whether your father would be coming to visit. To see the new factory and all that.'

'That, Putul, I'm afraid I don't know about. But I am coming.'

'You?' Putul was surprised.

'Yes, me. Who else?'

'Business?'

'Oh no! I'm not in the firm. I had a job with a bank.'

'Had a job with a bank? What happened?'

'I quit last week. I've decided rather than become a banker and spend the rest of my life in a dark suit, I'd like to do something else, so guess what? I'm coming to India!'

Putul was stunned. 'You're not coming to . . .' he fumbled for the words, '*discover* yourself or something, are you?'

'Oh no, not discovering myself at all!' John laughed. 'More like discovering my ancestors, really. My grandfather, his father and goodness knows how many fathers before them, all worked in India.'

'Oh yes, I remember. Your father told me last Christmas. Said it was one reason why he chose to join my uncle in the joint venture.'

'Yes. That and the profits, of course,' John laughed again.

'I suppose so,' Putul felt uncomfortable. He didn't like being reminded of the families' business connections. He preferred to think of their friendship as one that was merely catalysed by the business relationship. 'Where did your grandfather work?'

'A place called Sonapukur.'

'Sonapukur? That's just a couple of hundred kilometres from here.'

'You know it?'

'Sort of. A friend of mine, Dhiren Ghosh is the senior police officer there. Wait,' a thought struck Putul. 'If you're going there, you must stop in Calcutta. I'd love to see you and so would my uncle, I'm sure.'

'I'd love to do that,' John replied. 'It won't be too much trouble, will it?'

'Trouble? Of course not, none at all! Come whenever you please, we've got plenty of space.'

'Thanks, Putul.'

'Oh, don't mention it. When're you coming?'

'Next Friday, believe it or not. I've already booked my ticket.'

'So soon!'

'Yes. It is OK if I stay with you? It's not too short notice, is it?'

'No, no, John.' The Scotsman gave him the flight details. Putul replaced his receiver slowly. John was coming to Calcutta! Wonders would never cease. He went down to tell his uncle. He would be pleased.

CHAPTER EIGHT

I got to the big house by bus. I decided to wait until after ten, so as to avoid the office crush and it worked. Less than half an hour after leaving home I was climbing the stairs and ringing the bell.

'Who is it?' Priya Mashi called down. I recognised her voice immediately. I call her Mashi even though she's not my mother's sister.

'I, Meena!'

'Meena? Meena!' I could hear her trip over her sari in her hurry. I stifled a smile – I have never entered that house without answering that question, hearing that response and having that effect. Even when as a child I visited the house so often – and had actually stayed with her for a couple of weeks when I was ten – that they might as well have given me a key.

Priya Mashi appeared with two children in tow. She had obviously been in the kitchen – she is always in the kitchen, and always has children with her. Not one is hers, and every one leaves her care before they are ten. Her husband left her barely a year after their marriage – the events and reasons for his leaving have never been clear to me, but I do know she returned to her father's house and became the resident aunt-parent to everyone else's offspring. And very successful she is at it too, at one time or the other she has had a hand in bringing up almost all the children in the extended Sen family and now has an ever widening circle of 'grandchildren' who are routinely left in her care. These two were, I guessed, part of that new generation.

We went straight to her 'entertaining room' (her own name for it, it also serves as bedroom for her brood). I knew, immediately, where to sit – on the huge double bed with my legs tucked under me. There is no other way to sit there, since if I sit on the edge my legs dangle uncomfortably high off the ground. Priya Mashi bustled in and out and produced sweet *sandesh*, savoury *shinghara*, and tea. Taking the plates and cups from her, I placed them on the nearby window sill rather than on the distant and unstable little table she would have put them on.

'Meena,' she clasped my hands in hers, 'it is wonderful to see you again!'

'Priya Mashi, it's good to see *you* again. It's good to be home.' Priya Mashi smiled happily.

'So there is to be a marriage in your family?' Priya Mashi, like everyone else, knew of the search for a bride. 'You know, I was beginning to think your parents had decided not to get either of you married. Or that they were going to allow you to decide for yourselves. Not that there is anything wrong with that,' she laughed, 'it's just different from the way my generation did things. Times have changed, haven't they?'

'Not for my brother, at least!' I grinned.

'Yes, yes, of course. Your Dada is a very capable young man – even I, a mere housewife, can see that. But it is good that he has decided that his elders are better placed to choose a bride for him. It is nice for us older folk to be of use . . .' she broke off as her brother entered.

I moved to pay my respects, to *pronaam* him. He stopped me.

'Ai, don't do that, Meena. Save it for my father,' he pointed upstairs. 'He's expecting you.'

'Expecting me?' I was surprised. 'Does he know I am here?'

'Oh yes, he does. Those two young spies,' he indicated to the two children who had reappeared in the doorway, 'came up and told him we had a visitor. You'd better come up right away. He gets very agitated if he does not see his guests as soon as they arrive. He tends to latch onto the names and imagines that he has been waiting to see them for years.'

I hopped off the bed and followed him up the stairs. The old man was in his long-handled chair, by the window. He was too deaf to hear me enter, but Raja Mama drew his attention to my presence immediately.

'BABA, MEENA IS HERE,' he shouted. The old man turned slowly. I touched his feet and stood back. He peered at me through milky eyes.

'Meena? You have come back?'

'Yes . . .' Seeing the blank look on his face, I realised I would have to raise my voice too. 'YES. HOW ARE YOU?'

'Oh, as well as can be expected at my age, as well as can be expected. Come, sit down near me.' Raja Mama helpfully pushed a chair toward me. The old man patted my hand.

'So, Meena, how was your trip? Raja here tells me you have been abroad?'

'YES, DADU. I WAS IN ENGLAND,' I saw no point in explaining that I had travelled a bit further afield.

'Good, good. You know, in my day – or even in your father's younger days – women didn't travel, certainly not alone. But things have changed, haven't they?'

'YES, DADU.'

'Yes, they have. And women, like you, go out and work too. Are you working?'

'No, Dadu . . .' I remembered his deafness and raised my voice, 'NO, DADU, NOT RIGHT NOW. MAYBE SOON.'

'Good, good! Where did you go? England?' His tone grew reminiscent. 'You've been in England, eh? How did you like it?' He didn't wait for an answer. 'You know, you aren't the first one in the family to go abroad. The first one to go was my cousin. You won't remember, you weren't born then. He went to England a long time ago, in the twenties . . .'

'BABA, IT WAS THE THIRTIES. NINETEEN THIRTY-FIVE, TO BE PRECISE!' Raja Mama interrupted wearily. This was obviously not new to him, 'HE WENT IN NINETEEN THIRTY-FIVE.'

'That's what I was saying. My cousin – your uncle . . .'

'HER GRANDUNCLE. SORT OF.'

'Granduncle? Whose granduncle?! I am talking to this young woman about my cousin, the one who went to England in the twenties . . .'

'IN THE THIRTIES, BABA. NINETEEN THIRTY-FIVE, TO BE PRECISE.'

'That's what I said! Anyway, this cousin went to Oxford . . .'

'LONDON, BABA, LONDON. NOT OXFORD. DEFINITELY NOT OXFORD!'

'Don't interrupt, Raja! As I was saying, my cousin went to study engineering . . .'

'MEDICINE. NOT ENGINEERING.' Raja Mama sighed.

'What are you talking about? I am talking about this young woman's uncle . . .'

'NOT HER UNCLE, HER GRANDUNCLE, BABA,' his son shook his head despairingly.

'Uncle, granduncle! What is this nonsense?! He went in the twenties to study engineering in Oxford . . .'

'IT WAS THE MEDICINE IN THE THIRTIES IN LONDON!' Raja Mama's face told me it was time to leave. As I slipped out, I looked back. The old man had not noticed my departure. He was back in his own world, staring out of the window.

Downstairs Priya Mashi was waiting for me.

'Didn't last long, did it? It never does, these days. He can only concentrate for a short time. Then something someone says triggers a memory and, before you know it he is lost in his own world. Recently he has been talking about his cousin who went to England. Did he tell you about him?'

I nodded. 'He did.'

'Raja insists on trying to correct him when he gets his facts wrong. I keep telling him it's useless, the old man is happy, remembering things the way he does. Raja says that correcting him will keep him closer to reality but I can't see how,' she shook her head. 'All he does is stare out of the window. What he sees I don't know. His eyesight is no better than his hearing. But tell me about your brother's wedding, Meena.'

I smiled, 'There is nothing to tell yet, Mashi. Nothing has been decided, other than that he is to be married.

'Don't your parents have any girls in mind? They must, surely?'

'Those they do are unsuitable. Anyway, it wouldn't be any fun if they weren't – half of it is choosing the bride, isn't it?'

Priya Mashi laughed and I joined in.

'Before you know it, it will be your turn . . .' Priya Mashi looked at me quizzically.

'I'm not thinking about marriage now, Mashi. Too many other things to do!' But I blushed scarlet. She smiled and changed the subject. Not completely, but sufficiently.

'Putul came to visit us not so long ago. I told him it was time he got married too. But it made no impression on him. Sometimes I wonder about that boy . . . he's so, so *lethargic*!'

'I think you mean apathetic,' I corrected her without intending to. Then quickly added, 'I must admit he infuriates me, I can't be around him for very long without wanting to strangle someone. Him preferably!'

'Aii, don't say that, child,' she admonished. 'Just ignore him.'

'I do – at least, I try to. Fortunately I don't see him very often.' We chatted on and, before long, it was time for me to go – Ma would be waiting for me to return before she had lunch. She always did, unless I told her otherwise. I therefore bade Priya Mashi good-bye and, promising to return, left.

That evening Baba had news for us. A bride had been found! Well, a Potential, at least. Not through Pishi (thank goodness) but through Putul's uncle, Sailen. He'd got in touch with Baba to say that he'd been talking to his accountant, one Mr Banerjee. And it turned out that that gentleman had a daughter for whom he was seeking a match. Though a Banerjee, neither he nor his wife were bothered about caste, they wanted nothing other than a good groom. That was fine by us, but what of the girl, both Ma and I wanted to know. Well, Baba said, he didn't have too much information on her but Putul's Sailen Kaka had told him that she had been to college, had a degree in political science from Jadavpur University and was now doing her Master's there. Her family was very respectable – her father an accountant and her two brothers, both older than her, had good jobs. One was a college lecturer and in Calcutta, the other, having completed a PhD in the States, had got a job with an international company there. Neither was married yet. The family wanted their daughter to be settled first.

Before Baba could tell us more, Durga came in to say Dada was on the telephone. I went to take the call.

'Meena?' Dada's voice was still recognisable down the crackly Calcutta line (we are still on one of the old exchanges).

'Hello, Dada,' I greeted him excitedly. 'What's up? When'll you be home?'

'Well, not for a while – I'm going to be late tonight. I'm going out with some colleagues for dinner. Could you tell Ma that I won't be home for dinner?'

'Of course I can. This is a surprise, dinner suddenly?' I was curious.

'Oh yes, it just came up . . . someone had a bright idea and we thought it would be nice . . .'

'Where are you going? Somewhere interesting?'

'Going? I don't know yet . . . we might just get some food and have it at someone's place . . . maybe Punjabi food . . .'

'Punjabi? That sounds wonderful! Can I come?'

He took me seriously. 'Join us?! Oh no, that would be . . .' He sounded confused.

'Would be . . .' I was puzzled. 'Oh, never mind.' I wanted to get back to my parents. 'You can tell us all about it when you get back.'

'Yes . . . Bye . . .'

'Wait!' I managed to stop him hanging up. 'We've got some news for you – but it'll have to wait till you get back, I suppose.'

'News? Yes, it will have to wait . . . sorry, Meena I have to rush . . . tell me when I get back!' The 'phone went dead. I was puzzled. Dada is not usually one to let a secret pass without attempting to pry. Maybe he was in a hurry, he sounded like it. I went back out onto the verandah. Ma grumbled good-humouredly about the food but nothing else was said. We were more interested in the girl Putul's uncle had found than in Dada's dinner engagement. Baba was persuaded to call Mr Banerjee immediately.

He was on the 'phone for about ten minutes. When he came back he was beaming broadly. He had spoken to the girl's father and had been impressed. A friendly gentleman, very friendly. He wanted us to visit them soon, that very same evening, if we could! Ma and I both demurred – Dada wouldn't be able to come! Well, said Baba, he had explained that and Mr Banerjee had replied that perhaps it would be better if the preliminary meeting did not involve Dada meeting his daughter, Sushma. They – his wife, himself and the brother – would like to meet the rest of the family first. Ma sent for Durga and dinner was served early. I was almost too excited to eat but Ma insisted so I managed some rice and fish.

After dinner we changed, I put on a fresh cotton sari, Ma one of her silk ones, Baba a clean shirt and we set off. Baba had the car – the good old Austin was, for once, not in the garage. A good omen, said Ma archly. We drove down to Gariahat, still crowded (does it never quieten down?) and turned up towards Jodhpur Park, where Baba said the family lived. After Gol Park, the traffic eased and we fairly flew (if you can call the

Austin's speed flying) across Dhakuria Bridge towards our destination. When we reached our turning we discovered Baba had forgotten to get a precise description of the location. This meant that we had to spend some fifteen minutes driving around looking for the house – houses in that area aren't always consecutively numbered, some are numbered according to the plot they stand on. However, after a considerable amount of jumping in and out (on my part) and straining of eyes (by everyone), we found the house.

It was a modest looking bungalow with a low wire-mesh-topped wall separating its small lawn from the street. Baba parked outside since the drive was completely blocked by a black Ambassador. It looked like an accountant's car. We stood outside, uncertain – the gate was locked. Should we bang on it? Should we shout? Was there a bell? A light came on in the house and a small figure came out.

'Who is it?' A child's voice.

'Mr Sen and family,' Baba answered.

'Mr Sen? Wait – I will go and ask.' The door closed. A few minutes later a young man came hurrying out, unlocked the gate and pulled it open.

'Mr Sen? I'm so sorry! The boy is too cautious! We had told him . . .' he ushered us up the drive and into the house. We were in a large, bright living room. 'I'm Ranjan, Ranjan Banerjee. Sushma's brother.'

'Sushma's brother? The professor?' Ma was interested.

He laughed. 'Yes, I'm the teacher.'

'And what do you teach?'

'English literature,' he remembered himself and patted down the cushions on some chairs. 'Please sit down, my parents will be with you directly.'

'Oh, that's all right.' My mother was in a talkative mood. I wondered what could be causing it. Was she nervous? We all sat down, all except Ranjan who hovered over us.

Trying not to be too obvious, I looked around the room. Neat, whitewashed. No more than a couple of years old. The chairs were cane, as was the coffee table Ranjan set in front of us, cane topped with glass. A smart cabinet containing an equally smart new television and stereo stood in a corner. Most of the walls were covered by bookshelves filled with books that looked more like novels or poetry books than accountancy texts. I recognised some of the spines – novels mainly – but the rest were too far away to make out. A veritable library! If Dada married into this family, I thought, I just might be able to get to take a closer look.

Ma was still interrogating Ranjan. I examined him unobtrusively too. Medium height, darkish. Those awful squarish black-framed glasses that are so common, but a pleasant, open face which, though not handsome, was very animated. He waved his hands a lot and didn't seem to be able to stay still, pacing the room, adjusting this and that all the while.

'You teach English? Where?' my mother was asking.

'St Aloysius's.'

'St Aloysius's? That's not so bad. I have a cousin who studied there. A long time ago, though. How long have you been teaching there?'

'A couple of years. I did my BA there, then an MA at Calcutta University and was lucky enough to be offered some part-time teaching soon after I finished.'

'Part-time? So you are part-time?'

'I was. They made me full-time after a year . . . here is my father . . .'

Mr Banerjee came in. A small grey-haired man of the same darkish complexion as his son. I was slightly surprised to see that he wore a *dhoti*, because, for some reason, I thought he might be more, well, westernised. His wife, a cheerful looking woman dressed in a simple silk sari, was about the same height as him, just over five foot, but twice his girth.

'*Namaskar*, Mr Sen, Mrs Sen,' Mr Banerjee greeted us. 'Please, do sit down.' We resumed our seats. 'I see you have met our son, Ranjan. He's not the candidate, though.' He smiled. Mrs Banerjee sent Ranjan to arrange for some tea.

'Now, Mr Sen. Shall we get down to business – if I can call it that?' Mr Banerjee chuckled and rubbed his hands together.

'Certainly,' Baba replied politely. 'There is a lot to discuss – where shall we start?'

'Perhaps some ground rules? I prefer to get that sort of thing out of the way.' The chuckle again. 'Your cousin, Sailen Sen, has probably told you that we do not hold with caste?'

'He has,' my father replied. 'We are not particularly religious ourselves . . .'

'No matter, no matter,' Mr Banerjee interrupted. 'We just want it to be clear that if the marriage is agreed we expect to share the costs of the wedding. Which is to say, we will pay our share. May I be blunt?'

'Of course,' Baba looked slightly puzzled.

'Well, I do not hold with dowry. We will have none of that. If the couple are compatible, I will of course contribute as much as I can but I would like to make it clear that I do not like dowry . . . and I am not saying this just because it is my daughter, the same will hold true when it is my son's turn . . .'

'Mr Banerjee!' Baba was speechless. I could not tell whether he was offended or angry or both.

'Mr Sen, Mr Sen, please do not take this amiss! I mean no offence. It is just that recently a friend of ours had a – shall we say "disagreement"? – with another prospective family . . .'

'I'm sure my husband understands – he is not offended, only surprised that it was raised at all,' Ma said soothingly, glaring at my father. 'When we were married there was no question of it either. We may not be atheists but we do come from a fairly educated background,' her laugh took the sting out of the remark. Everyone looked suitably mollified.

Mr Banerjee cleared his throat, 'I'm not used to making arrangements for marriages and I am not very tactful, I see. I apologise again for any offence.'

'There is no need,' Baba had recovered his composure, 'it is good that we clear that up straight away. It is the sort of issue that can lead to unnecessary and avoidable complications and misunderstandings later. Is there anything else you would like to clarify?'

'Yes, a couple of other things, actually,' said the accountant. 'First, horoscopes. I do not approve of them and would be grateful if you spare us them,' he paused, 'though, of course, if you wish to have one drawn up I will not object – I would just prefer not to have anything to do with that sort of mumbo-jumbo.'

Baba pursed his lips. 'Mr Banerjee, we have educated our children as best we can, as rationalists. We too have no faith in horoscopes but it may be necessary – to please others in the family – to have their horoscopes checked. However, I assure you that we will take our decision without recourse to such – mumbo-jumbo,' he smiled mischievously, 'and if one practitioner of such mumbo-jumbo – I like your term – finds fault with the match, should we decide to go ahead I'm sure we can find another. A second opinion, so to speak?'

Mr Banerjee chuckled. 'A second opinion, I like that. Yes, that I will accept, I definitely like the idea! My wife and I married against the advice of the horoscopes and, I am happy to say, we have had no problems.' Mrs Banerjee smiled mildly at her husband as he said this.

'And the other point?' Baba prompted.

'Oh yes,' Mr Banerjee, still chuckling happily at the vision of competing astrologers, continued, 'the other thing is: my daughter is doing her Master's and it is possible that she may want to teach or do further studies. I hope that would be acceptable to you?'

'Yes, certainly!' Baba replied. 'We would be very pleased to have a daughter-in-law who takes her education seriously. Our daughter, Meena – I'm sorry, I should have introduced her earlier – is a poet and continues to write with our full support. In fact, she has just returned from a tour of the UK sponsored by the British Council.'

All eyes turned to me. I wished I were somewhere else, somewhere far away. 'Yes, Baba. But I'm not the candidate, please . . .'

Mr Banerjee chuckled and rubbed his hands together again. 'She's right, you know. We should leave the poor girl alone – though I'm sure my son would be most interested in hearing about her work,' Ranjan had re-entered but, having missed the previous exchange, looked baffled. 'Ranjan, she is a poet. My son is very interested in poetry. But let's stick to the subject. I suppose you'd like to meet Sushma?'

'Well, yes . . .' Ma said expectantly.

'She should be here in a minute – Ranjan, is she bringing the tea?'

A slight figure, about the same height as the elder Banerjees entered, carrying a tray. I could not see her face. 'Can I take a photograph? This is a one off!' Ranjan was grinning broadly. Sushma glared at him.

'Now, Ranjan, leave your sister alone,' Mrs Banerjee said.

'Go on, prepare your lessons or whatever it is you have to do.'

'Can't I stay, Ma? Please?' he begged.

'Oh, do let him stay, Mrs Banerjee!' Ma interceded for him. She really did like him!

'Oh very well, then. But only because Mrs Sen has asked – and you must behave yourself. Get a chair and sit down.' Ranjan obeyed, smiling cheerfully.

'Now, Sushma, tell us something about yourself,' Sushma looked up and blushed. For the first time I saw her face properly. She was fairer than her brother and quite good-looking. The family resemblance was clear in the open friendly face. Her nervousness was obvious and natural. After all, who wouldn't be? I shivered slightly at the thought that some day I might find myself in the same position.

'Mrs Sen. What shall I say? What do you want to know?' Her voice was slightly husky.

'I don't know – everything!' Ma laughed. 'Oh all right, let's start with the usual – can you cook, sing that sort of thing?'

'Oh my parents are better judges of that . . .' she appealed to them.

'Yes, she can cook,' her mother answered. 'Not very well, yet, her studies don't allow much time for it, but she has studied the harmonium and can sing Rabindrasangeet.'

'Not very well, either,' Ranjan slipped in mischievously. His father quelled him with a look.

'Don't be rude, Ranjan, she can. Our son is jealous – he has no musical talent. He attempted to learn the flute and had to give up. Sushma is not an artiste but she is very competent. She is more interested in her studies, though. Stood first in her BA class,' Mrs Banerjee said proudly.

'Is there anything you would like to ask us, Sushma?' Baba intervened. He could see the poor girl was embarrassed.

'Me? No, nothing!' She blushed again.

'Oh yes, she does,' Ranjan seemed incapable of keeping quiet, 'she wants to know about your son – she told me so herself!'

'Quiet, Ranjan . . .' Mr Banerjee gave him another stern look.

'Don't mind him, it's quite all right,' Baba said, 'I'm sure she does want to ask us lots of things but is too shy. Let's see if I can make it any easier. He's a good boy, and an engineer. At least, he trained as one, he's in management now, like everyone else. He earns a decent salary and is . . . I don't know, he's a good boy!' he ended lamely.

We stayed for about half an hour. Ranjan and his sister left after about ten minutes, leaving the elders (and myself, for I had nowhere to go) to discuss the suitability of Dada and Sushma. While they were talking I mulled over what I had seen. She seemed very nice, and the family seemed the sort Dada might be quite comfortable with. They were very well educated – Mrs Banerjee, it turned out had a BA too, in Bengali. Their elder son, Utpal, was an electrical engineer who had gone to the States on a scholarship to do his PhD, found a job in a multinational and stayed on. He now lived somewhere in New York (or was it New Jersey? I don't remember, both were mentioned). Ranjan had, quite early on, decided he didn't want to study science and had done English instead. A cheerful but stubborn fellow (his father's description, not mine), he had refused to even apply to US colleges and universities and chosen Calcutta University instead. His real interest was poetry. And he claimed to enjoy it. Sushma was a quiet girl, very studious and hoped to get a job teaching sometime and, if things went well, to do a PhD. The family appeared to be as pleased with us as we were with them and, when we left, Mr Banerjee and Baba agreed to call each other to confirm the next meeting. A second preliminary meeting. I had so enjoyed this first that when we got back I completely forgot to ask Dada about his dinner. We all did and he volunteered no information. In retrospect, perhaps I should've asked. But it is always easier with hindsight, isn't it? At the time, we were too busy thinking about the future.

CHAPTER NINE

As soon as he saw it Choto realised that he had been more than a little over-optimistic about Nawab's car. It was at least fifteen years old and showed its age all too clearly. It wasn't really even a car but a Trekker, a vehicle halfway between a Jeep and the ground. Without the advantages of either, the sturdiness of the Jeep or the immobility of the ground. It had the classic Trekker body – flat and low, bolted onto a flimsy chassis. It had never been pretty and now, after years of neglect, it looked ready to be either stripped down or dumped. But neither fate had been granted it, instead here it was, in service as the 'car' that Nawab had promised him. Still, it was better than nothing, it was a start.

There were more surprises in store – immediately after presenting him with the keys, Nawab had explained that they were no use, the vehicle started by crossing the two loose wires hanging below the dashboard. It was not a smooth ride either – when it went over a pothole it rolled like a ship at sea or a tank in a trench and was about as comfortable. The first time he hit one of the many holes he would have to negotiate he was almost thrown out, only managing to stay on board by clutching the steering wheel. The brakes too were barely functional. But he had never driven a vehicle that braked properly and, besides, it was not capable of any great speed – when he used the accelerator all it did was belch clouds of black smoke which, if the wind was behind, swirled in and smothered passengers and driver alike. On the plus side, it was an unlikely target for thieves. And the engine sounded moderately healthy.

He did not complain. It was, after all, a chance to earn a living, his first to show his mother and girl that he could provide for himself. A few months, maybe a year, and he would have enough money saved to convince a bank to finance his own vehicle, perhaps even get a taxi licence. First he had to make the vehicle profitable. Nawab had offered him a grace period of two months on the rental. Naturally, he would have to pay it back later but at least he did not have to pay it immediately. And he had advanced, at low interest, sufficient for a tank of petrol. He also provided Choto with his first job that same morning, transporting no less than ten loads of junk – although the owner assured him it was valuable scrap metal – from his side of Dhakuria Bridge to Park Circus. They started at eight, but the loading and unloading took time and traffic jams did not help. In the end, Choto worked late into the evening, only finishing at nine. He was too tired by then to argue when the contractor cut a third off the agreed price 'because it had taken so long', or to notice that what he received after the reduction barely amounted to the price of the petrol. Choto was still euphoric – he was in business, a real business with a future. He was a driver *with* a car.

Having started visiting relatives, Putul found that there were also family friends who demanded his presence. Hari Ganguly was an old friend of his uncle's, the owner of no fewer than six shops specialising in electronic goods. Putul arrived at his house late on Sunday morning. Nothing much had changed, the high gate was opened by the same *durwan* he had seen when he first visited at the age of three. He crossed the broad, flower-bordered lawn to the porch where Hari Ganguly sat reading a newspaper.

'Hullo, Hari Babu,' Putul began. Although the businessman was older than Putul's father would have been, he called him Hari Babu, having got into the habit of addressing him thus when very young. Hari Ganguly had found it amusing to be called 'Hari Babu' by a child and had prevailed upon Putul's uncle and aunt to allow it. And, out of respect and mindful of his position and wealth, they had agreed.

'Putul, Putul. How very nice to see you!' Hari Babu said, rising to embrace him. 'How are you, my boy?'

'Very well, Hari Babu, very well. And yourself?'

'Pretty good, considering. Pretty good. But don't stand there, come and join me. I am having elevenses.' Hari Babu beckoned the servant waiting silently by the door of the house. 'Bring a fresh pot of tea – or do you prefer coffee?'

'I'm not particular – tea'll be fine.' The servant turned to leave.

'And bring some more biscuits,' Hari Babu called after him. 'Now, Putul, tell me all about your stay. How it was, what you learned – if anything!' He smiled. 'And how it feels to be back.'

'Oh, there's not a lot to tell,' Putul trotted out his standard response. 'I went to do my studies, I did them and now I have returned. It's good to be home.'

'Nonsense, boy. You can fob off your aunts with nonsense like that, but not someone like me. I expect more details. You went to study economics, you must have learned something? Was it just a waste of money sending you there?'

'Maybe it was,' Putul laughed, 'just study, study, study.'

'I don't for a moment believe that all you did there was study. And if you insist that it was, I shall be convinced that you are a lazier person than I thought, hey? Here's the tea –. milk, sugar?' The servant placed a cup in front of Putul. He sipped cautiously.

'It must be most fascinating to see how they run their economy out there – first hand, I mean. After all, I can only read about it. Our journals,' he prodded the newspaper on the table disapprovingly, 'are full of no news from the outside world except of England. Colonial mentalities die hard, and never harder than in India.'

'You think so?'

'Of course,' said Hari Ganguly comfortably, 'Just look at us, drinking tea at eleven in the morning! Why, we didn't even drink tea before the English came, did you know that?'

'Really?' Putul selected a biscuit.

'Oh yes, definitely. They brought it as a cash crop. However, it is not tea that enslaves our minds – though it might our taste buds. It's a lot more than that.'

'Our minds are enslaved?'

'Look at all these changes they are making to our economy,' Hari Babu explained. 'Of course it's good for me as a business-man – there are lots of new goods to sell – but the real reason for "opening up" the economy is that we are blindly following what the colonial powers and their successors, the international financial agencies, say.'

'And is that bad, Hari Babu?'

'Is it, Putul? Is it? Of course it is! Look around you, everything we make is in imitation of what the West produces. Our cars, our televisions, what goes onto our televisions, everything is either "made under licence" or copied. We, as a nation, have lost our identity.'

'Our identity?' Hari Babu required more encouragement than Dhiren and Putul was, in this case, perfectly willing to supply it. Hari Babu was an interesting speaker. Almost a politician. 'How?'

'Open your eyes and look around you. We grow more like the West. The better off consume more and more every day and what they consume is not indigenous. Why, we even get hamburgers now!'

'Are you recommending that we return to some kind of Gandhian utopia?' Putul tossed in another morsel.

'In a way, yes. Up to the point that there was more truth in what he said than in what he practised.'

'What do you mean by that?'

'That Gandhi proclaimed the gospel of Indianness but lacked the courage and the conviction to implement it. The men who wrote our constitution and those who have succeeded them, like Gandhi, pay lip service to Indianness while pushing ahead with whatever suits them, not what is good for the people of our motherland. Their creeds, including socialism, are alien: Russia and Communism is no more Indian than burgers and churches. They fill our children's heads with a mish-mash of what the colonialists wrote about us – or what *their* colonised minds have invented!'

'Is there an alternative, Hari Babu?' Putul helped himself to another biscuit.

'An alternative? Come, come, surely that is obvious? We must teach our children – and ourselves – about what it is to be Indian. What it really is, not what some washed-out Western liberal or Communist tells us it is. We must look to our past, to the civilisation that flourished in our land before it was invaded.'

'Before it was invaded? Surely you mean subjugated by the British?' Putul exercised his normally dormant intellect. 'Strictly speaking they never invaded us, did they?'

'No, I mean invaded. Most recently by the British and before them, by the Muslims.'

'The Muslims?'

'Yes, they too are aliens, at least inasmuch as they have embraced an alien creed. A religion that may well be suitable to the barren desert lands of the Middle East, but it is neither of, nor suitable to, India. We have a more ancient history and civilisation of our own, and books that go further back in time than those of the barbarian invaders. Their books are good, but they are for their contexts, not ours. We have our own culture, Hinduism, and a language of antiquity and complexity and beauty to match, Sanskrit.'

'I don't speak Sanskrit . . .' Putul nibbled his biscuit.

'The loss is yours. My point is fundamental. This country has, for too long, allowed foreign ideas and ideologies to define its present. It, and the people within it, have lost their sense of identity and it is high time that it was reasserted. We, as a nation, need to look back into our past, to the glories of our civilisation, the glories that attracted foreign attention, the glories that have suffered, been denigrated and overwhelmed by that same foreign attention. Remember, Putul, that in my youth I was as ardent a nationalist – in the sense that it was understood in those days – as the next man. I was a passionate Gandhian, then a Nehru socialist, and I·worked hard and rejoiced in the self-sufficiency that we seemed to be attaining. I even stood shoulder to shoulder with those who demanded the protection of the rights of the minorities, the rights of those whose forefathers had abandoned our own culture for those of foreigners. And then I realised that my own sons know nothing of their culture, their history and that their ignorance was the direct result of their father's laxity in promoting pride in it. And so I have decided to rectify it in my own small way.'

'How?'

'First, my grandson is learning Sanskrit and is having all the ceremonies performed for him that I, in my Nehruvian socialist blindness, denied my son. I now give a portion of my income – not so much as to endanger my grandson's inheritance, of course – to those who promote Indianness, Hinduness. They will, I believe, help give those who live in this *Bharat* of ours – Hindu, Muslim, Sikh, Christian, Brahmin, Kshatriya, Sudra – a sense of their heritage and its superiority over imported fashions and ideologies.'

Putul blinked. He had not known that Hari Babu held such strong political views, 'Who are they?'

'The party that supports Bharatvarsha, the Hindu Sangh. To show my commitment I am sponsoring their rally transport later this month,' he rose, 'and now it is time for me to prepare for my worship. You will excuse me . . .'

Putul's next vist was to another family friend. Soumen Rai was a politician, a member of the ruling party and an MLA, a member of the Legislative Assembly. He had been at school with Putul's father and uncle and, while they were building up their business, he had joined the Party, working his way up the ladder from cub-journalist to Central Committee member. Now an MLA, a member of the Legislative Assembly for the constituency that included the village of Sonapukur, rumour had it that he would soon be 'promoted' to a parliamentary seat – a rumour he refused to either confirm or deny.

Soumen Rai's house was not unlike Boro Dadu's, four-storied, many-roomed, but of grander design. Entering through a rusting wrought-iron gate Putul found himself in a huge colonnaded courtyard overhung with grand balconies that ran the length of each floor. But the paint was peeling, the courtyard was draped in ropes and washing, weeds sprouted from the brickwork and the fountain, and a small tree had taken root at the base of one of the mock Greek columns.

Putul's destination was a flat in a secluded section cordoned off by an unpretentious but fully functional sliding gate. Soumen Rai believed in keeping a low profile, meeting ordinary visitors in modest rooms overlooking the courtyard, admitting only close friends to the inner sanctum with its plush, air-conditioned interior. Putul had to wait outside Soumen Rai's office for about ten minutes. Soumen Rai was busy, on the telephone. 'Bishness,' the man at the door informed him. Putul took a seat. Eventually the door opened.

'So, Putul, you've returned,' Soumen Rai greeted him. 'The Prodigal Son, eh? Now bileth-qualified, ready to take on the system, eh?'

'I don't know about that, Soumen Jeta.'

'You don't know yet but you will soon, boy. So, how was England?'

'Interesting. I'm glad to be home, though.'

'Glad to be home? That's the spirit. Too many educated people are abandoning the country. Brain-drain and all that. And what are your plans now that you are back?'

'Well, first I have this article to finish. I promised it to my professor in Glasgow and have been working on it since I got back but it isn't quite done,' Putul tripped out his excuse again.

'Article, eh? Very impressive,' Soumen Rai drummed on the desk, 'not for Indian consumption though, is it?' He didn't wait for an answer, 'And what about when you finish?'

'I'll be joining the family business, I suppose,' Putul said resignedly. Why did everyone keep asking? Why couldn't they leave him alone?

'Family business, eh? Now what is it your uncle is into these days? Joint-ventures, auto-spares, isn't it?'

'Yes, I met Sailen Kaka's partner in Scotland. His son and I shared a flat.'

Soumen Rai nodded. 'Good, good. Strengthens the ties. Now you're back, I'm sure you've noticed, business is booming here.'

Putul nodded. 'Yes, things have changed over the past few years.'

'Yes, and our state is leading the way. In the current climate, I'm sure there's no dearth of interest in someone like you. You know, you should consider it, my boy.'

'Consider what?' Putul was lost.

'Consultancy, that sort of thing. Branch out on your own. Lots of people want economic advisers these days. You could combine your interests, business and consultancy. Never did my family any harm!' Soumen chuckled.

'You're in economic consultancy?'

'In a way, my boy, in a way. We have interests – not myself, of course. My brother, for instance. People like to have a construction firm that knows the way things are going.' He leaned back in his chair and ran his fingers through his thinning hair, his spectacles and the *dhoti* lending him the air of an ancient professor.

'And how does he know the way things are going?' Putul inquired.

'He's my brother, boy. My brother, my flesh and blood. Sometimes times are hard and we help each other out. Hardly ever has labour problems, my brother. And even if he does, he's too valuable a man to have on board to cancel a contract. You see, the unions know which side their bread is buttered. Power isn't only derived from their members, it pays for union leaders to pay heed to those in public office. You might call it two-way democracy!' He smiled cheerfully. 'The unions know our family is on their side. Myself and my brother. So do those who need work done – if you are building something you want a contractor who has a good relationship with his workers and can deliver, eh?'

'I'm not sure I follow, sir . . .'

'Never mind, boy. Just take a tip, you could make people pay as much for your knowledge as they will pay for your goods. And it's always handy to have uncles – even if the ties are affection, not blood, eh?'

Before Putul could reply there was a knock on the door and an old man came in.

'Yes?' Soumen Rai addressed the new arrival.

'Your car is here, Babu,' the old retainer bowed.

'Ah yes, the car. I have a meeting, Putul. An industrialist whose name I shall keep to myself because you might be too impressed. Besides, Party business is for Party ears only, isn't it? Now, stay and have a cup of tea. This fellow will get you

123

one. It's been nice talking to you, my boy. Good of you to come round. Keep in touch, eh? You never know when I might be able to help you!' Patting him on the shoulder, Soumen Rai left the room.

The morning after his first job, Choto realised that he had been done. Nawab's 'contractor' had effectively left him out of pocket! Unless things improved dramatically, he wasn't going to earn enough to pay for repairs, leave alone the rent on the vehicle, or anything else! He resolved, therefore, to make sure that he was never again brow beaten into taking an un-economic fee. But determination is easy, action is not. The next day had brought no work, the rent was mounting. So when Nawab asked if he would transport materials for the same contractor he accepted immediately. And agreed to charge a lower price than his 'fixed' one, because the con-tractor was now 'a regular customer'. This job turned out to be as great a financial disaster as the first. After Choto had paid for the repair of a burst tyre, he found he had not broken even. He would have cried but instead, when Chandu and Aziz insisted he buy them a bottle to celebrate his 'success', he borrowed more from Nawab to pay for the treat. So far, being in business was more expensive than being unemployed. Choto drowned his sorrows in the fiery liquid. And as he did, he regretted it – he would have to spend the night outside again. But his luck had to change, tomorrow would be better.

CHAPTER TEN

Somewhat to our surprise, Mr Banerjee called Baba the day after our first visit – would the second meeting be possible that weekend? Dada was asked and agreed to be available that Saturday evening. He had shown only faint interest in the proceedings so far. Ma and I put it down to nerves. In the intervening days I found it difficult to contain my excitement and Ma banished me 'permanently' from the kitchen because I kept bringing up the subject.

Saturday dawned fine and bright, even the smog omitting to descend. Dada continued to feign indifference and went for his customary morning row at the Lakes when Baba went to the *bazaar*. He brought back ingredients for a near-festive lunch, and Ma and Durga did their best. But I hardly noticed what I ate.

Finally, at six o'clock sharp, the doorbell rang. Ma smoothed down her sari and opened it. The Banerjees. The parents – and Ranjan. I guess I shouldn't have been surprised to see him, after all I had been to see his sister. But I was. Dada, finally showing his nervousness, perched nervously on the edge of his seat. I volunteered to make tea. When I returned, Ma was interrogating Ranjan again.

'So what exactly do you teach, Ranjan?'

'Literature, Mrs Sen,' he grinned.

'She knows that!' his mother intervened.

'Yes, I'm sorry. I teach all sorts of things. As the youngest member of the staff I don't get much choice.'

'Really?'

'Well, not really,' he said apologetically, 'I have to teach some papers but I do get some choice and do get to do some things I like.'

'But you still haven't told me what you teach?'

'Old English, Shakespeare's *Twelfth Night*, Synge, Hardy for the novel paper, that sort of thing.'

'Did you study them for your MA?' Ma persisted.

'No, I did American literature, I'm afraid. The novel was my preference.'

'Ah, which is your favourite novelist?'

'Updike. Not on the BA syllabus.'

'Would you like to teach him?'

'Teach him? Maybe. No, my interests have changed – I'm more interested in what they call New Writing these days.'

'New Writing?' The term was new to Ma.

'Kenyans, Australians, Indians who write in English, that sort of thing.'

'Ah, like Rushdie,' my father joined in. 'What do you think of him?'

'A professional assessment? Or a personal one?'

'Personal.'

'Oh, I think he is a very good writer.' Ranjan side-stepped neatly.

'My son is a diplomat, no?' Mrs Banerjee tried to steer the conversation back to Dada and Sushma. 'How about you, Arun?'

'What about me?' Dada was ill at ease.

'What sort of books do you like?' Mrs Banaerjee sounded encouraging.

'Oh, novels . . .' Literature is not his thing. 'No, politics . . . I prefer magazines, to tell the truth . . .' Liar, I thought to myself. You only read thrillers and spy stories.

'Very commendable,' Mr Banerjee said approvingly. 'Too many young men have no interest in what is happening around them.'

The conversation moved onto politics, the role and strength of the Party, the situation in Delhi. My father and Mr Banerjee dominated, with Dada occasionally contributing a remark. Ranjan, however, did not join in – instead he sat back and looked out across the park. It was a pretty sight, the sun setting behind the trees, the cricket players packing to go, the lovers and old folk moving in.

I plucked up the courage. 'Ranjan, aren't you interested in politics?' He looked at me, startled.

'Interested? Oh yes, I am. But not in the parties. They're so much the same . . .' His father and mine had stopped talking and were looking at him, 'But what would I know? I'm just a poor teacher, my preferences only stretch to disliking the Hindu Sangh more than the others. Not that it matters.'

'Of course it does.' Baba wasn't going to let him off so lightly. 'Tell me, why do you so dislike them?'

'Because they stand for everything I do not. Bigotry, a synthetic glorious past, Brahmin ascendancy. At school I was taught that India's strength was "Unity in Diversity" and they want to turn it into a fascist pseudo-theocracy. That's not what India is about, it's not what Hinduism is about either. We have enough problems as it is, without creating new ones, don't you think?'

Baba looked at him with a new respect. 'You are smarter than I thought . . .' He stopped. Ranjan, however, did not seem to mind.

'Ah, that is a façade I maintain. Saves a lot of bother. Now, I know this is not my house but would anyone like some more tea?'

No one did. Mrs Banerjee looked pointedly at her husband and at the dark sky. Taking his cue, Mr Banerjee said it was rather late – Sushma would be waiting. They took their leave.

When they were gone Ma served dinner. The talk was, predictably, all about the Banerjees. Ma was definitely pleased with what she had seen. Baba admitted to being impressed and said that he could see no problems. We all looked at Dada. He was non-committal. If it was all right with everyone else, he had no objections. Ma suggested that it might be an idea if he met the girl and Baba agreed. He said he would phone Mr Banerjee the following day to discuss it.

I was back on Park Street, back for my book. Once again the person who knew about it wasn't available, and would only be back after an hour. I wanted to scream but settled for discreetly clenching my fists. And, as I did I realised someone was watching me. Annoyed and embarrassed, I swung around and glared.

'It is Meena, isn't it?' The voice was familiar. So were the glasses.

'Ranjan!' I reddened. 'Oh, I'm so sorry, I didn't recognise you!'

'Oh, that's all right, I'm used to that sort of thing. Forgettable face, you know.'

'I'm sorry!' He looked so mournful I had to laugh. 'I didn't mean that. It's just that I didn't expect to see you.'

'You come to Park Street and you don't expect to see me?' He raised an eyebrow quizzically. 'Where else would I be?'

'What?' I was confused, then I realised he was pulling my leg. 'I wasn't looking for you, I came for a book.'

'But you don't seem to have one – look out, there's someone trying to get past . . .' He touched my elbow and guided me out of the way.

'No, my book hasn't arrived,' I explained, 'or they don't know if it has. And won't know for at least an hour – the only person who might know is never around when I come.'

'Ah, so that's the story of your life, waiting for something which never arrives. Are you going to stick around here? Or can I take you out for a cup of tea?'

This was amusing. Twice on Park Street, twice an unexpected meeting, twice an offer of tea. What next? Flury's?

'I wouldn't mind a cup – where?' Willing myself not to laugh out loud if he suggested Flury's.

'Flury's?' he said. In spite of myself I smiled. 'Is that funny?' he asked.

'No, no, it isn't,' I regained my composure. 'The last time I was here for this very same book, the same thing happened!'

'The same thing? *I* offered you a cup of tea? I don't remember that . . .' He smiled.

'Not you!' I laughed. 'Someone else! Oh, never mind, come on – are you going to get me the cup of tea or not?'

We walked down to Flury's, stopping once for him to buy a pack of cigarettes. Once again there was a couple of foreigners in Flury's, faded T-shirts and shorts. I pointed them out to Ranjan.

'Shall I go and speak to them? Excuse me, were you here ∴. . when was it?'

'I won't tell you!'

'Oh well, I'll have to go and ask them "Do you do this sort of thing often? My companion has been watching you and she thinks . . ."'

'You will do nothing of the sort!' For a moment I thought he was serious.

'Oh, all right then,' he conceded. 'It's just that it might have been interesting. Especially if they *were* the same people. Maybe they don't like Indian food, or they are pining for the cakes of home . . .'

'Look, just order the tea, please.' But I was smiling.

'Two teas – would you like a cake?' I shook my head. 'Very sensible, makes girls fat. Makes men fat too, come to think of it, so I won't have any either. Are you sure you are Bengali? Am I sure I am? If we are, why aren't we having sweets?' I frowned at him. '. . . I'll get the tea!'

He came back shortly with a pot and sat down.

I took the initiative, 'Well, what are you doing wandering around Park Street?'

'I teach down the road, remember? I'm the St Aloysius's professor, I work in this *para*.'

'What I meant was, why aren't you teaching or something?'

'Ah, teaching – am I supposed to do that?' He grinned. 'No,

amazing though it may be, I don't teach all the time. Sometimes we are allowed out and I prowl the streets . . .'

'You weren't *prowling* the streets,' I pointed out, 'you were in a bookshop.'

'Prowling the streets, prowling bookshops, what's the difference?' He dismissed my objection airily. 'I was browsing. I do that a lot, I was just looking to see if there was anything I had missed.'

'And was there?'

'Oh yes, lots. Only I couldn't afford a single book. Guess I'll have to go down to Free School Street and look at the second-hand bookshops instead. I'm more likely to find something within my budget there. Or in Mullick's on Rash Behari Avenue . . . do you know it?'

'I do live near there, you know.'

'Ah, but you may be a philistine. Maybe you don't read?' He grinned.

'Nonsense. Mullick's used to be one of my favourite shops.'

'It was one of mine too!' he said triumphantly. 'How come I've never seen you there?'

'Maybe because you were there at a different time . . .'

'Come to think of it, I probably was. Different years, probably. You're a bit younger than I am, aren't you?'

'I won't admit any age!' We both laughed. He looked thoughtfully at me.

'Say, what are you doing? I mean, after you finish with the bookshop?'

'After the bookshop? Oh, I don't know. I suppose I'll go home.'

'Come with me to a film instead – I've got two tickets for a film at the British Council.'

I was quite taken aback. Should I say yes? A film would be nice and he did seem very pleasant. I could ring Ma and tell her I'd be late.

'Come on – it'll be great!! I'll have to give the ticket away at the gate otherwise. Tell you what, if you don't mind riding on the back of my scooter, I'll drop you home after it too. So you won't be home too late. Come on, I'm safe – I'm almost family, soon to be your brother-in-law, you know.'

'Oh, OK. I'll have to find a 'phone first though.'

'The bookshop?' he suggested.

'They wouldn't allow us . . .'

'I know, the post office on the corner of Russell Street.'

He was right. The post office had a telephone. Ma was surprised to hear me, I normally announce my plans at the beginning of the day and stick to them so I don't ring often. I didn't tell her who I was going with. I saw no reason to, she didn't ask. I merely said I'd met a friend and was going to the British Council for a film. When she heard I was being dropped home, she raised no objections either. After all, why should she? I'd been abroad on my own and survived.

Ranjan was in the bookshop looking at a book called *The Buddha of Suburbia*.

'It's by the same author, Hanif Kureishi,' he showed me the cover.

'Same author as what?'

'Oh, *My Beautiful Laundrette* – you know, the film we are going to see.'

'Is it? Is he any good?'

'Oh yes, I've read this one. Thoroughly enjoyed it.' He looked at his watch. 'We'd better go. The film starts in forty minutes.'

It is just a short walk so we weren't in a hurry. On the

way he stopped to talk to a lame man who looked like a beggar.

'Who was that?'

'That? Oh, someone I know. He's been here for years. I used to walk past him every day when I was in college and got to talking to him. We're old friends.'

At the British Council he presented the tickets to the guard. A small group of people hung around, looking hopeful. Ranjan shook his head at them ruefully.

'I used to do that, you know.'

'Do what?'

'Hang around the gate if I didn't have a ticket. It's sort of a tradition – if you don't have a ticket, you turn up anyway. Pretty often someone has an extra – as I almost did today – and they give it to someone waiting. Next time you need a ticket someone else might give you one.'

After the film we headed back to the college for Ranjan's scooter.

'Is Britain like that?'

'Like what? Oh, yes, in some ways.'

'Hmm, I've often wondered . . .' He sounded wistful.

'Have you ever been there?'

'What, on my pay?' He laughed. 'Not a chance. Don't think I ever will, either. My salary'll never stretch to that sort of expense!'

'Would you like to go?'

'Like to? Yes, for a visit. Not to stay, I'd miss home too much. Did you? Miss home, I mean, while you were away?'

'I did and I didn't. It was all so new that I usually didn't have time to miss home. It surprised me, I've never been away from home for so long before. Have you?' I turned the question on him.

'Oh, I've been away from home for long periods. I was in boarding school in Darjeeling – a while ago,' he smiled.

'Did you like it?'

'I guess I did. But when I got back to Calcutta I decided I wasn't going to go away for so long ever again. And, as you can see, I haven't.'

'Don't you ever get the urge to travel?'

'Yes, of course. Doesn't everyone at one time or the other? And I've been to Madras, Bombay, that sort of thing. I've seen the Taj Mahal and Mahabalipuram. I think my most realistic travel dream is to go to Kanya Kumari.'

We were near St Aloysius's. 'Would you like to travel abroad? Other than to England, I mean?'

'Oh yes, I would. In fact, I wouldn't mind giving England a miss. I'd like to go to – oh, I don't know, Rome, Paris, Prague . . . but what's the use of dreaming? I'm too lazy to even apply for a scholarship . . . here's my scooter.'

It was an old machine and spluttered geriatrically as he started it. I asked to be dropped off a short distance from home. On the way we didn't say much to each other, scooters aren't built for conversation and, anyway, once I'd put on the spare helmet, I could hear nothing. So the next chance I had to speak to him was when I got off. And all I could think of was the forgotten book.

'Oh no!'

'What is it?' He was all concern.

'I forgot the book! I'll have to go back again . . .'

'Surely that isn't such a problem?'

'Well, I don't like having to go all that way. I didn't even want to go today.'

'Ah, but if you hadn't, you wouldn't have got to see the film. You never know who you'll run into next time.' Without waiting for my answer, he revved the scooter and, with a wave, sped off.

When I entered the house, my parents and brother were just sitting down for dinner.

'How was the film, Meena?' Ma asked.

'Oh, not bad. Interesting in its own way.'

'Who did you go with?' Dada asked.

'A friend. Someone you don't know ... well,' I added under my breath. I don't know why I didn't tell them. I wanted to change the subject. 'Baba, do you have any news?'

'News? Of what?' Baba pretended great interest in his food.

'You know what!' Ma snorted. 'What else has this family been talking about for the last week? Arun's wedding, of course!'

'His may-be-wedding,' I interjected. Ma snorted again.

'Well, I spoke to Mr Banerjee today,' Baba took a sip of water, 'and he is as happy as we are with the way things have gone so far. We both think that it is perhaps time for the two young people,' he smiled at Dada, 'for the two young people to meet. What do you say, Arun?'

'If you want ...'

'No, it's what you want that matters.' Dada inclined his head in acquiescence. 'How about we all go to visit them sometime next week? In fact, how about a week from today. Would that suit everyone?' I had no objections, Ma nodded her agreement. Dada examined his plate carefully and then nodded too.

'Good,' my father was pleased, 'I'll ring Mr Banerjee to confirm after dinner.'

When I went to bed that night, I realised that I was excited not about Dada's meeting Sushma but about visiting the Banerjees myself. This wouldn't do, I told myself sternly. It wouldn't do at all.

When Putul came down for breakfast on Monday his uncle was waiting for him at the table. Putul knew this was not a good omen, it was already well past eight.

'Sailen Kaka!' Putul tried a hearty greeting. 'Good morning – starting late today?' He helped himself to a cup of tea and a slice of toast. His uncle watched him, waiting for him to sit down.

'Good morning, Putul. I was hoping to catch you before I left. What are your plans for the day?'

'Oh, this and that,' said Putul nonchalantly, 'I'm going to do some work on that paper.'

'Ah yes, I nearly forgot. The article. How is it coming along?'

'Pretty well,' Putul lied, 'but it is rather more complicated than I expected . . .'

'You have been working on it for quite a while now, Putul. Over a month,' his uncle said pointedly.

'Oh yes. It isn't easy!' Putul's laugh was forced. He did not like the look on his uncle's face.

'So I see,' Sailen Kaka leaned back in his chair, 'it must be quite something.' Putul realised he had no intention of leaving for work until he'd had his say.

'Well, you know, academic work, Kaka. I have to get it completely right, you know. I can't afford to make a single mistake,' Putul tried to sound convincing.

'Perseverance and an attention to detail are admirable, Putul. As is hard work.'

'Thank you, Kaka – I am working hard.'

136

'Putul,' his uncle leaned across the table, 'I was *not* complimenting you. I was suggesting that perhaps you should put some more effort into . . .'

'Oh, I am, I am,' Putul interrupted hurriedly. He did not care for his uncle's tone.

'Putul, I think you are being deliberately obtuse.' His uncle looked annoyed. 'We – your aunt, the rest of the family and myself – are very glad to have you home. And we appreciate that after such a long spell away, after such a long spell studying, you need a break. But you must also look to your future.'

'Sailen Kaka, I am . . .'

'Not your immediate future, Putul,' his uncle cut him short, 'I hate to be repetitive but someday the company will be yours to run, so it is about time that you started coming in to see how it works, to acclimatise yourself. And, perhaps even to get involved in it. When exactly do you plan to do that?'

'As soon as I finish the paper?' Putul said hopefully.

'I don't think that's such a good idea,' his uncle said sharply.

'You don't?' Putul said almost wistfully.

'No. The sooner the better. In fact, why don't you come in this afternoon?' There was no saying no, Putul realised. This was the end of his vacation.

The visit to the office of Shiva Enterprises was all Putul had hoped it wouldn't be and worse. First he had to run the gauntlet of clerks' desks, each one of whom seemed to remember him from his childhood, and remarked on how he'd grown. When he finally made it to the air-conditioned comfort of his uncle's office he found a welcoming committee of 'senior' management': four men, all his uncle's age. After pleasantries he was treated to a 'quick review of the past year'. Figures, charts, books, ledgers. He hid his yawns and feigned interest. The major task in hand, he was told, was the operation of the new factory, Anglo-India Autospares, the joint-venture with the Stewart firm. It had come on line two months previously but was still not operating at full capacity. Senior Manager Number One announced that there had been some 'teething problems with suppliers'. Number Two pointed out that that might have been precipitated by the cash flow problem – none of the suppliers had been paid. Manager Number Three insisted that even if the supply problem were resolved there would remain the problem of an inexperienced, untrained work force – a full report was needed. Putul might like to 'help coordinate efforts'? He was co-opted in spite of his feeble objections.

The worst came at the end, just as the meeting was drawing to a close, when a message came in from their man in Delhi. Some parts for the new plant had arrived but were held up, something about duties and paperwork. He could not resolve it himself, he needed the signatures, authority and preferably, the presence of someone senior, someone who could impress upon officialdom the importance of the parts. Putul's uncle took it upon himself to fly out, announcing that his nephew would accompany him. It would, he told Putul, be a superb opportunity to get acquainted, not only with the business but with the bureaucracy that surrounded it. Putul tried his best to wriggle out. His reply failed to satisfy his uncle who was, in any case, in no mood to entertain further excuses about the incomplete paper. Try as he might, Putul could not escape.

He was going. His guest, John, his uncle said, could be picked up at the airport and could stay at the house. They wouldn't be away for very long.

He was going. His great John, his uncle said, could he picked up at the airport and could stay at the house. They wouldn't be away for very long.

CHAPTER ELEVEN

❖ ❖ ❖ ❖

Putul rang John to tell him the news.

'So you won't be in Calcutta when I arrive?'

'I'm sorry, John, I won't. But I'll send the driver round to the airport to pick you up.'

'No,' John replied. 'Don't do that.'

'What do you mean?' Putul was surprised.

'Well, I'd like to find my own way around.'

'But, John, you must stay with us. My uncle would very much like to meet you. And it'll be no trouble, my aunt'll be here. She'll look after you. I should be back by the end of the following week.'

'Thanks for the offer, Putul, but I'd rather try travelling around on my own for a bit. I've been thinking about it and I fancy being on my own first. I'll stay in Calcutta for a couple of days and then I'll go to Sonapukur. I'll stop by to see you on my way back. Which should be around the time you return. I don't expect to be spending more than a few days there.'

Putul tried to insist but John would not budge. Putul gave in and agreed, on condition that John contacted them as soon as he got back to Calcutta.

'Well, I must say it is quite unusual,' Sailen Kaka said as he and Putul drove to the airport. 'I was looking forward to meeting John. Especially after his family were so good to you.'

'I stayed with them for just a few days,' Putul pointed out. 'But that's the way John is. Determined. When he gets an idea into his head nothing will change his mind.'

'It's a pity you can't learn from him. Decisiveness is something you could do with.'

Putul ignored the barb.

John had done some homework. An English friend who had been to Calcutta had briefed him.

'There's no bus to the terminal (or there wasn't when I was there) so you'll have to walk across the tarmac – it gets really sticky in summer, the tar melts! It's all a bit shabby inside, and the luggage takes ages to appear on the ancient carousel. Once you're through customs you'll have to force your way through your first crowd. It's not very big by Calcutta standards but it is a lot more physical than you might expect. Beware of the ranks of taxis and the hundred eager hands pulling you to their vehicles – believe me, the bus is the best. It's cheaper and takes you straight to a hotel. Go straight to the tourist bureau at journey's end, it's just to the left of the entrance, opposite the reception desk. They'll be able to direct you to a reasonable hotel. Remember to make it clear that you neither need nor want five-star. Check what the current taxi fares are, by the way, the guide-books are invariably out-of-date and it saves haggling over the price at the other end!

'Take the first couple of days easy. Try to get a feel of Calcutta, get used to the temperature, the food, the traffic, everything. Water – boil your own or stick to the bottled stuff – check the seal carefully, people aren't above refilling them! And if in doubt, stick to tea. If you decide to go off the beaten track, let someone know where you are going.'

John had mentally filed it all away. It was his first trip to India, and he wanted to be both independent and safe. When he stepped out of the plane he was, in spite of all the preparation, taken aback by the dense, warm air. And the terminal – shabby was a description that erred on the side of caution. But he wasn't here for the airport, but to follow the trail of his grandfather. Perhaps his ancestor had once landed right here. He smiled at the thought. It was unlikely, people didn't fly much in those days, did they?

His friend's information had been accurate – he was glad he'd been told to look for the bus. The bus-fare was less than a third that of the taxi. It made him feel he was off to a good start, spending his money wisely as soon as he landed. In the five-star hotel at the end of the bumpy ride, the tourist desk directed him to another hotel a short taxi ride away. There, a wizened old man showed him up to a room that was basic but clean, the sheets on the bed worn but freshly laundered. After a wash, John went down to ask for food. The old man directed him to 'a little restaurant across the road'. John found it without difficulty. A restaurant it was not, but it did offer hot food, and shade from the burning sun. It was, he decided after his second Limca, an ideal place from which to watch the people of the city. There was plenty to see, traders with carts, children going to school, children not going to school, hurried and not-so-hurried office workers, women out shopping, jay-walking gangs of young men, and women, rich, poor – it was quite a sight after the bleak winter streets of Europe.

The next day John explored the area around his hotel. By the time he returned he was quite sure he knew every street and alley in a two mile radius. He was proud of himself too, having found cheap food to keep him going. If he continued to spend money as prudently as he had begun, he would be able to stay for six months or more! His stomach was holding out well. He remembered that he hadn't written his parents, to tell them of his safe arrival. Tomorrow would do. He drifted off to sleep, lulled by the dim blue night light, the shadow of the slowly turning fan on the ceiling, the sounds of the city – a radio playing unfamiliar music, the hoot of an owl, the rumble of motor vehicles and carts, distant dogs barking, a cat-fight (for all the world like a baby being murdered), voices . . .

Choto was trying not to worry. The damn Trekker was not turning a profit – far from it! The more he thought about it, the clearer it became he was digging himself further and further into debt. He shared his fears with Chandu.

'Ai, Choto! Relax, *bhaai* – you can do it,' Chandu reassured him. 'You want the work, no? If you give it up what will you do? Don't worry about the paying now, *bhaai*, worry about it when the time comes. Things will improve, *bhaai*, you are just starting. Give it some time . . .'

At home, Durga was not so sure. She did not hide her double displeasure, displeasure that he had walked out on the job the Sens had arranged, and displeasure that he was beholden to Nawab. If that weren't bad enough, she managed to extract the terms of the 'lease' from him. She could not believe her ears.

'My son is a fool!' she exclaimed. 'A complete idiot! Choto, Choto, can't you see that there is no chance of Nawab losing from this deal and every chance of you doing so? Are you a fool? That man, Nawab, is dragging you down – leave him and his cars alone!'

'Ma, it isn't so bad,' Choto tried to comfort her. 'Things will work out fine. You will see, Ma. NawabDa may seem like a bad man to other people but I am like his own *bhaai*, he will look after me.'

'He may say you are his brother,' his mother retorted, unimpressed, 'but there are those in this world for whom brothers are only to profit from – and that *goonda* of yours, that thug, Nawab, he is one of those, believe me! I have seen his kind too often . . .'

'No, Ma, that is not true, not the way it is at all! If NawabDa wanted to cheat me then he would not have given me time to get myself set up, would he? He would not have taken the risk of never being paid . . .'

'And if you did not make enough, could you *not* pay him?' Durga snapped. Choto stared at her, aghast.

'Not pay NawabDa? No, Ma I could never do that, I could not let him down! He has shown he has faith in me, I cannot fail him, can I?' Durga threw up her hands and stormed out to buy oil for their meal. Choto did not wait for her return. He headed off to his tree, to find Chandu.

'Choto, Choto,' his friend said when he told him the story, 'all mothers are like that, otherwise they wouldn't be mothers, would they? They need something to worry about and maybe they don't want their children to succeed because that way they can always treat them like children, isn't it?' He called for two cups of tea. Choto accepted his gratefully. They sipped the hot sweet tea in silence for a while. Then Chandu spoke, 'Choto, you know you really need to get this car business started properly.'

'Of course, I do,' said Choto, 'but where am I to find customers? And how? I can't go out on the róads and try to pick up people – the police would grab me immediately. And no one will issue a licence for this . . . machine, even if I could afford to pay for one. So what am I to do? I have no idea where to start!'

An idea struck Chandu and he smiled, 'Well, as it happens, I have an idea, a real good one. I know some boys in the Party office and just yesterday they were saying how they needed to get some people and equipment out of the city. I don't know where, but I'm sure they were planning to hire something. It may just be that they will be able to fit it all in the Trekker, hey? And if it is a good distance, then you'll make a decent amount of money, no?'

'Yes,' Choto agreed half-heartedly, 'but why would they choose to travel in my Trekker? They're Party, they have their own people.'

'Not these boys,' Chandu said confidently. 'Believe me, I know them well enough. In fact, since you are such a close friend of mine, I'll go down to the office right now and see if I can't fix something for you . . .' He looked inquiringly at his friend. Choto shrugged. It was worth a try. Chandu gulped down his tea and, promising to return soon, left to talk to the Party boys.

He was not gone for long, getting back before Choto had had a chance to finish a second cup of tea.

'Aii, Choto, you are a lazy one!' he greeted him, beaming broadly, 'You need something and someone else has to go and get it for you, no?' He slapped him on the back.

'So, what happened?' Choto sounded as casual as he could.

'What happened? *Shala*, you can thank your Chandu Uncle. He can do everything. You have a customer – and what a customer, the party, no less! It was so easy, I went in there and sorted it out in seconds. I just walked in and there was Sadan and the others discussing – guess what? – getting some cadre and "equipment" out to Basanpur district in time for some rally. And, just as I expected, they haven't got transport. They're too small – besides, Sadan says what they are doing is nothing to do with Central Office so they aren't getting any help from them. In fact, for some reason they don't want Central Office involved at all, it's all a bit hush-hush. Anyway, there I was, right in time to do everyone a favour: them, you and myself! They get the transport, you get the work and I . . .' He winked at Choto. Choto knew what he wanted. Alcohol. Chandu liked his drink. After all, that's what friends are for, isn't it? as he often said.

'OK, when do I start? Where do I go?' Choto pressed him for details.

'You start now,' his friend replied. 'They want you down at the Party office to discuss everything as soon as possible. So now it's between you and them, nothing to do with me. Except my commission, of course!' Choto nodded and Chandu called for another tea, rubbing his hands in gleeful prospect of alcohol soon to come.

Down at the Party office, Sadan explained the task. Choto was to get him and two other comrades to Sonapukur village, two hundred kilometres away in Basanpur district by Sunday evening. Why? Because on Monday the Hindu Sangh were going to be shipping their cadre out of Sonapukur for a rally across the border in Bihar. Which was why Sadan was going: he had no intention of letting the Hindu Sangh's absence from Sonapukur go unnoticed – there were some 'tasks' he had been meaning to carry out for a while, and this would be a good time for it, he felt. Since they had so much stuff to carry, it would be easier to travel by car. Was Choto willing? Choto was. All he needed to know was that there would be reasonable payment and security – he didn't want to get caught between the Party and the Hindu Sangh. Of course, he *was* a supporter of the Party, but if this village was, as Sadan had suggested, Hindu Sangh, he needed to be sure. Sadan reassured him. It was just that there were a few Hindu Sangh supporters with whom he, Sadan of the Party, had some scores to settle. Political stuff. So he needed to visit in their absence. All Choto had to do was leave Sadan and his team in the village and wait in nearby Basanpur town. Choto agreed, breathing a sigh of relief. It sounded a bit shady but it was work. He didn't want to know what their business in Sonapukur was, he just wanted to be certain that he was going to be safely out of the way if anything cropped up. The price clinched it – it was considerably more generous than what Nawab's contacts had paid.

John breakfasted at the eatery across the road and caught a taxi to the tourist bureau. The woman there was all charm – he wanted to go off the beaten track? That was easily done, but why? After all, there were so many interesting places to see – why, only last week a French television crew had been to . . . he *really* wasn't interested? Well, what sort of thing *was* he interested in? She was sure she could find something – how about going to some beaches? Wildlife sanctuaries? Climbing? Trekking? Historic monuments? Sonapukur, he said, Sonapukur! Where was that? Oh, Basanpur District. Why on earth did he want to go there? Nothing there. Just fields or something. Why not go to Bolpur, to Santiniketan, the university founded by the world-famous poet and Nobel Laureate

Rabindranath Tagore? John shook his head vigorously. No, he didn't want to go to Santiniketan. Where he *did* want to go was Sonapukur, in Basanpur District. How could he get there? There was an organised trip to Santiniketan . . . No? Well, in that case he could take a train to Basanpur, and from there he'd have to find some other transport. Maybe a jeep? There was sure to be one around. The only other thing she could tell him for certain was that there was a dak-bungalow in Sonapukur, but she couldn't book it for him. She could, however, tell him where to go to book it. He took her scribbled instructions, paid for the maps she offered, and went to look for the Railway Booking Office. He queued for a form, filled it in and queued again to submit it. A couple of hours later he had his ticket. He put it away carefully. He was on his way.

The evening of our visit to the Banerjees both Dada and Baba came home a little early to 'freshen up' before going out again. We ate quickly.

The Austin was still in a good mood (it hadn't been in the garage for over a month!) and, since we made the journey without the detours that had slowed us down on our first visit, we arrived promptly. This time the boy recognised us and opened the gate to let us in without challenge. Inside, in the library-living room, Mr and Mrs Banerjee rose to greet us. So did Sushma. In spite of myself, I was a little disappointed. Of Ranjan there was no sign.

After the usual pleasantries, Sushma was sent to make tea.

Settling her sari around her, Ma initiated the conversation proper.

'And how is Sushma?'

'Very well – but nervous, of course!' Mr Banerjee chuckled and rubbed his hands.

'Nervous?' Ma laughed. 'You should see Arun, he has given up talking to anyone . . .'

'Please, Ma!' Dada flushed scarlet.

'Oh but it is true, isn't it, Meena?' Ma continued relentlessly. 'He hasn't said a word to anyone for days – he just goes to work, comes back, has his meals, maybe reads a bit, then off to bed. We hear not a peep out of him!' She smiled affectionately at him.

'Please, Ma!' Dada pleaded, reddening.

'Arun, tell me about your job,' Mr Banerjee took pity on Dada.

'Well, I'm in the production division of a tyre company . . .'

'Tyres, eh? And what did you study at college?'

'Mechanical engineering, actually,' Dada was more comfortable now. 'It isn't as bad as I thought it might be. I got used to it after a while – the company has a good training programme.'

'And do you enjoy it?' Mr Banerjee asked. 'Good prospects?' Aha, I thought, a shrewd question.

'Oh yes, I like it very much. As for the prospects – well, like in every commercial organisation, they are as good as you make them.'

'And are you making them good?' Mr Banerjee chuckled. 'Don't worry, you don't have to answer. I'm sure you are. In fact, your father and your uncle tell me that you are doing well.'

'I suppose so – there is a chance,' Dada broke off abruptly. We all looked at him, puzzled.

'Chance of what?' Baba asked curiously.

'Oh nothing,' Dada said hurriedly, 'I'll tell you later . . .'

'Oh no, do tell us now, Arun – the Banerjees are almost family already,' Ma insisted.

'Well,' he began slowly, 'there is a chance that I might be going to Bombay.'

'Bombay? But why Bombay!' I couldn't help bursting out.

Dada avoided my eye. 'Prospects, that sort of thing. Nothing's definite yet.' I stared at him.

Sushma reappeared with a tray. Tea, biscuits, sweets – I jumped up to help but she had already put it down and had begun to pour.

'Did you hear that, Sushma?' her father asked. 'Arun might be transferred to Bombay.' Did I see Sushma's hand tremble?

'Bombay?' She did have a nice voice. Dark is how I think of it.

'Yes, Bombay,' said her father uneasily.

'Come and sit beside me, dear,' Ma beckoned Sushma over. She shot an inquiring glance at her mother who nodded.

'Tell Arun about your studies, Sushma,' Ma patted her knee encouragingly.

'Oh, there's nothing much to tell.' It was her turn to blush.

'Go on, Sushma, tell them something about it,' her father urged, selecting a biscuit and nibbling it fastidiously.

'Yes, Sushma – I'm sure Arun is very interested,' Baba looked at Dada, 'and even if he isn't, we are.'

'I'm doing an MA in politics. It's . . . it's well, very interesting,' she said.

'Politics? And what is your particular interest?' Baba asked.

'My speciality? The politics of the former Soviet Union. I'm interested in the new constitutions that are being written. Although I don't get to look at that much right now, my MA is more historical. If I get a chance, I'd like to research that for a doctorate.'

'A doctorate?' Ma asked quickly.

'Oh, yes,' Sushma was not the slightest abashed. Talking about her studies seemed to relax her, 'I'd really like to do one but it isn't easy. I'll probably get myself a teaching post first and then, after a few years, try to do a doctorate somewhere.'

'Somewhere?' Ma noticed the vagueness.

Mr Banerjee coughed uneasily. 'Sushma has been toying with the idea of applying to that place in Delhi – what's it called?'

'The New National University, Baba.' Shushma examined her hands.

'Yes, whatever it is called. But it's just an idea, isn't it, Sushma?' A pleading note had crept into his voice.

'Yes, Baba, it's just an idea. I could do it elsewhere, I suppose.' She kept her eyes on her hands.

It all was a bit uncomfortable, like we'd stepped into a family quarrel. To ease the tension I changed the subject, 'Your parents have told us that you sing?'

'Yes, a little. I studied Rabindrasangeet when I was younger,' she sounded grateful for the diversion. 'Though I haven't had much time for it recently.'

'Rabindrasangeet?' Ma pricked up her ears. 'Tell me, Mr Banerjee, have you visited Santiniketan?'

'Have we visited it? Of course, of course,' Mr Banerjee's good humour returned. 'We know it well – my wife's brother teaches there and we often visit him.'

'He teaches there?' Ma's eyes widened. 'Oh, that is nice! What does he teach?'

'English,' Mr Banerjee pursed his lips, 'I have never understood why he chose it.'

'But surely there is nothing wrong with that?' Having been quiet for a while, Baba re-joined the conversation.

'Oh no, not really, I suppose. After all, that's what my younger son does too.'

'You don't approve?' Baba's tone was easy.

'My husband thinks that there are more useful things they could do,' Mrs Banerjee volunteered. 'And I must say I agree with him – at least a little. We hang on to English a bit too much, I think. So it is a bit of a pity that both my brother and Ranjan chose it and not something else.'

'A pity? But surely Ranjan has, at least, a good profession and respect – a professor is not just anyone?' Ma was puzzled.

'Oh, it is a good profession, with respect, if not money. But, as my wife said, I cannot help feeling that he could do something more useful for his country,' Mr Banerjee growled.

'Like your elder son?' Ma said, forgetting.

Mr Banerjee's face darkened. 'My elder son? No, I am disappointed in him. India educates him, he goes abroad and, as soon as he is offered a job there, he takes it and stays away, giving nothing back!'

'But surely he has just taken the opportunities available to him?' Ma blundered on, unable to extricate herself.

'Taken the opportunities, yes. But what of it? Where will this country be if everyone who gets a chance leaves? All our skilled people are going abroad,' Mr Banerjee broke off as his wife put a soothing hand on his arm.

'Would anyone like more tea?' she said sweetly. Grateful for the interruption I held out my cup. She poured. An uneasy silence reigned.

'I bumped into Ranjan the other day,' I began and stopped. Why did I say that? Here of all places!

'You did?' Ma looked at me, astonished. 'You never told us?'

'Oh, it was on Park Street, when I went to get the book. I didn't get it, you know, they still haven't got it in,' I mumbled desperately. But Ma had remembered something else.

'Oh yes, he teaches around there – St Aloysius's, isn't it?'

'Yes, he does,' Sushma confirmed.

'It's quite good, isn't it? My nephew,' she was referring to Baba's sister's son actually, 'did his high school there. Where is Ranjan, by the way?'

'Ranjan?' Mrs Banerjee poured her husband another cup of tea and helped herself to a biscuit, 'he's busy with something in the college. Debating society or something?'

'Not the debating society, Ma,' Sushma corrected her, 'He gave that up when he finished college. It's the drama society these days.'

'Drama society?' Ma took a biscuit from the plate Mrs Banerjee extended to her.

'My son finds these things to interest him. One year it's debating, the next it's drama. He flits about, like a gadfly. Or is it a butterfly? Sushma used to be quite active in the university music society – weren't you?'

'Yes, Baba,' she said quietly. 'But that was years ago, when I was still in first year.'

'Was it that long ago?'

The conversation meandered on. Dada, I noticed, hardly said anything, merely agreeing or making appropriate noises. Sushma, on the other hand, did involve herself a bit, although mainly to change the subject when it turned to her. I myself lay low, trying not to think about Ranjan. Instead I thought about Dada. What if he went to Bombay? The house would seem empty without him, he's always been around. And what of Sushma? Would she go to Bombay too? Or would she stay in Calcutta to finish her studies? If she did, would she stay with her parents or with us? It would be odd to have another woman in the house – Ma and Durga would probably welcome it. The more I thought about it, the more I liked the idea. If she stayed with us, her family would certainly come to visit. That made me think of Ranjan again. Fortunately, my parents were ready to go.

CHAPTER TWELVE

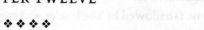

They set off on Sunday morning. Choto and Sadan in front and two others in the back. Their first stop was an alley behind Sealdah Station. Choto honked his way down, scattering the early-morning traders and shoppers, before drawing up, as directed, in front of a Ration shop. The Party boys disappeared into it, returning a short while later with two coolies who loaded a tea chest and some smaller boxes into the back of the vehicle. These they covered with old gunny sacks and tarpaulin. When they set off again, Choto was conscious of the Trekker lurching more than usual. The extra load, he guessed. Fortunately his passengers appeared to think it normal. He whistled softly as he dodged through the crowded streets. Half an hour later the crowds eased a bit. They were outside the city. Choto hadn't been so far afield for years. It smelled unusual too. Sort of burning. Suddenly he realised the smell was coming from the Trekker! Hiding his concern, he nonchalantly put his foot down on the brake pedal.

'*Baap-re-baap*!' his mild exclamation as the car swerved, narrowly missing a lamp-post before coming to a halt, was overshadowed by the louder and more colourful phrases of his companions.

'What's going on?!' Sadan demanded, shaken and angry.

'I don't know. Nothing!' Choto said hurriedly. He didn't want Sadan to see he was worried. 'I need to check the tyres.'

'If you need to check the tyres, why not stop normally?' Sadan raged, 'You could have killed us!'

'*Arré*, I'm on board too, aren't I?' Choto replied, as coolly as he could. 'Do I look like someone who wants to die? It was just a little rough, happens sometimes. Don't worry, it won't happen again!' He hoped he was right. They got out. Sadan grumbled as he watched Choto poke the tyres, but soon gave up and went to join his comrades who'd found a tea-stall. A swarm of children descended, Choto tried to disperse them but no sooner was his back turned, than they pressed in again. He gave up and opened the bonnet. He had no idea what was wrong! He poked harder. Half-an-hour passed, he was no closer to enlightenment than when he had started. One of the watching urchins offered to fetch a mechanic. Announcing, in case Sadan was listening, that he had done all he could he agreed and the child raced off.

Ten minutes later the mechanic rode up on a battered bicycle. He was a slim young man, about the same age as Choto but with an air of experience and world-weariness that Choto was instantly envious of. The expert peered at the engine, probing it with an oil-stained finger and a rag. He sucked his teeth, pursed his lips, shook his head, cleaned his ear with a matchstick. Inspiration came – he spread a cloth on the ground and wriggled underneath to spend a quarter of an hour muttering darkly to himself. Choto was uncomfortable, he could feel Sadan's eyes, dissatisfied, disapproving, boring into his back. The mechanic surfaced and scratched his head.

'How long have you had this vehicle?' Choto noticed that his eyes were slightly bloodshot. Tiredness? Alcohol?

'Oh, a week, a month,' Choto replied vaguely. The other's eyes widened in surprise.

'You *bought* this a month ago? How much?'

'Oh, no, I didn't buy it – I'm the driver.' Without meaning to he glanced towards the group at the tea-stall, hoping they could not hear. His interrogator followed his eyes and mis-understood.

'One of them's the *malik*? He owns this? Bought it recently or had it a while?'

'No, the owner's not here,' Choto corrected him, 'it belongs to someone else. He's had it for a while, I'm not sure exactly how long . . .'

The mechanic lost interest in the question of ownership. 'When was it last serviced?'

'I . . . I had a tyre changed about a week ago,' Choto replied, adding hurriedly, 'I don't know. I'm just the driver.' It stung to have to repeat it, but it would have hurt even more to admit he had not had anyone check the vehicle. Perhaps he should have – but, even if he had thought of it, how could he have afforded to pay someone to do it?

'Well, it looks like there's plenty wrong with it. It's in bad shape. Very bad shape. You've been lucky for – oh, months, by the look of it.' He spat blood-red *paan* in the Trekker's direction. 'You're lucky to be alive – though perhaps this thing can't go fast enough for anything to make a difference!' he smirked. Choto's ears burned but he said nothing.

'You need to get it patched up at least,' the mechanic continued. 'If you want, I can send someone over, but it'll take a couple of hours. Got to get the parts, you know. Not easy out here,' he gestured at the roadside stalls. Choto shrugged. What could he say? He agreed to the repairs and went over to explain to his passengers. Sadan was not pleased. He swore fluently. Then, when he calmed down, he did some calculations. Even with a couple of hours' delay, they could be at the village around eight. After dark. Perhaps just as well, he said, it would probably be quieter. Choto breathed more easily.

The mechanic returned an hour later, by which time Choto had begun to worry that he was running out of nerve-calming *bidis*. The mechanic was accompanied by a small boy this time. A child of no more than ten who rode a bicycle too large for him, so that each foot lost touch with its respective pedal once in every revolution. The pair dismounted, and leaned their bicycles against the Trekker. Choto resisted the urge to object as he would normally have done. This was not the time to worry about the paintwork. Far more important was getting back on the road. They tut-tutted around the car, the younger boy imitating the mannerisms of his mentor before disappearing under the vehicle for a while, resurfacing to confirm the earlier findings. Then he wobbled off on his oversize cycle. Half an hour passed. The mechanic squatted silently in the shade of the Trekker while Choto paced.

The boy returned and slipped under the car again, this time more purposefully. He banged and thumped for a while, occasionally calling out for another tool. After a while he resurfaced and reported to his boss. The latter listened carefully and approached Choto. The Trekker, he declared, with much shaking of his head, was ready to leave. Choto broached the sensitive subject of price. How much for parts? The boy shuffled and looked at his toes. The mechanic coughed. Parts are expensive. Yes, but how much?

'You know how important it is to use the right parts?'

'Yes, yes! Just tell me how much!' Choto said impatiently.

'Well, they're new parts,' the mechanic picked his nails. 'From a good company, they cost money.'

'Yes?' Choto could barely restrain himself.

'One hundred and fifty rupees.'

They haggled, they bargained. Eventually they settled on a total price of one hundred and twenty. Choto would have dearly loved to bargain further but Sadan was getting restive. Besides, he'd had to ask for an advance to pay for it, an advance provided with such bad grace that Choto felt ashamed, no better than a beggar.

At least they were on the road again, dodging in and out among the giant lorries which hurtled down the highway, oblivious of potholes. The Trekker, Choto realised ruefully, commanded no such respect – to clear even a bullock cart he had to drive round it, or lean on his horn for ages. But he made up for some of the lost time and got the Party cadre to their destination at around ten. Sadan suggested he stayed with them, but Choto was determined. Sadan shrugged. If that was what he wanted. Choto climbed back into the Trekker and drove down the dark roads to the town they had passed a short while earlier. He found a quiet spot near the railway station, parked and settled down in the back. He was too tired to be hungry, too tired to be troubled by the unfamiliar quiet of a small railhead. He fell asleep almost instantly.

John was wakened by the plaintive bleeping of his alarm.

Monday morning. Sleepy-eyed, he splashed water over his face, ignoring his already rusting razor. He rubbed his hand over the rough stubble, wondered briefly whether to keep the beard when it grew. A car horn sounded outside and, minutes later, the manager knocked on the door. His taxi was waiting. John shouldered his rucksack, stuffing the last of his belongings into the side pocket. Under his T-shirt, his money-belt pressed reassuringly against his stomach. A quick glance around the room revealed no forgotten items. He was ready.

In the mayhem of the station he found the departures board. But no mention of his train. He panicked briefly, then it flickered and new trains and times appeared. There it was. Platform 6. He plunged into the mass of humanity and was borne along its tide, first one way then the other. Inch by inch he fought his way to the platform but once there found the train's doors locked. A man in uniform appeared, slapping lists of names and unlocking doors. John followed him from carriage to carriage, from list to list, until he found the one that bore his name.

Entering the carriage wasn't easy. His rucksack, usually so convenient, took on a life of its own, restraining him at every step. Eventually he made it to the seat that matched the number against his name, only to find it was occupied by no fewer than three people. He waved his ticket at them and they laughed and got up – then, to his surprise, helped him stow his bag overhead. In spite of their friendliness he was relieved to see them disembark when the whistle sounded.

The train had left 'just half an hour late!' exclaimed one of the other occupants of the carriage. In English. John eyed him surreptitiously. A young man, no doubt, trying to impress the other passengers. His companions, maybe? Another man and two women of similar age. The comments in English continued, not addressed directly to John, but the choice of language, and quick glances he cast, gave him away as surely as if he had said 'excuse me, can I talk to you?'. John smiled quietly to himself, watching the countryside roll past the iron-bars of the window. Finally the English-speaker plucked up courage to tap him on the shoulder.

'Where you go?'

'To Sonapukur.'

'You like our country?'

'Very much. It is very interesting.'

'But it is hot for you, no?'

'Er, I suppose so . . .'

'Food also?'

'Hot, you mean? Yes, but I like it that way.'

His interrogator translated this to the other passengers who nodded vigorously. One of them whispered in the English-speaker's ear.

'Why are you going to Sonapukur? To the mission?'

'Mission? No no, family reasons. My grandfather used to live there.' The translation was greeted with exclamations and some laughter.

'How will you get to Sonapukur?' demanded the English-speaker.

'Hire a jeep. The tourist office told me I could.'

His companion shook his head. 'Very difficult, cost much money!'

'I'll have to see.'

'I am going to Sonapukur, too. I can arrange one for you. You want me to help?'

'Maybe,' John said warily.

'Very good price. Only two hundred rupees.'

'No thanks!'

'Why?'

'It should cost around a hundred,' John said firmly even though he had no real idea.

The translation caused much mirth among the group.

'You are my friend, no? I can get you jeep for one hundred and seventy-five.'

'Forget it!!'

They bargained cheerfully, John haggling as best he could. Finally they settled for one hundred and fifty. John wasn't sure it was the best deal but he felt he could afford it – unless he had to hire jeeps every day. The entire compartment began a game of translating and learning new words. John enjoyed it, they were pleasant company.

They arrived in the late afternoon, two hours late on a three-hour journey. Just before they stopped John gave his new friend a fifty rupee advance to secure the jeep – and then, as soon as they were out of the carriage, he lost sight of him. Slightly dazed by the crush he was pushed and carried along to the exit. Offers of rickshaws came from all sides. John brushed them away and clung to the gate to maintain his position in the flood. He scanned the crowd desperately. But there was no sign of his new friend. Annoyed, he found the station-master's office. The station-master, a fat, sour-looking, middle-aged man with a pencil moustache and red *paan*-stained teeth listened to his tale and shrugged his shoulders.

'What you want from me?'

'Just help to find this man,' John said testily. What did he think?

The station-master snorted and returned to his paper. His clerk, aping his superior, snorted too. John persisted and eventually the junior official got up and led him outside.

'You see your man here?'

'No, that's the whole point . . .'

'You see many men here, no?'

'Yes?'

'But not your man. Your man has gone, just like that!' The clerk looked triumphant. John groaned. What a fool he had been! He shouldered his rucksack and hurried away from the grinning clerk.

Outside the station the road was a mad flow of gaily decorated vehicles, vans, jeeps, cars, trucks, all heading one way. And every one full of people, young men. The only attempt at order was the loud but ineffective attempts of groups of youths who swaggered around, shouting and pushing all who were in their way. Not wanting to fight his way through them, John stopped. Something tugged at his sleeve. He shook it off.

'Sahib!' Sure it would be another tout, he did not even look round.

'Sahib!!' The voice was insistent. John turned.

'You?' His companion from the train!

'Yes, it is me – you were expecting someone else? Come, sahib, I have found you a jeep!'

'But I thought you had . . .' John stopped. It would be churlish to tell him that he had, until a minute before, written him off as a thief.

'Sahib, I could find no jeep. Not for that price today, not for any money. It is very busy, very busy – but I gave you my word, so I looked for one and – see!' He waved proudly in the direction of a battered . . . what was it? Never in his life had John seen anything like it. It vaguely resembled a jeep – but what on earth had they done to it? Surely he couldn't be serious? His new friend was dragging him towards it. This was their transport!

'Sahib, why did you leave the station?' the procurer chattered on. 'I was coming for you. But because of this rally every jeep is going the other way and no one wants to go to anywhere else unless you pay lots, lots of rupees. But I promised you, so I came outside to look and then I found this man. He is not from here, he is from Calcutta. He is here on work – he does not tell me what – and he is taking us to Sonapukur. For just one hundred fifty. So I was coming back for you. But you were leaving! Why?'

'I didn't think you . . .' John mumbled.

'Sahib!' his companion stared at him. 'You thought I took your money and ran away! You think I am a thief! Sahib, I may be many things, I may be good-for-nothing but I am not a thief!' John flushed, he had not intended offence. Suddenly his companion began to laugh, a chuckle that grew into a full-throated roar.

'Sahib, sahib, now I understand! I went away with your money so you thought I was a thief. Oh Sahib, I work at the mission, I am not a thief. But now I see why you thought I am a thief. Perhaps I am a fool – I should have told you where I am going. Or maybe I should not have come back,' he spluttered. Relieved, John smiled too.

When their merriment had passed, his guide made the introductions. The driver was Choto, from Calcutta. He was Francis, compounder at the Mission hospital on the Sonapukur Road. Would John mind him giving him a lift? Of course not. Perhaps he could stop at the mission on his way back? Yes, of course, he would be welcome, and he, Francis, would be most honoured if he did stop by.

As they bounced along the road Francis pointed out sights that he thought would interest John: a herd of buffalo wallowing in a pond, a heron, a bullock cart. John tried to respond but found it difficult, he was too busy concentrating on trying to stay on board. Francis did not notice, he continued his patter. There was a village and there a big house. His friend lived there, that was the house of a doctor. John grunted agreement, hanging on for dear life while the huge people-carriers bore down on them, swerving away only at the last minute. One thing he did notice, however, was that all of the vehicles were decked out in banners. Some showed a trident with the words 'Hindu Sangh' and others advertised 'Ganguly Electronics'. The passengers rent the air with loud shouts. John asked Francis for an explanation. Francis dismissed them as 'hooligans'.

'Come on, Francis, what are they saying?' John pressed him.

'It is all politics, sahib. I do not understand politics.' He tried to change the subject, 'Look, a kingfisher!'

'But even if it is politics, you must understand,' John insisted.

Francis gave in, 'Sahib, they are shouting praises of their heathen gods and politicians . . .'

'And the banners?' John was pleased he was getting some information, 'What's the trident?'

'Trident? No, no, they call it a *trishul*,' Francis replied.

'*Trishul*? What is it?'

'Oh, it is a symbol of one of their gods.'

'Which one?' John persisted.

'Shiva.' Francis would not look at him.

'And what is he the god of?'

'Destroyer of the world . . . look!' A shout of relief almost. 'The mission! My home! Stop, driver, stop!

Choto didn't like conversations with strangers, especially with a couple as odd as this. A weedy Christian and a grubby looking foreigner. The Christian hadn't said anything about his companion being a foreigner. If he had, Choto would have insisted on a higher fee. After all, these foreigners could afford it – especially one who looked so disparagingly at his vehicle. So what if it was a decrepit pile of junk? The foreigner didn't have a choice, did he? thought Choto angrily. His brief stay in the town had convinced him that his was the only vehicle to be had – the Hindu Sangh had commandeered or hired all the rest. Reassured by the thought, Choto straightened his back and drove more confidently. Even if his was the most battered car on the road he wasn't going to let anyone think he couldn't handle it. They jolted along, occasionally even able to challenge some of the other users of the road, the bicycles, the stupid mopeds, the damn bullock carts.

The Christian called to him to stop so he pulled over and let him out in front of a big gate. Mission Hospital or something, he couldn't read too well. With just one passenger on board, there was no point hanging around, Choto decided. Might as well get it over with. He kicked the accelerator and stole a backwards glance. The foreigner was clutching the frame. Good, he smiled to himself. The white man was scared. As he turned to face forward again he saw what was transfixing the European. Another truck heading straight towards them. Bloody fool! He leaned on the horn, first a single blast, then two longer ones. The truck and its cheering human cargo did not change direction. Choto held out as long as he could. Then his nerve failed him, the other vehicle was way too big. He wrenched the wheel sideways. The car hit the side of the road and, with a sickening lurch, careered down the embankment. He stamped down on the brake pedal. No response. His passenger was being tossed about in the back, falling towards him . . . slammed against the wheel by the heavy body, Choto tried to turn the wheel again . . . in the split second before the car hit the tree he thought of his mother, Nawab, Gowri, Sadan, the Party boys . . . his neck snapped before the petrol tank exploded.

CHAPTER THIRTEEN

Dhiren's day started early, much earlier than he had
intended. He woke in darkness to the sound of
someone banging on the door of his small Calcutta
flat. He groaned and rubbed his eyes. Groping for his watch, he
saw by the light of a stray moonbeam that it was two o'clock.
He rolled out of bed, tightened his *lungi* around him, and
staggered, sleep-drunk, to the front door. He swore loudly as
he tripped over a chair. The banging stopped for an instant
then began again with renewed vigour. Whoever was outside
was taking no chances.

'stop it! i'm coming!' The banging ceased and did not
start again. Dhiren stood at the door, hand on the big wooden
bar across it, about to raise it. Belatedly, caution surfaced and
he paused: 'Who's there?' he asked.

'It is I!' The reply was quick but polite.

'What kind of a damn fool answer is that?' he snorted his disgust. 'Who the hell is "I"? Have you got a name?'

'Sorry, Ghosh Babu.' The voice was apologetic, 'It is I, Ranjan Das – Inspector Das, sir.' Inspector Das? His Sonapukur inspector? What the hell was he doing in Calcutta, rousing the dead at this time of night? He had left him with strict orders not to leave his post. Dhiren lifted the bar, placed it carefully out of the way and undid the latch to reveal Das on the doorstep, in full though slightly rumpled uniform. He looked worried. Dhiren glared at him. 'This had better be important, Das.'

'Oh, it is, sir. Very important, sir. May I come in, sir? If you don't mind, of course, sir?'

'Mind?' Dhiren looked at him blankly for a minute. 'Oh no, come in, come in,' he switched on the light and waved him inside. Das stepped in but remained standing by the door.

'I'm afraid, sir, it's very important, sir,' he said. 'You'd better get dressed and come with me, sir.'

'Come with you? What is this? A coup?' Dhiren's voice rose derisively. He'd never heard such nonsense.

'No sir. Of course not, sir. But it is very serious, sir,' Das insisted. 'There's been an accident, sir.'

'An accident? Where?'

'On the Sonapukur road, sir. I think you ought to come immediately, sir.'

'Look, Das, calm down and tell me why I need to be there. You're a policeman, too, damnit, and I'm off-duty!'

'Sorry, sir. Not really, sir. Off-duty, that is, sir. I shall explain, sir – a Trekker went off the Sonapukur road, sir, while the rally vehicles were passing, sir. It wasn't a rally vehicle, sir, it was going in the opposite direction. But the occupants, sir, both were killed, sir. One unidentified, believed to be from Calcutta, sir, and may have some link with the Party, but nothing significant, sir. That was the driver, sir. And the passenger, sir. That's more serious, sir. A foreigner, sir. Male, Britisher, sir.'

'British? An Englishman? On the Sonapukur road? What the hell was he doing there?'

'Going to Sonapukur, sir,' replied Das.

'Don't be so bloody literal, Das,' Dhiren groaned. 'Where else could he go on the Sonapukur road? Tell me what happened. And where the hell were you? I left you in charge!'

'I was keeping an eye on things in Basanpur town, sir. I didn't expect any trouble up the road, sir.'

'Didn't expect trouble! You incompetent imbecile!' Dhiren realised he would have to sort things out himself, 'Wait for me here – no, outside! You've got transport?' A thought struck him, 'And the superintendent, does he know?'

'Yes, sir. To both questions, sir. I have a jeep waiting downstairs, sir, and the superintendent knows, sir. I telephoned him immediately, sir.'

'You did what?' Dhiren swung round in the doorway of his bedroom. 'You telephoned the superintendent! Why? Are you mad? Why didn't you consult me first?'

'I tried, sir. But you don't have a 'phone here, sir.' That was true – Dhiren had been meaning to sort it out but hadn't got round to it.

'So I called the superintendent, sir,' Das continued. 'He told me to tell you to get in touch as soon as you got back, sir. If you will pardon my saying so, sir, he did not sound pleased to hear that you were out of the station, sir.'

'Well, of course he bloody wasn't! You can hardly expect

him to be thrilled. Damn, damn and double damn! Get out!'
Das stepped out, closing the door behind him. Dhiren hurried
off to dress. He found a recently-pressed unifrom in the
almirah, donned it, splashed water on his face and ran down
the stairs, still rubbing his eyes. Das was waiting in the jeep.
They accelerated down the empty streets. There was a long
drive ahead.

When I went into the bookshop on Tuesday, I was glad to find
that the person I needed was in for once. But she had bad news.
She was very apologetic – she had been in touch with the
suppliers, even with the publishers, but it appeared there
wasn't a single copy of the book to be had, for love or money,
in the entire Eastern region. If I wanted she could try the other
regions or try to order it from abroad? No, it wasn't that
important, I said, secretly thinking I should try College Street.
They were better at finding things – only it is such a pain
battling one's way down it. I sighed and turned to see the face I
half-expected.

'Ranjan!'

'Who else?' Grinning from ear to ear. 'At least this time you
recognised me. Maybe I'm not so forgettable, after all. You are
already doing wonders to my ego, Meena!'

'What are you doing here?' I could think of nothing else to
say.

'The same as always,' he said archly. 'Browsing for books I
cannot afford, that sort of thing. Any luck?'

'Luck? What with?'

'Your book. Your reason for venturing down into the wilds
of Park Street.'

'Oh, that book! No, it seems I'll have to look somewhere
else.' It was on the tip of my tongue to say College Street but I

thought better of it – out of the corner of my eye, I could see the assistant eavesdropping unashamedly.

Interpreting my concern correctly, Ranjan steered me towards the door, 'Shall we go somewhere else?' Out on the street he said, 'A cup of tea?'

'Not Flury's, please!' I couldn't help smiling.

'No, not Flury's. I can't afford to make a habit of it. How about Sangan?' A small place on Russell Street. 'It's quite nice, they've put little tables out on the lawn and there's a bookshop attached – well, in the same compound, at least.'

I didn't have anything else to do so I agreed. We crossed the busy road and headed down Russell Street.

'Now that was a good guess, wasn't it?' Ranjan said chattily.

'What was?' I feigned innocence.

'That you would come to the bookshop in the afternoon today,' he pushed his glasses up his nose.

'You mean you were waiting for me?'

'Don't say it like that. It sounds predatory, like I was waiting to pounce,' he complained.

'I didn't mean that . . .' I gave up. He laughed.

'Well, I suppose it was a bit of luck too. I couldn't have come earlier, anyway, since I was teaching. Very depressing, Hardy. Then I said to myself, well, why not? She might be there, and if she isn't, you can read a book instead.'

I ignored the first part. 'Read a book? How do you manage that?'

'Oh, I hide in a corner. Or used to when I was a kid. Sometimes they caught me and threw me out, especially one grumpy old fellow. I'd slink off, not to be seen again – for a day or two. Then I'd be back, hoping they'd forgotten. Which I don't think they had, but they never let on. It was cheaper than buying books, anyway.'

'And you still do it?' I was amused at the idea of this college professor skulking furtively in a corner, book in hand.

'No, I'm too big to hide anymore,' he said sadly, 'but I do often read a short story or an essay while I'm there. I read fast so they don't notice.'

We were at the gate – both the bookshop and the teashop-cum-snackbar are behind a very ordinary-looking gate, the big metal sort which swings open to let a car through and has a sort of cat-flap for people. This gate was, unlike most others, wide open to attract customers. I knew it fairly well, the bookshop-cum-snackbar is a quiet haven that I have escaped to more than once when waiting for appointments in the area.

Ranjan led the way.

'How about something savoury? A samosa or something?' He studied the menu. 'They do *dosas*, too.'

'A samosa would be nice. No *dosas*, they're too filling.'

'Good idea. I never have a *dosa* outside a South Indian place, anyway. No, that's not true, I do, but only rarely. But, enough of my eating habits – what'll you have to drink? Tea or a cold drink?'

'Tea, please.' He beckoned a waiter over and ordered tea and samosas.

'Nice place, isn't it?' He looked at me expectantly.

'Oh, it's all right,' I agreed. 'I don't go out of my way to come here, but if I am around it is very handy.'

'It's different for me,' he replied, thoughtfully, 'I come here quite often, whenever I'm not lurking in Park Street book-shops. The problem is my students are beginning to discover it too – don't look now, but that fellow over there, with the big nose and glasses, wearing a *khadi kurta* and jeans, he's one of mine. Keeps throwing what he thinks are surreptitious glances in my direction!'

I looked, quickly. The boy, who was staring at us quite openly, blushed and averted his eyes quickly.

'Now you've gone and ruined it,' said Ranjan ruefully.

'Ruined it?'

'Ruined his fun and my reputation. To say nothing of yours.'

'What do you mean?' The tea and samosas arrived. Ranjan bit into one and puffed loudly.

'Ouch. Watch out, these things are hot!'

'What do you mean "ruined your reputation and mine"?' I repeated.

'Well, it'll be all over the college in about ten minutes. I think the students use telepathy. "Ranjan Banerjee, professor of English, seen sharing samosas with unknown and as yet unidentified female." Not that you will remain unidentified for long if they can help it. And then your reputation will be mud, too. "Meena Sen seen breaking bread with penniless professor." I can see it all, I can see it all.' He shook his head in mock dismay. I had to laugh.

'Are they really like that?'

'Oh no, they're not, they're a lot worse. Those that feel they can will try to pump me and anyone else they think might know for information. Weren't you like that? I certainly was!'

'Yes, I did that too,' I admitted. 'Won't do you any harm though, will it?'

'Me? No, none. I may lose some of my female fans but that's about it. Not that I have many to lose!' I laughed too.

'Come on, have a samosa,' he held out the plate. I took one and bit it cautiously. It was hot – both in temperature and spice.

'It's funny, you know,' he said, 'when I was in boarding school we were desperate for female company and now, faced with roomfuls of girls, I can't wait to get away!'

'Did you like it?'

'Being without any girls around? Not really, though since we didn't know any we weren't too sure . . .'

'I meant boarding school.'

'Yes and no. I remember being very lonely there at first. I cried into my pillow. Of course, I never told anyone and no one ever asked. I got used to it after a while and enjoyed myself but it must have been terrible for my mother. Not seeing her sons for months on end and them growing further and further away from her,' he paused, 'though I don't suppose it's that different for day-scholars in some ways. The moment boys reach a certain age they try to run away from their families.'

I didn't know whether to agree. It would've been disloyal to Dada to say 'yes', even though I knew he had been through such a phase. I pursued the original subject instead. 'And what did you like about it?'

'The mountains and the stars, most of all. You know how on a clear new-moon night you can see lots of stars?' I nodded. 'And have you noticed how many more you can see when you're outside the city?' I nodded again, wanting him to continue. 'Well, in Darjeeling on the rare occasions we had cloudless nights, the sky absolutely teemed with them. And there were shooting stars galore too – sometimes it looked like a shooting gallery. No, not really,' he hastily corrected himself, 'not that many, but there were plenty even at full moon. For a poor little city kid from the plains like myself, it was a revelation. I felt that I could almost reach out and touch them. And the sounds of the night! After lights out, I would lie in my bed and listen to them. Not just the crickets and dogs but the jackals or whatever they were, the owls and those strange thumps and grunts that always seemed to be around. Sometimes I used to scare myself so much, imagining that they were bears, even though I knew well there were none left in the area, I couldn't sleep!' He laughed at the memory.

'You said the mountains too?'

'Oh yes, the mountains. Kanchenjunga suspended above the clouds. We didn't see it often, since we lived literally in the clouds, but every now and then it would clear up and there it would be. No wonder some people consider it holy. Everest isn't a touch on it. Some day I'll go back. Don't think I could live there, though,' he suddenly became practical, 'I'm too much a city person now, but I'd love to spend time just looking at that beautiful mountain again.'

He sipped his tea. 'Now, I've told you lots about myself, it's your turn.'

I shook my head resolutely. 'My childhood wasn't that interesting.'

'Go on, tell me something,' he pleaded, 'if not about your childhood, how about your travels?'

'I'll tell you about my last day in Scotland – will that do?'

'Just the last day?' He seemed disappointed. Then he brightened up, 'OK, we'll start with that, then some other time you can tell me more.'

Would there be another time? I didn't know for sure but I hoped so. 'It's a deal.' He leaned back in his chair and I reached into my bag for my notebook. His eyes widened when I pulled it out but he said nothing.

'The last week in Glasgow – which was the last stop on my travels – was desperately cold. The city froze with a vengeance. The light dusting of snow first crystallised, then melted just enough to freeze again into sheet ice. Stretches that had seemed mere inclines before became hills I had to ascend painfully, hauling myself up inch by inch along the railings.

Every morning and evening I turned on the radio and listened to the weather forecast, and after a short spell – probably only a day – of snow-inspired wonder, my heart sank with every falling degree Celsius. Nothing had prepared me for it, nothing I had read, nothing I had been told. It was a winter to remember Europe by! The morning I left the cold water pipes did their worst and solidified,' I broke off and added, 'you know, while I waited for bowls of boiling water from the hot water tap to cool so that I could brush my teeth, I was blowing steam, and half-expecting it to freeze!'

I wetted my throat with tea and returned to my notes, 'When I left the house, the icy streets hampered my every step, laden as I was with bags and hampered by three layers of clothes. The Underground itself billowed as though aflame, but it was only warm air encountering the Arctic cold. Fortunately, the trains were unaffected and for the first time in my life, probably, I was grateful for being crushed against so many other human beings. A Calcuttan liking being squashed! Can you imagine that? The smell of other bodies, which I normally find so unpleasant, became a welcome indicator of life, that my senses continued to function,' I paused and looked at my companion. He nodded encouragingly. I continued.

'At the airport lounge I had to sit on my hands to warm them. But the heating was good and they soon returned to normal. In fact, after I'd had a coffee I had to retreat to the wash-room to shed some of my extra layers. That relief was, however, short lived, the interminable wait at Heathrow returned numbness to my limbs – this time caused by the sheer fatigue of waiting in a sterile lounge surrounded by deadened or anxious adults and over-excited children. (At what stage in life does one cease to perceive an airport as an adventure?) Some of my fellow passengers dozed warily, starting at every announcement and casting worried looks at their watches or at the flickering departure lists on screens above our heads. But it was so cold outside that the airport was enveloped in thick fog, and no plane could land or take off. Five hours late, they called my flight, and, after the long flight, you can imagine my relief when I stepped out of the customs area and saw my brother waiting patiently for me!'

I stopped, embarrassed by my own words. Ranjan nodded slowly. 'Meena, that was wonderfully interesting. You should polish it up a bit and, hey presto, you'll have an essay worthy of publication . . . some day!' He grinned.

I blushed. 'It's just something I've been scribbling, that's all!' I looked at his watch. Five o'clock! Oh no, I had to run. I made excuses, Ranjan tried to offer me a lift but I declined. As we parted at the entrance to the Metro, he called after me.

'I'm usually in that bookshop on Wednesday afternoons . . .' I didn't hear the rest, it was lost in the bustle of the crowd that bore down on me.

At the family gathering on the verandah that evening our first topic of conversation was the fiasco of Durga's son's visit to the Biswas office, news of which had reached us. Ma was annoyed (fortunately, Durga was out of earshot) and announced that she had expected no better from him. He was, in her opinion, a lazy layabout, an unworthy son. And if she, Ma, had her way, he would be given a good hiding and sent to work in a factory. I smiled at this – Ma likes to make sweeping statements that conceal the fact that she is so gentle that she rarely even raises her voice. Baba was more conciliatory, saying he would have liked to hear the young man's story from his own mouth but, as that seemed unlikely, he felt he could not recommend him for any other positions. I felt rather sorry for the young man but said nothing, being more interested in what I had overheard Baba tell Ma when he came in – that he had spoken to the Banerjees again.

The conversation rambled onto Baba's business, the unusually warm weather. 'Can you believe it in January?' Ma raised her eyebrows. Finally, I could bear it no longer.

'Any news on the wedding front?'

'Should there be?'

'I don't know, I haven't been talking to anyone!' I retorted.

'And I haven't been making any phone calls,' Ma said, smiling. 'Has anyone else?'

'Well, you might say I have and that things have been bleaker,' my father pretended resignation. 'There have been times when I have despaired of finding anyone, you know.'

'And now? What about the Banerjee girl, Baba?' I demanded. 'Please?'

'Go on, tell her, the child is dying to know!'

'Don't you think we ought to wait for the party concerned?' Baba asked.

'No!' I could not contain my impatience. 'You can tell it all again when he gets here!'

'And have to repeat it all?' he considered. 'Oh, very well then. It may improve with the telling,' he stretched his legs. 'Last time we met the Banerjees we agreed that we would talk again – you remember?' I said nothing, there was no need to. My father continued, 'Well, I did. Mr Banerjee and his wife appear to be very happy with what they have seen, and say that they would be very happy to agree to a match, if we accept.'

'So it is all agreed? We do accept, don't we?'

'Well, Sushma seems altogether quite suitable to me. Intelligent, well educated and even artistic. Her family is perfectly respectable, too – your Dada will have an accountant for a father-in-law, and an engineer and a college professor for brothers-in-law. There is even a family connection, Mr Banerjee being Sailen's accountant. Can't say I see any reason not to accept – can either of you?'

'Baba, don't be silly, of course we can't!'

'Ah, but perhaps your mother might think differently?' He turned to her.

'Ma,' I challenged her, 'do you have any objections?'

'Hmm,' she said, prolonging my agony, 'let me see: education, OK; looks, OK; family, OK. Compatibility? Well, she isn't very talkative but then Arun isn't a great talker either. Might make for a quiet marriage but that isn't necessarily a bad thing, is it?' She watched me itching with excitement, 'Oh very well, Meena, no, I don't have any objections.'

'Yes!' I could've jumped for joy.

'Hold on, hold on!' Baba interrupted me. 'There is one other opinion we need to get, don't you think? The party affected, so to speak?'

'Oh, he'll agree! I'll make sure he does,' I could see no reason for him objecting. After all, he'd agreed to everything so far. 'Have you set any date for the wedding yet, Baba?'

'No, no, of course not, Meena,' he replied, 'I thought I'd wait till I'd spoken to Arun. Wouldn't be such a bad idea, don't you think?'

'But Dada will agree, won't he? Why shouldn't he?'

Ma took pity on me. 'Well, we can start planning as soon as

your Dada says yes . . .' As she spoke Dada entered the twilight verandah. 'Here he is!'

'I'm getting married,' Dada said quietly as he sat down. His face was nearly invisible in the half light.

'I know!' I half-shouted. Then his words sank in. I stopped, puzzled, 'How did you know? Baba just told me . . .'

'Baba? No, he . . . you,' my brother turned to Baba, 'have no hand in this.'

Baba stiffened.

'I am getting married. But not to the Banerjee girl. I've proposed to Seema and she's said yes. We want to get married in June. She is going to tell her family this evening.'

'Seema? Who's Seema?' There was bewilderment in my mother's voice.

'Seema from my office. You know, I told you about her.' Dada's tone was quiet, patient but I detected more than just a hint of nervousness in it.

'The Punjabi girl?' My father's voice was hushed.

'Yes.'

'But when?' I was speechless.

'Before we go to Bombay.'

'We go to Bombay? *We?*' Ma demanded.

'Yes. Once we are married we will go to Bombay, we're both going to Bombay,' my brother replied.

'Both?' Ma again.

'Yes. She was offered a job with Anglo-India, the Shiva Enterprises subsidiary, first. That's why I decided to ask for one there too. It came through today.'

I couldn't understand it.

'Shiva Enterprises?' Baba said numbly. 'But Sailen said nothing to me.'

'I asked him not to. I'm sorry, I'm tired, I think I'll turn in, if

181

that's all right with you. Please have dinner without me.' He stood up and went indoors. We stared after him, dumbstruck.

Dinner that night was one of the most uncomfortable meals I've ever eaten. Baba, Ma and I sat around our table, playing with our food, avoiding each other's eyes. It took Ma half an hour to say anything. And when she did it was only to announce that she was going to bed. Baba followed her shortly afterwards, leaving me to clear up before retiring. In my room, I threw myself on the bed. My head was spinning. I told myself there was nothing wrong with his choosing his own partner but . . . Trying to analyse my feelings, I rationalised that my reluctance was a mixture of loyalty to my parents and disappointment that he had given me no inkling of these developments in his life. The problem, I told myself, was not the idea of his choosing his own partner and excluding us all from a process that we believed we were part and parcel of, nor the idea of his choosing as his partner a non-Bengali, it was that he had deceived us into believing that he was both amenable to and enthusiastic about the idea of an arranged marriage – a deception that had led us to make preparations for one. It was an untruth that had made our father ask questions of other people's families, to answer questions about our own, and even to volunteer information that he would not normally have revealed to any but the closest of friends, if at all. Surely, neither Ma nor Baba would have objected to his choosing his own wife? But maybe that's why he hid it from them and from me . . . but then why agree to the arrangements being made? Surely that was unnecessary? He could have just said 'No', or 'Not now'.

Couldn't he have stopped it all earlier? Couldn't Sailen Kaka have told us? Before we approached the Banerjees. But how would Sailen Kaka have known that Dada was planning to elope? What would Baba tell the Banerjees? And what could we say to all our relatives? How could Dada have done this to us? I cried into my pillow.

CHAPTER FOURTEEN

❖ ❖ ❖ ❖

Hari Ganguly had just finished his morning reading
from the Gita when the telephone rang. The servant
told him it was 'an Inspector Das from Sonapukur
Thana'. Hari Babu frowned – he didn't recall anyone by that
name. No, come to think of it, he did. He was one of the
subordinates of that amiable (if a bit stupid) friend of Sailen's
nephew, Dhiren Ghosh. He'd spoken to him once when he'd
tried to get in touch with Dhiren about the traffic arrangements for the forthcoming Hindu Sangh rally.

'Hari Ganguly, sir?' Hari Ganguly remembered the man had
an infuriating habit of 'Sir'ing constantly. Damn the man –
half his conversation was salutations.

'Yes, Das, yes!' he responded testily. He wanted his tea,
'What is it?'

Ghosh Babu would like to have a word with you, sir.'

'Well, put him on then,' Hari Babu heard a click and Dhiren clearing his throat.

'Hari Babu? Dhiren Ghosh here.'

'Hullo, Dhiren,' Hari Babu said warmly. A friend of Putul's deserved a welcome, 'Where are you? This is most unexpected, I haven't heard from you for a while. Not since we discussed the rally.'

'That's what I'm calling about.'

'The rally? No problems, are there? You said you had everything under control?'

'Well, Hari Babu, there's been an unforeseen – unforseeable – development. An accident on Monday, involving a truck . . . one of the transports you have been sponsoring. No damage to the rally vehicle, I'm glad to say – we haven't identified precisely which one it was yet, but we do have a good idea – but there were casualties.'

'Casualties? Ram, Ram! How many?'

'Two. One Indian, a driver from Calcutta, we believe and a young Englishman. God knows what he was doing here but both of them were killed.'

'Killed? Ram, Ram! That is terrible. But what has all this got to do with me?' Hari Babu said more quietly. So what if he paid for the truck? 'You say none of my vehicles has been identified so why call me?'

'It's not quite as simple as that, Hari Babu. There is a non-partisan witness who insists it was due to reckless driving on the part of your vehicle.'

Hari Ganguly groaned. Couldn't Ghosh run his own *thana*? 'Witnesses? Ghosh, you don't need witnesses for this sort of thing – it's your job to sort things out!'

'Wish I could solve it so simply, Hari Babu. But this one's

185

from a local mission and won't back down. Says it's his Christian duty or something like that.'

'Christian duty!' Hari Ganguly was furious. 'Discredit him, you fool. Christian missionaries accusing Hindu patriots! You can't allow that sort of thing, Ghosh!'

'It might just be a problem, Mr Ganguly,' Dhiren dropped the familiar form of address, 'the mission is pretty well regarded around here. They're not conversion freaks, more social work types with supporters in high places.'

'Foreign influence, external interference, Ghosh . . .' barked Hari Babu.

'Look, Mr Ganguly,' Dhiren interrupted impatiently, 'I don't have time to discuss this on the 'phone right now, I've got the superintendent and goodness knows who else breathing down my neck. I'd advise you to get down here as soon as you can to sort out your side of things. I've got other things to do!' The telephone slammed down. Hari Ganguly's brow creased. This sounded serious – first time he'd directly funded anything and now this! With his advertising banners all over the convoy, this was just what he didn't need. Ghosh had been right to call him. He needed to sort things out.

He dialled Soumen Rai – in spite of political affiliations, the two men had known each other for many years, having met through their mutual friend, Sailen Sen. At the time Soumen was a lowly Party cell organiser and Hari had had only one shop. A relationship, not quite a friendship, more symbiotic, had developed. Hari had supplied PA equipment for Soumen Rai's Party events and, in return, Soumen had made sure that whenever there were strikes Hari's business did not suffer. When, in recent years, Hari Ganguly had shifted allegiance to the right-wing Hindu Sangh, he had drifted apart from Soumen Rai, the rising star of the Leftist

Party. But the link had never been properly broken and until recently Hari Babu had continued to provide the Party with PA equipment at nominal cost. Now Soumen Rai was the MLA, the elected representative, of Basanpur district and Hari needed to talk to him. After all, whatever their current differences, didn't Soumen owe him something for services once rendered?

'Soumen?'

'Hari? How are you?' Soumen's voice was guarded. Hari Ganguly was someone he could live without these days. A Party member could not afford to be too familiar with Hindu Sangh supporters.

'Yes. Have you heard the news?' Hari Ganguly ignored the coolness in his old acquaintance's greeting.

'What news? I hear a lot of news, Hari.'

'The accident, Soumen,' said Hari Ganguly patiently.

'What accident, Hari?' the politician was perplexed.

'In Basanpur. Near Sonapukur, I believe. A vehicle went off the road and killed both its occupants. One a foreigner.'

'WHAT!' Soumen Rai was stunned. 'But the police have said nothing to me!'

'So you haven't heard?' Hari Ganguly couldn't resist a little smugness. 'You should talk to your policemen more often, Soumen.'

Suspicion was beginning to dawn in Soumen Rai, 'What has it got to do with you, anyway?'

'It's a long story, Soumen. We need to talk.'

'So talk!' Soumen had no desire to be observed in Hari Ganguly's company. The latter's current political affiliation was too unsavoury.

'Not now, not here. Sonapukur. On Friday, Republic Day,' Hari Ganguly hung up on the spluttering Soumen Rai. This was good, he had the MLA dangling. Hari Ganguly rubbed his hands happily. Things might work out, after all. Soumen's party would want it hushed up, of that he was sure, and the police would almost certainly be amenable. Now he needed to make another call. To Dhiren's superior, the superintendent.

When he got through the superintendent was no happier than Soumen Rai at being called. But he knew it did not pay to be uncivil to a man with political connections, he had a career to think of. So he controlled his temper and listened patiently to his infuriatingly cheerful caller. Hari Ganguly explained his interest and hinted that his contacts were sufficiently powerful for him, Hari Ganguly, to make it extremely difficult for the superintendent to continue in his position untainted if he did not sort out 'that unfortunate incident'. His political friends would be extremely concerned if anything untoward surfaced in the course of the investigation. He was sure that the superintendent understood? Not that he wished to prejudice the course of events, far from it. No one had more faith in the police than he had. After all, hadn't they apprehended the Nepal border smugglers? They hadn't? Hari Babu expressed astonishment. He had heard that the superintendent had had the ringleaders in his grasp. He didn't mean to say that they had managed to evade him? Now that wouldn't look good if a new government, a Hindu Sangh government, came to power, would it? Especially since they would want officers who were not just above suspicion but able to deliver law and order. The superintendent cleared his throat. He would do his best. Dhiren Ghosh had been away from his post when the convoy was passing but he would sort him out. Sri Ganguly did not want any hasty action? Of course not. He would ask Ghosh to ensure it was cleared up speedily. Sri Ganguly could rely on him. And how was the superintendent's family? Doing well? The superintendent would give them his regards, wouldn't he? And the matter they were discussing, minimum fuss, of course? Of course. A pleasure talking to the superintendent, he would see him on Friday. The conversation over, Hari Ganguly called for tea. It was, he mused, rather like a garden – careful cultivation could bear good fruit.

Dhiren was busy. The damned accident business was turning out to be a huge headache. The bloody thing was positively snowballing! To begin with there was that damn foreigner. Why couldn't they stay at home? Never brought anything but trouble – either they were robbed or they had no money to begin with. Now this one had gone and got himself killed extremely inconveniently. If it had been only the driver – Kartick or whatever his name was – he could have got rid of the case easily. But thanks to the Englishman, he would have to investigate the whole damn thing. What did they think he was going to find? A black box? A credible witness? There was only that fool from the Christian mission who was determined to say that the bloody truck had been on the wrong side of the road. What if it had? If he tried to bring a case on the basis of that and the fellow disappeared – after all, he just might – he'd be left with no proof and the whole thing would collapse and the Sangh would be after his head. On top of that, the party was annoyed because the Trekker was ferrying party cadre on a mission that had no clearance. All that was left was for the press to sniff it out. He'd have to talk to the mission. Get the witness to shut up. After all, if their fellow kept talking he might end up quiet quicker than he expected. And that would be another complication. Far better to get him out of the way sooner rather than later.

Dhiren was a creature of habit. Ever since his schooldays he'd found lists handy, seeing things written down made them so much easier to deal with. He found a clean page in his notebook. A plan of action. Not too explicit, of course – even though he would keep it under lock and key. He chewed the top of his pen for a while and began to write:

1) Go to church
2) Check car
3) Write letter

He stopped. A bit short, but it did sum things up. 'Go to church' meant go and talk to the mission. 'Check car' meant examine the accident wreckage. 'Write letter' meant file a report. No, it was a bit sketchy. Too sketchy. He didn't like it. He needed to discuss that report. Damn. And, perhaps he should change the order –

1) Check car
2) Go to church
3) Ring Dada
4) Write letter

That was better. 'Dada' was his euphemism for the superintendent. The first step was to take a look to see if the accident couldn't be ascribed to anything other than a bloody fool of a truck driver forcing the Trekker of the road. If it could, things might be easier. Dhiren bit his lip. That day of all days. Every other day – the days he'd been here since his return, all the days before the incident – had been all right. But just that one day had caused all this. No point brooding, better off going down to the accident site to see what he could find (if anything). He summoned the constable. An old fool with a penchant for salaaming. Which he did as soon as he entered.

'Salaam, sahib.'

'Tell the driver to bring the jeep round the front,' Dhiren ordered.

'When, sahib?'

'When do you think?! Tomorrow? No, now, you idiot, now!'

The constable salaamed again and left. Presently the jeep drew up. Dhiren straightened his uniform and climbed in. He had an awful premonition he was going to have to make this trip several times. He hoped not. Damn and double damn.

When they reached the site he ordered the driver to remain in the jeep. An order the latter was only too happy to comply with – he did not see the point of tempting fate by visiting the scene of death. Dhiren walked round the shell of the burnt-out vehicle, prodding the wreckage with a stick. Nothing, just twisted metal. Then he got to the front, the section wrapped around the tree, and something caught his eye. Something newish by the look of it, jutting out of the wreckage. He leaned over and tugged at it. To his surprise a fragment broke off. That was odd. He didn't know that much about the undersides of cars but it did seem a bit too easy. Brushing away the soot he turned it over and read the words inscribed on it. 'Anglo-India'. It meant nothing to him. Perhaps he'd better send it off for analysis. He returned to his jeep.

Back at the *thana*, Dhiren packed the fragment in a box and sent if off to Calcutta. Task of the day done, he sat down to read. Or rather, tried to – he plucked first a novel (his favourite writer, Agatha Christie), then a magazine, but he could not concentrate. Damn. He crossed the compound to his bungalow, poured himself a stiff shot of whisky, unfolded the day-old Calcutta newspaper and tried the crossword. But even the first clue eluded him. What the hell, he thought, draining his glass, may as well get well and truly drunk. Might not be able to once things hotted up. He refilled his glass and turned on the radio.

'This is All India Radio. The news, read by . . .'

His accident wouldn't be in it, nor would his transfer if it did happen. Even though that would be real news, not this stuff about Zaire or Congo or wherever. All India Radio, pshaw!

A cough interrupted his reverie. Das, damn him. What the hell was he doing in the bungalow? He had told him, time and time again, never to disturb him unless it were urgent.

'Yes, Das?' Wearily. He didn't bother to conceal the whisky. If the fool insisted in wandering in without knocking, he would have to get used to the idea.

'There's a 'phone call for you, sir.'

'A 'phone call? Can't you see I'm busy, Das? Look, take a message, tell whoever it is that I'm out and not to be disturbed!' It usually worked. But this time Das was obstinate, he wasn't covering this time.

'I'm sorry, sir. I think you'd better take it, sir.'

'You think I'd better take it?' Dhiren growled dangerously.

'Yes, sir. I don't mean to be rude, sir, but I think you'd better take it, sir. The superintendent says he wanted to speak to you, sir.'

Dhiren jumped up. 'The superintendent! Why the hell didn't you say that earlier? Get out of my way!' He pushed the unfortunate inspector aside and rushed across the compound.

The superintendent was angry. He'd been holding on for ten minutes. He hated that – and his wife was muttering darkly in the background about people who couldn't leave their work in the office. Damn that Ghosh! First he was out of station when there was a rally on, then he took his own cool time getting to the 'phone. Who the hell did he think his boss was? His father?

'Good evening, sir!' Dhiren spoke as smartly as he could.

'Ghosh? Where the hell were you?'

'Err, I wash having my dinner, shir,' Dhiren slurred, whiskily.

'Your dinner?' the superintendent snapped. 'Then why are you slurring? You drink for dinner, Ghosh?'

'No, sir! Just a pre-dinner aper . . .' Dhiren tried to sober up.

'Shut up and listen, Ghosh! I don't have time to discuss your habits or your diet – I'm calling because the lab got back to me.'

'So soon, sir?' Dhiren's surprise was unfeigned.

'Yes, yes. I told them to check out anything you sent them immediately. The minister – never mind which one,' he pre-empted his junior, 'is breathing down my neck! But that's none of your business, what is is that the lab says the part was faulty and may well have caused the accident.'

'Thank God, sir,' Dhiren breathed a sigh of relief.

'Thank God?' The superintendent exploded. 'What do you mean "Thank God"! You think this is the end of the matter?'

'No, no sir,' Dhiren stammered, taken aback by the super-intendent's vehemence, 'I just thought, sir, that if the part was faulty then, sir, we could leave the . . . the politicians out of it, sir!'

'Of course we leave the parties out of it, you idiot! We leave them out, anyway. But it isn't that bloody easy.'

'Isn't it, sir?' Dhiren was genuinely confused. 'I don't

understand, sir – surely we can ascribe the accident to mechanical failure?'

'Mechanical failure? You fool, you know who made that part?' The superintendent felt the urge to smash the 'phone. Didn't that Ghosh understand anything?

'No, sir . . .' Dhiren remembered the inscription. 'Yes, sir! Someone called "Anglo-India", sir. Surely that isn't important, sir?'

'Not important, Ghosh! Of course it bloody is. Know who Anglo-India is? Shiva Enterprises. Which means Sailen Sen, you damned idiot! And know who he is? Contributor to the party, friend of Soumen Rai, Hari Ganguly and the minister! And to top it all, it's one of the bloody new joint-ventures! You think we can go plastering it all over the place that Anglo-India makes faulty parts? "New joint-venture claims first two victims" in the papers? You think the minister would want to see that as a headline? Or the bloody investors he's so keen on bringing in?'

'What can we do, sir?' Out of his depth, Dhiren was completely sober now.

'Do? I don't know yet.' He took a deep breath. 'Look, Ghosh – ring me tomorrow morning and we'll discuss this. No, wait a minute, that witness, the mission fellow. Have you spoken to him yet?'

'No, sir . . .' Dhiren hoped this would not incur further wrath.

'Just as well. Speak to him tomorrow, find out if he might have been mistaken.' The superintendent chose his words carefully. Dhiren understood. It was what he had been intending to do anyway. At least he was on the right track.

'Anything else, sir?'

'Else? No, nothing for now, Ghosh. Just speak to that

fellow and let me know. I'll ring you tomorrow. Afternoon . . . no, make that evening. Sevenish – I'll be in the office if you need me before. And don't speak to anyone else about this, or leave any messages, we don't need any leaks or anything. Do you understand, Ghosh?'

'Yes, sir. Goodnight.' The superintendent was gone. Dhiren walked slowly back to his bungalow. He really needed another drink – things were getting worse. Just when he thought they couldn't.

The morning after Dada's announcement I slept late. I'd lain awake half the night, trying to figure out what it all meant – why things had turned out the way they had. But nothing made sense. And when I awoke, I was none the wiser. There was no sign of Ma in the kitchen. A subdued Durga brought me tea and *moori*. I ate in silence. She spoke quietly of her own problems, of her son and his 'job' with the *para mastaan*. She feared that he was getting the worst of the deal, that he was being used and that no good would come of the venture. I tried to concentrate and offer words of solace but could not. After a while she noticed and left me alone. Ma returned from the market but was also unable to lend Durga a sympathetic ear. She gave up completely and the only sounds heard for the rest of the day were of cooking and cleaning. And the incessant background noise that fills the Calcutta air – crows, children, hawkers, dogs, the world outside our window.

That evening Ma and I drank our tea in silence on the balcony. Baba only arrived around dinner time – he dumped his briefcase in the room and came out to join us. Ma passed him a cup. He put it on the floor beside him. After a long silence, he said, 'I rang Mr Banerjee today.'

'So soon?' Ma asked even though she knew the answer.

'Yes, I wanted to get it over with.'

'How did he take it?'

'Very badly, I'm afraid,' Baba's tone was heavy. 'He was most disappointed. They – Mr and Mrs Banerjee certainly – were quite happy with Arun,' Baba seemed to find it hard to utter my brother's name, 'and they were not pleased to hear that we were withdrawing. I told him the real reason, I had to.'

'What have we done to deserve this?' Ma began sadly. 'What have we done to deserve this? Our son leads us on, deceives us! Why? Have we not done all we can for our children? And this is how they treat us? Where did we go wrong? All we wanted was his happiness, yet he kept us out of his life even while he was under our roof? Why?'

Baba remained silent. Ma continued. 'Why? Why? How could he, how could he? And your cousin, Sailen? He could have told us.'

'What if he knew nothing of the girl?' Baba said grimly.. 'No, this is Arun's doing. He should have told us. Whom did he tell? No one. No one who told us, at least. Perhaps this is something that all of their generation wish to inflict on their elders. How could anyone have foreseen it?'

Ma turned on him angrily. 'Why do you talk of them, of others? Is it not sufficient that our own son has turned away from us? What do we have to do with other people's children, other people's lives? We gave Arun everything. You slaved and made sacrifices that he will never know and this is the reward we get. This? That he shames us in front of all the world?' She stormed off into the kitchen. I sat frozen in my seat, unable to get up and put my arms around her, unable to comfort her. Instead my treacherous heart thought only of Ranjan. Oh, I wished I were far away, that I had not come home just when I did. I was grateful for the cover of darkness.

CHAPTER FIFTEEN

Dhiren did not sleep well. The mixture of alcohol and tension produced strange dreams, nightmares. One recurred. Of a firing squad. The first time he woke from it in a cold sweat. Don't be stupid, he told himself, they don't sentence police officers to firing squads. But when he did fall asleep again, he was back in the yard and soldiers were taking aim. When he got to the office he was tired and nervous. He rang for the constable. The fool salaamed again.

'Stop that!'

'Yes, sahib!'

'Get the jeep here – immediately!'

'Yes, sahib!' Another salaam was on its way – but the constable saw the murderous look on his superior's face in time and restrained himself.

On the way to the mission, a thought struck Dhiren. Sailen Sen. Wasn't that the name that the superintendent had mentioned? Where did he know it from? Sen, Sen . . . not the sari shop . . . why did it remind him of Putul? He had it, Putul's uncle, his guardian, that was Sailen Sen! Of course, Putul had talked about a joint-venture and, come to think of it, the name he mentioned was Anglo-India. If his own future hadn't been at stake, Dhiren might have smiled. As it was, he pursed his lips meditatively. What a small world – everyone in everybody else's pocket.

His thoughts were interrupted by the driver.

'The mission, sir. Do you want me to go in, sir?'

'Yes, yes, of course,' Dhiren snapped.

The gate opened at the driver's blast and the jeep drew up at a long, low verandah. A small woman in a blue sari came out to greet him.

'Ghosh Babu?'

'Sister Aruna. Good morning.' The woman stepped back to allow Dhiren to climb down.

'This is most unexpected.' If she was surprised it did not show. 'To what do we owe the pleasure of this visit?'

'Business, I'm afraid,' he tried to sound casual. 'Is there somewhere we can talk in private?'

'Of course. My office.' She led the way to a whitewashed house behind the main building. Dhiren took in the room with a practised eye. Spartanly furnished, with nothing more than a table for a desk, two metal chairs and a neat stack of files. An electric bulb hanging from the ceiling. No sign of a fan but the room was cool.

'Do sit down,' Sister Aruna indicated one of the chairs, taking the other herself. 'Before you start, Ghosh Babu, may I offer you something – a cup of tea, perhaps?'

'No tea, thank you, Sister. I wish I had the time. A glass of water would be nice though.'

'Certainly.' She poured him a glass from an earthen pot. 'Would you like some sweets?'

'No thank you, Sister. Never eat while I'm on duty.' She smiled politely at his joke. He hurried on, 'Can we get down to business, Sister?'

'Of course, Ghosh Babu. How can I help you?'

'Well, it's about that accident, Sister.'

'The one outside? It was tragic, wasn't it? That lorry, you know.'

'Yes, I know. I've read the report. And the witness's statement. One of your people, I believe?'

'Yes, one of ours. Francis saw the whole thing. Your people took a statement,' her tone was polite but firm.

'Of course, of course. Forgive me. Would you mind reminding me how he came to be on the spot?'

'But surely you know already, Ghosh Babu?' Dhiren did not reply. She sighed. 'Very well, I will repeat it, if you want. Francis arranged the Trekker in Basanpur town and had just been dropped off. The Englishman was going to Sonapukur – Francis was waving good-bye when the accident happened.'

'So he had been in the vehicle himself?' Dhiren used his most professional tone.

'Yes, he had,' she looked at him suspiciously. 'Would you like me to call Francis to tell you his story himself?'

'No, Sister – at least, not yet. You see, there are a couple of things I would like to discuss with you first. I think you are better placed to decide than he is.'

'I'm not sure I follow you,' Sister Aruna's eyes narrowed. She was getting the idea.

'My apologies, Sister,' Dhiren sounded contrite. He had been thinking on his feet and had decided on a softly, softly approach. 'You see, Sister, the vehicle was not a licensed carrier.'

'And so? The accident took place all the same.'

'Sister, please hear me out,' Dhiren smiled winningly. Sister Aruna subsided. 'Well, as the vehicle was not licensed, your man – Francis?' He raised his eyebrows inquiringly. She nodded. 'Francis,' he continued, 'was, in effect, involved in an illegal transaction,' the missionary opened her mouth as if to speak, 'please, Sister, please. Besides, if he were waving at the driver, he may have been guilty of distracting him and,' he continued inexorably, 'be – how shall I say it – culpable of causing, however unintentionally, the accident.' Dhiren allowed his voice to trail off. He wanted to see the reaction. He was not disappointed.

'Ghosh Babu, I am astounded! Are you suggesting that an innocent bystander might be . . .' Words failed her. Dhiren waited patiently, feigning concern. She struggled with the words, 'An innocent bystander be made a scapegoat! Ghosh Babu, I have always had the greatest respect for you, but I cannot believe what I am hearing!'

Time to play the second card, thought Dhiren.

'Sister, I would not dream of such a thing. I am, as you are well aware, as concerned about justice as you are. But there are issues more powerful than I involved. You must understand that that was no ordinary lorry. It was involved in political activity. The occupants – if they can be traced – will deny any wrongdoing and may, if there is an attempt to bring them to court, be inclined to take matters into their own hands.' He introduced a pleading note into his voice, 'Sister, if I thought there was any chance of being able to prove negligence on the part of the lorry I would do so. But I am afraid that it will be Francis's word against that of a number of others. Simple arithmetic often prevails, and the other witnesses may recall events differently. They are, I have been reminded recently, members of a powerful organisation.' The policeman paused. 'Sister, your mission does magnificent work here, and I am sure you value Francis – who, I am told, is a compounder. It would be a great pity for all of us if the accident were to result in unwelcome attention,' Dhiren's voice trailed off again. He did not want the threat to be anything more than veiled. After all, it was not his duty to pressurise honest people.

Sister Aruna looked at him sadly, 'Ghosh Babu, if I did not know you, I would think that you were leaning on us out of choice. But I know you better than that. You will pardon my saying so – but I think that you are at worst pompous, but not crooked. I will, therefore, interpret what you have just said as an attempt to save your own skin.'

Deflated, Dhiren added miserably, 'And Francis's, and the mission's.'

'Very well, Francis's and the mission's, too.' Her voice grew softer, almost sorrowful. He did not move. She continued, 'Very well, Ghosh Babu, I will think it over. There may be something in what you have said. Can I have some time?'

'Of course,' Dhiren mumbled, 'but I need to speak to my superiors this evening.'

'I will send you word this afternoon, Ghosh Babu,' she said firmly, 'and now, if you will excuse me, I have a clinic to run.' He stood up as she left.

Dhiren spent an anxious few hours in his office, tidying files to keep him busy. At three o'clock the 'phone rang. He fairly jumped at it.

'Sonapukur *thana*. Ghosh speaking.'

'Mr Ghosh. Sister Aruna here,' her voice was quiet, 'Francis Gomes has decided to go on leave.'

Dhiren swallowed. 'Has he decided to retract his statement?'

'Mr Ghosh, I said Francis has gone on leave and will not be able to assist in any further investigations. Nothing more.' Dhiren took a deep breath.

'I understand, Sister. Thank you.'

'Thank you, Mr Ghosh. I hope you find it easier to live with this than I do.' She hung up before he could say any more.

Live with it? What choice did he have? He would have to. His career was on the line.

The superintendent was punctual. He rang at precisely seven, calmer than he had been the night before. He allowed Dhiren to blunder through his account of the day before intervening.

'Well done, Ghosh. A sorry business, this. I am glad that you have managed to clear up that side of things. Unfortunately that is not the end of it. I will be coming to Sonapukur myself to see what can be done. Soumen Rai will also be coming. Please make arrangements for us.'

Dhiren tried to sound businesslike. 'When can I expect you, sir?'

'Sometime in the next few days. Probably Friday – I know it is Republic Day, but these things can't wait. We don't have time to waste.' The 'phone went dead. Dhiren was alone with his thoughts.

Sailen Sen had left Delhi in a hurry – his old friend Soumen Rai had been uncharacteristically insistent on his returning to

Calcutta immediately. He had not wanted to leave when negotiations were at such a delicate stage, especially as it meant leaving Putul in charge. Fortunately only technically in charge, since there were experienced company men to keep him on the right track. Thank God for that, he thought fervently. On his own, Putul would almost certainly have made a complete mess of things. The boy was bone idle. It was his aunt's fault – she had spoiled him. 'After all,' she had said, 'the poor boy has lost both his parents. Such a tragedy is a lot to bear.' Mr Sen had had to bite his tongue more than once. It would have hurt her – they had not been blessed with children of their own. He would have liked it if the boy had shown more responsibility but there was nothing to be done now. If only Soumen had been willing to explain on the 'phone.

The doorbell rang. Mr Sen hurried to open it, waving away the servant who padded up.

'Ah, Sailen.' It was Soumen Rai. 'I'm so glad you could get back so quickly.'

'It wasn't exactly convenient, you know,' Mr Sen said sharply.

'Nothing is, Sailen,' Soumen Rai answered ominously. 'Shall we go to your study?' Mr Sen led the way to a comfortably appointed room. His guest dropped himself into a chair and mopped his brow.

A servant, sent for water for the guest, returned. Soumen drank thirstily while Sailen Sen waited impatiently.

'Ah, I needed that,' he said when he had finished. 'A warm January, isn't it?'

Sailen Sen did not reply. The politician continued, 'Sailen, would you mind closing the door? I would not want us to be disturbed.'

'No one will come in here without my permission,' Mr Sen responded curtly.

'If you say so, Sailen, if you say so,' the politician leaned across the desk. 'This is a matter of great delicacy – and of great urgency, you see.'

'Soumen, I have known you for years and never have you got on my nerves so much!' Mr Sen exclaimed. 'Will you please come to the point?'

'Come to the point? But of course, Sailen, of course. How's business?'

'Business?' Mr Sen was annoyed. What on earth was this about? 'It'd be doing better if I were not bothered by needless interruptions.'

'Needless interruptions? But all interruptions aren't needless? By definition, some of them are necessary.' Soumen Rai played with a pencil, pursing his lips meditatively, 'Do you mind if I smoke?'

'Would it matter if I did?'

Soumen Rai lit a cigarette and blew the match out carefully.

'Right, Sailen. Let's get down to business. Is your plant in production yet?'

'Only just. Which is why I was in Delhi. Look, for God's sake, will you please tell me what this is all about? If you wanted to hear about my business you could've waited until I got back.'

'I'm sorry, Sailen. I should have been clearer,' Soumen Rai said soothingly, 'you see, this matter of both urgency and delicacy involves your new factory. One of your parts has been involved in an accident. In fact, it might well have been the cause of the accident.'

Mr Sen blanched. 'Accident? Where? When? Is it serious?'

Soumen Rai ignored the first two questions, 'Very serious. Two dead, I am told.'

'Two dead? Oh my God! Are you sure it is the part that is at fault?'

'It looks pretty certain. The laboratory says preliminary investigations point to it.'

'Good god! We've barely started production. Is there nothing that can be done?' Mr Sen was dismayed. Bad publicity could ruin him – and his British partner, Stewart, would be most unhappy.

'Sailen, that could normally be done. But this case is a bit more complicated. You see, one of the victims was British . . .'

'British? Oh no!'

'Oh yes. Name of John Stewart.' Soumen Rai dropped his bombshell casually.

'John Stewart?' Sailen Sen was puzzled. 'I know a Stewart.'

'The same.' Soumen Rai blew a smoke ring.

'What do you mean?'

'He's the son of James Stewart, joint proprietor and director of Ango-India. The deceased was, I believe, also a friend of your nephew's.'

'James Stewart's son? My partner's son?' Sailen Sen was aghast. 'But where?'

'On the Sonapukur Road. Apparently. Stewart Junior was, police sources inform me, going to Sonapukur to visit his grandfather's last posting. Turned out to be his – the jeep he was in swerved off the road and poof!' Soumen Rai saw no reason to include details of the rally. It was none of Sailen's business.

'The boy was coming to my house and then he changed his mind and now this . . .'

Soumen Rai looked at his friend sadly. 'Sailen, I am doing all I can. The minister is also keen that there is no mention of the Anglo-India part in the report. We will see what we can come up with,' he carefully did not elaborate who 'we' was, 'and will let you know. Right now, perhaps, you might want to contact the family. Sort things out, that sort of thing. Delicately, I would suggest. Very delicately.'

Soumen Rai left Sailen Sen with his head in his hands. What was he to do? Perhaps he could get more information from the police. Wasn't that friend of Putul's, Dhiren Ghosh, the officer in charge of Sonapukur? He must know about it.

When I walked into the living room the evening before Republic Day, I was surprised to see my father deep in conversation with Raja Mama. They looked serious and I was about to leave but my father stopped me.

'Your Raja Mama is here because he needs some advice. You may as well hear what he has to say.' Baba did not say it but I knew what he was thinking. He no longer wanted to involve Dada.

'Yes, Baba,' I said meekly.

Raja Mama shifted nervously, 'Hullo, Meena. I . . .' he faltered.

'Please, Raja. Meena is as capable of assisting as I am.'

'Very well then,' Raja Mama acquiesced. 'You see, we – that is to say my father – has always admired SailenDa's business sense. So he has always supported his ventures. And the most recent one of Shiva Enterprises, Anglo-India, is no exception. My father invested considerable sums of money in it – both to help Sailen out and for the family's benefit. SailenDa's other businesses have always been successful and we were happy with the returns. But this time it seems we did not take

207

adequate precautions. It was, after all, a family matter, so there was no need to involve lawyers or others. Only now it appears we may be ruined . . .'

I looked at Baba.

'Perhaps you should tell us more,' Baba encouraged Raja Mama.

'You have not heard? SailenDa has not spoken to you?' He looked surprised. 'It appears that an Anglo-India product has been involved in a fatal accident which, if it comes to public attention, may mean the end of Anglo-India and Shiva Enterprises. It is a very serious matter!'

I finally had something to say. 'Is it that bad? Surely, if the product is faulty, it can be rectified?'

Raja Mama looked at his hands, 'Oh yes, it can. But that costs money and the company is far from being profitable yet so any further expenses may be impossible to finance. We have no more to invest. Sailen has used up all his money and it is unlikely that the government or banks will be willing to back an already tainted firm. We really do not know what to do! Even if we were to ask Sailen to return our capital he probably would not be able to, since I doubt he has the ready money. The only way would be to sell off his holding in Anglo-India – and that would almost certainly be at a loss. Do you see my dilemma? If we ask for the return of our capital we will both not get as much as we have invested and we will force him out of business. Which we do not wish to do. But if we do not, we may well lose all our money anyway! We . . . I am in a quandary so I have come to you . . .' for the first time in the conversation he looked at me, '. . . for advice.'

What could I say? What did I know of finance! How I wished Baba had not dragged me into this.

'Baba, what do you think?'

To my relief Baba decided to take over. 'Have you spoken to SailenDa yet, Raja?'

'Yes, he rang me to tell me the news.'

'And did he say anything else?'

'He was very honest with me, as he has always been. He informed me of the options I have outlined – of asking for the return of our money, of risking waiting to see what happens. He also told me that because of the manner in which our money was invested in the company it is unlikely that we will be considered creditors if Anglo-India or Shiva Enterprises goes into liquidation. I think he is acting honourably but it still leaves me in a very difficult situation.'

'Yes, I can see that,' my father frowned, 'and what does he advise you to do?'

'Well, he said it was up to me. But he did say that there is a possibility that Soumen Rai would be able to restrict the damage.'

'Soumen Rai? Of the Party?'

'The same. He is taking an interest in the affair. I do not know why, I did not ask. They have known each other for years.'

Baba pondered this. 'On the one hand, it would seem most advisable to withdraw as much as you can as soon as you can and invest it safely somewhere else. On the other hand, Soumen Rai is involved. So perhaps something can be done. Soumen Rai has influence. He has the chief minister's ear and can make things happen – if he decides. He will exact his price, of course, but that it is not your concern. It is Sailen's. So, if I were in your position I think I would rely on Soumen Rai. For the sake of family unity, if nothing else,' he looked solemnly at Raja Mama. 'But the final decision must be yours, because in the end, if Soumen Rai fails you may lose catastrophically.'

When Baba had finished Raja Mama rose, and put his hands together in farewell.

'Thank you for your help. I will think it over, and, God willing, make the right decision.'

Alone with Baba after he left, I broached the question that had been in my mind all along:

'Baba, how long has Boro Dadu's family been investing in Sailen Kaka's businesses?'

'For as long as I can remember, Meena. When Putul's parents died, Sailen decided to take the risk of expanding his business and all the members of the family were invited to support him. I had my own business to build up. But it turned out well, Sailen's business acumen has kept your Boro Dadu's family afloat all these years – which probably explains their decision to risk so much on this venture.' He looked at me sadly. 'Meena, if you are wise you will always maintain your independence. And, in the end, perhaps others around you will respect you for it.'

How I wished that Baba could have heard himself. Perhaps then he would have been able to come to terms with Dada's choice sooner rather than later.

The telephone rang.

'Sailen Sen speaking.'

'Ah, Sailen Kaka. Dhiren Ghosh here.'

'Dhiren?' Putul's uncle heaved a sigh of relief. 'Just the person I need to speak to!'

'You need to speak to me?' Dhiren said guardedly.

'Yes, Dhiren,' Mr Sen put on his bluffest tone. 'I was hoping you would call. Soumen Rai has been to see me.'

'He has?' Dhiren was relieved. 'Then, Sailen Kaka, I assume you know why I am calling?'

'I have a fair idea . . . the incident, in your *thana* recently. The incident that might involve my company . . .'

'Yes, quite. I am calling about that . . . incident . . .'

'Dhiren,' his friend's uncle interrupted him, 'before we go any further, can I ask for your absolute discretion?'

'But of course, Sailen Kaka!' the policeman was puzzled. 'You are like my own family.'

'Yes, Dhiren, we are very fond of you. You're like one of our sons . . . a brother to Putul, no?'

'Yes, Sailen Kaka. Can we discuss the matter in hand?' Dhiren was surprised. Although Putul's uncle had never shown any dislike of him, neither had he shown any particular enthusiasm for him, or any of Putul's companions.

'Before we go on, can I ask you a small favour?'

'If it is in my power.'

'It is not much, Dhiren, not much at all. Just that nothing of this incident is communicated to Putul until the right time.'

'Nothing to Putul?' Dhiren breathed more easily. 'Is that all? If you wish, Sailen Kaka, if you wish. But why?' The danger past, his curiosity was aroused.

'I would prefer to keep my reasons confidential for now,' Sailen Sen replied. 'Let us just say he is in Delhi right now and I would not wish his concentration disturbed. Naturally, I will let you know when it is appropriate to break the news to him. Can you trust me to do that?'

'I can, sir,' Dhiren slipped unconsciously into an official response. 'And you can rely on me, sir . . . Sailen Kaka.'

'Thank you, Dhiren,' Mr Sen relaxed. He had bought time, for a while. However, it was imperative that matters were sorted out quickly. Dhiren explained what was being done and assured him he would call him after the meeting with the superintendent, Soumen Rai and Hari Ganguly. Mr Sen was surprised at his friend's involvement but kept quiet. There was no need for Dhiren to know how ill-informed he was.

After Dhiren hung up, Mr Sen called for tea and pulled a pad of headed note-paper towards him.

'Dear Mr Stewart,' he began – and stopped.

Perhaps it would be better to address the letter more familiarly. After all, not only were they doing business together, Putul and John were friends . . . had been friends. He tore up the sheet and started again.

Dear James,

I do not know how to begin this. I wish to communicate to you and your family the sincerest condolences of ours. We have been business partners for some time now (whether you count the period of negotiation or not) and I have come to regard you with as much affection as I do my own family. However, I did not realise how close our families are – it came as a surprise to me that your son intended to visit us, perhaps to stay in my own house. If I had had any inkling of the dangers I would have done everything in my power to protect him. Sadly, the tragedy was unforseeable. I can only hope that you and your good wife will accept our deepest sympathies and regret that we were unable to prevent the unthinkable.

There is a small matter which, tragically, is linked to the accident that you might wish to be made aware of. I have made enquiries of the authorities [*Mr Sen felt uneasy about the prevarication but let it pass.*] and they inform me that they have not yet been able to ascertain the precise cause of the disaster. There appear to be conflicting reports, the most likely being that the driver of the vehicle – which was not licensed – was paying insufficient attention to the road and lost control. [*Mr Sen did not want to bring up the political angle – it might give the wrong impression of the situation.*] There is, however, a complication. It appears, from preliminary investigation, that another potential factor in the accident was a faulty part that bore the markings of our own enterprise. I do not wish to distress you overly in this matter so I hasten to add that there is neither conclusive evidence that the part was really a factor, nor that the part was really produced by Anglo-India. [*This was an inspired comment, thought Mr Sen, after all, it was at least conceivable that the part was a fake.*] I have been in touch with our factory and they assure me that all parts were made by machines you have supplied and to your specifications [*This was true, he knew it for a fact.*] and with the authorities'. I will, of course, keep you posted of any further developments.

Once again, please accept our deepest sympathies. If there is anything that we can do to help, please do not hesitate to ask,

I remain yours in shared grief,

Sailen Sen

He carefully folded the letter, inserted it into an airmail envelope from the packet in his drawer, moistened the flap and sealed it, writing the addresses on either side in a firm hand. Satisfied with his work he summoned the *durwan*.

'Take this to the post-office and have it sent off immediately . . . wait, here is some money,' he pressed a twenty rupee note in the man's hand. 'Hurry!'

He had done all he could for now. He might as well go back to Delhi.

CHAPTER SIXTEEN

❖❖❖❖

Things had never been so busy in the *thana* – at least as far as the old constable could remember. Not since the days of the Naxalites had there been so many important people coming all at once. Excitement in Sonapukur was a dacoity, some cattle-rustling, one or two cows going missing. But this was altogether different, this was the real thing. Soumen Rai, the member of the legislative assembly (MLA), visiting outside election year – and on Republic Day at that. There was also a strong possibility – if he'd overheard correctly – that they would play host to the superintendent and a very rich man who was somehow linked with another party. Impressed by all the titles, the constable had got the *jamadar* down at the bungalow to clean it and the *thana* up. He was all in favour of VIPs on such an important day. His only regret was that Dhiren Sahib wasn't joining in the excitement whole-heartedly. The constable couldn't understand it – he was an officer of the *Sarkar*, the government, wasn't he? Why worry about the politicians? All Dhiren Sahib needed to do was to sort out the investigation and then take the credit. But did he see this? No! He'd got it all wrong and was more interested in justifying his absence from the *thana* than with making the most of it all!

The constable scratched his beard. *He* was going to benefit from the VIPs' visits, he would make sure of that. To begin with, there would be good *baksheesh*. That was the way it had always been, politicians of different hues came and he took his reward from each and, astute judge of electoral fortunes, passed on the benefit of his influence to the one who would win. And thus gained their gratitude. After which he could rest assured that any supplication he made would receive a sympathetic hearing – and, if he did not over-stretch himself, he could use it for his protégés. And that in turn would increase his own prestige. He was well-known as a fixer of things – not on the scale of Soumen Rai, but in his own little way.

Dhiren Sahib had ordered him to make arrangements for all the visits. Now *that* was the way to do it. Treat every one of the VIPs equally but make it seem as if each were special. He'd asked for more instructions, details. To his amazement, the sahib lost his temper.

'How the hell am I to know when these . . . these *people* will come? They're politicians, come and go as they please. Be ready for them whenever! Do you understand me? Whenever!'

'Of course, sahib. But you must know when, sahib?'

'No, I don't. Nobody tells me – I'm just a police officer, not a travel agent. Just do as you are told!'

'Yes, sahib. Of course, sahib.' But he did need to know more so he had summoned the boys whom he'd done favours for before. They told him all he needed to know.

The superintendent came first, arriving in the morning and taking up residence in the bungalow. The whole thing, at first, then just Dhiren Sahib's quarters when the MLA appeared. By late morning the Hindu Sangh businessman, Hari Ganguly, sent word of his arrival. The other VIPs did not seem pleased. They closeted themselves in a room, behind a firmly shut door. Then Dhiren Sahib took the jeep into town to visit Hari Ganguly, as the driver later confirmed. He returned with a face like thunder and the three shut themselves in the office again. Around lunch time Hari Ganguly arrived and was ushered in. He was an oily man, the constable decided, fawning on him all the same (you never know when favours might be needed, or from whom). The negotiations began in earnest.

Leaning back in his chair, Hari Ganguly examined the ceiling, 'Dhiren, Dhiren, you've got yourself into quite a sticky situation haven't you?'

'Me? What about you?' retorted Dhiren.

'Ram, Ram. What did I do?' Hari Ganguly asked innocently. 'I merely provided, perfectly legally, vehicles for the transport of party supporters. Nothing wrong with that, is there? You, on the other hand, Dhiren, were not at your post when this accident happened. Now why was that?'

His face burning with anger, Dhiren began to answer but Soumen Rai interrupted.

'Now, now,' he said soothingly, 'we're not here to argue – we're here to discuss the issues, no?' Three heads nodded, the two policemen wary, Hari Ganguly faintly smug.

'Well, let's start at the beginning, shall we?' the politician spoke with authority. 'First, the events and the findings. The accident – no, the incident – took place when the Trekker swerved off the road and collided with a tree?' More nods.

'Now, the question that can be asked – I am not necessarily saying that it is relevant – is what caused the vehicle to swerve? Was that the cause of the accident?' He paused to let it all sink in, 'Let's deal with the first issue. What caused the Trekker go to off the road? According to a witness, the driver swerved because a lorry was bearing down on it . . . wait, Hari Babu,' he silenced Hari Ganguly with his hand, 'you will have your say . . . first let us hear what Ghosh has to say about that. He has, I believe, been following that up.'

'I have, sir,' replied Dhiren. 'I went to the alleged witness's residence but he appears to have vanished . . .'

'Vanished, Ghosh?' The superintendent frowned. '*Vanished*?'

'Sorry, sir, not vanished,' Dhiren corrected himself. 'He has decided to withdraw the allegation and has gone on leave. Under the circumstances his statement is no longer relevant.'

Soumen Rai beamed. 'He was not put under any pressure, was he?'

'Of course not, sir,' Dhiren played along, tried to sound faintly, though not impolitely, affronted. 'No, sir, he decided to return to his home village of his own accord.'

'Well, well,' said the politician, 'that is the end of that then. But that still leaves us with the question of what caused the accident.' He opened the file in front of him, 'It appears that a damaged part was found at the scene. It might be suggested that this faulty part caused the accident. However, there is no conclusive evidence to support this and plenty to suggest otherwise. The part in question is manufactured by a reputable joint-venture which operates to the highest possible standards, international standards, in fact. But the part was damaged, that is clear. The question now is "Why?"' He turned a page. 'The laboratory report gives no clues. There are two possible reasons. One is that it was fitted by an unqualified mechanic. Someone the driver found along the way. The other is that the part was fractured *during* the accident.' He looked round the table triumphantly. 'I'll discount the first, it would involve further investigation. I therefore suggest that the damage to the part was not the *cause* of the accident but *the result of it*!'

'The result of the accident?' Dhiren repeated, bewildered.

'Yes, the result of the accident. After all, the factory involved has strict quality controls. It is inconceivable that it would have produced a potentially dangerous part. Cosmetic faults, perhaps, fundamental structural ones, extremely unlikely. So the accident and the ensuing conflagration must have damaged the previously undamaged part. That seems to me the most likely explanation. In fact, I see no other.'

'Rai Babu, are you sure?' The superintendent spoke slowly.

'Sure? Of course not. But if we – if the police have any doubt they can send it back to the government' – Soumen Rai faintly emphasised the word – 'laboratory for further tests.'

There was a brief silence. The superintendent responded without looking up, 'No, I don't think that will be necessary. If there is another more likely cause . . .'

Soumen Rai smiled, 'Ah, there is, there is. I have asked my people to do some investigating of their own and they have found that the boy driving the vehicle had no licence. *No* licence! Is it any wonder then that he was unable to control the vehicle? A Trekker is not a bicycle – maybe he saw some girl or something, spun the wheel, lost control and hit the tree.'

'Yes, that is possible,' the superintendent sounded unconvinced.

'I didn't think you would doubt my word . . .' a dangerous note entered Soumen Rai's voice. Hari Ganguly was pleased – the party vs. the police. Wonderful!

'Doubt your word?' the senior policeman looked abashed. 'Of course not, sir!'

'Which leaves us with only one problem.' The MLA shuffled his papers, 'Why was the officer in charge of the area not available?'

Dhiren shivered. The politician continued, addressing him directly.

'Fortunately for him we have decided to take matters in hand. Let it be a lesson not to leave such important matters to subordinates.' He cleared his throat. 'The fact is that he was in Calcutta at my request, and on his superintendent's orders. Correct?' Dhiren nodded miserably. 'Good,' said the MLA. 'Now we have everything under control? No case, a simple accident. Untrained, unlicensed driver lost control of a vehicle which should not have been in the area, and killed self and passenger. Unfortunate incident, passing rally-goers will if necessary – and I hope it will not come to it – tell how they saw a car swing off the road, hit a tree and burst into flames.' Hari Ganguly inclined his head in agreement and the MLA continued, 'As the local MLA I will express sorrow and send my condolences to the families. The police will issue a statement to the effect that the vehicle was in the hands of an inexperienced driver, and everything will quieten down after a while. It will be just another accident, another unfortunate incident. No more.'

Dhiren bowed his head in acquiescence. He knew that some day he would pay for this.

Late in the afternoon a distant rumble is heard, breaking the silence of the hot day outside the schoolroom. The children's concentration is easily broken and the boys closest the window look out. '*Uro Jahaaj*! Flying machine!' they cry. Heedless of the master's order to return to their seats, the whole class rushes to the window. The machine lands, its huge blades raising a cloud of dust. The children rush up, only to be beaten back by men flailing batons. Amidst the confusion a police jeep has arrived and policemen in khaki uniforms surround the now immobile giant. They rush the crowd of children again. They scatter, only to regroup beyond the reach of the long sticks. A consular official descends and is met by Dhiren.

The body is in a room at the mission hospital. Dhiren orders the area be cleared. The party enters the building. Inside, Inspector Das, in his best uniform, salutes and leads Dhiren and the consular official to a room with the bodies. The corpses are charred but one is still recognisably European. The consular official signs the papers and the European's body is manhandled into the helicopter for the journey back to Calcutta. The other body will be cremated in Sonapukur.

In Delhi, Mr Sen waited anxiously in a hotel room. The meeting Dhiren had told him about should have taken place – he had promised to call him as soon as it was over. He poured a whisky. He was not a habitual drinker, his wife disapproved of it. However, he found it useful in his business dealings and occasionally indulged socially and privately. That day he had an excuse. He was nervous. He was, he assured himself, drinking moderately. This was only his second glass since he had returned two hours before. He sipped it slowly, trying to focus on the television news. But try as he may, his thoughts kept returning to the possible fallout of the accident. What if anyone, intentionally or unintentionally, let slip that Anglo-India (or Shiva Enterprises, for that matter) was linked to it? Until now it had merited no more than a small note in the papers, a news brief, nothing else. However, if there were any leaks or if the police decided to make an issue of it, Anglo-India might be in trouble. The opponents of joint-ventures would be overjoyed, accusing his enterprise and others of undermining the country by producing second-rate goods for quick profits. He did not agree. Even if his product was cheap, it was a patriotic contribution, an affordable alternative to expensive 'original' parts. He had been particularly pleased to find that agency, Swaraj, to promote it – it lent it a peculiarly nationalist aura. But now it could all unravel, the slightest hint of association with a fatal accident . . . it was bad enough having his own money invested in it, worse still that he had convinced his uncle, Putul's Boro Dadu, to provide capital. Now they too were at risk, even more so than he. After all, if worst came to worst, he could raise loans for the ventures which would eventually make good his loss from other sources but they . . .

He took a large mouthful of the whisky. The telephone rang. He reached for it, spluttering as he swallowed.

'Hullo?' He coughed.

'Sailen Sen?' Sailen? *Sailen*? That couldn't be Dhiren!

'Yes?' Who on earth was it?

'Ah, Sailen, Soumen here,' the politician was genial, 'glad to have caught you. Dhiren Ghosh told me where to contact you. Said he was going to call you, I told him not to bother as I want to speak to you anyway.'

'You want to speak to me?'

'Yes, yes. First, I'm sure you will be glad to know that we have settled everything. The police are now convinced that the accident was caused by careless driving.'

'They are?' Sailen Sen breathed a sigh of relief.

'Oh yes, very certain. Skid marks and all that. Besides, the driver didn't have a license. A terrible tragedy, but one that would have been very difficult, if not impossible, to avoid. Should it be necessary, the investigation will receive depositions from witnesses – you know, there was a passing lorry,' he did not elaborate, 'but both Ghosh and the superintendent are satisfied that the driver was responsible for the accident. A terrible tragedy. Terrible.'

'Yes, terrible,' Mr Sen repeated, numbly.

'Well, I am sure you are as relieved as the police that the cause has been established,' Soumen Rai carefully did not include himself or Hari Ganguly in the 'relieved' category. 'I will, of course, be reporting on my meeting to the party. I think they will be quite pleased with the outcome, too. After all, we have been long proposing the introduction of traffic islands on busy roads, to prevent vehicles from meandering from one side to the other.'

'Traffic islands?' What was Soumen Rai talking about?

'Oh yes. Definitely. Part of the road safety campaign that some international donors have been so keen on . . .' It dawned on Mr Sen that he was to be involved in this. Soumen Rai did not leave him in the dark long, 'But, of course, it was the brainchild of our illustrious transport minister. However, such innovations are expensive and the ministry has suggested that sponsorship might be an option . . .'

'Sponsorship?' Sailen repeated cautiously.

'In fact, it has just struck me – perhaps Anglo-India would be interested? After all, it would raise its profile. And it is related. If you were counting costs you might see the sponsorship of such a civic amenity as free advertising.' Mr Sen could almost see Soumen Rai beam.

'Yes, of course,' he said dully.

'Naturally, the islands would not be out in the far-flung areas of the countryside where there is neither traffic nor police,' Soumen Rai said airily. 'They would be in the city. Perhaps somewhere like South Calcutta. Imagine that, driving past Anglo-India advertising every day – it would be impressive, wouldn't it?'

'It sounds interesting, very interesting . . .'

'Well, take your time to think it over. No one wants to rush you, you know. Take your time, let me know tomorrow.'

'So soon?'

'Oh yes. Before I go to see the minister, you know. Terrible tragedy. The sooner it is cleared up the better, don't you agree?'

'Of course.' Dully.

'Good, good. But you must excuse me, I have a train to catch – wouldn't want to have to travel by road,' Mr Sen heard Soumen Rai laugh softly as he put the phone down.

He poured himself another drink. One last one, he promised himself. To celebrate. Anglo-India was safe. His reputation too. All he had to do was to find the money for the campaign.

An hour later he had an idea. He would consult his accountant, Mr Banerjee. Best ring him at the office. After the marriage fiasco Sailen Sen did not wish to talk to any other member of the Banerjee family. Still, business was business, and it was urgent.

The accountant was in. It was not going to be easy, he said.

He had the accounts in front of him and everything was tight, very tight. Anglo-India, as far as he could see, didn't even have enough to pay its suppliers. If they got wind of the problems there might be a stampede and bankruptcy would certainly follow.

Sailen Sen reminded him that the danger of the suppliers finding out only made it more urgent that they found the money for the scheme. Mr Banerjee leafed through the books, clicking his tongue noisily. He went through the options. Further delaying payments to suppliers was out, they might leave the factory without the raw materials it needed – and there was only so much political pressure could do to convince them . . . the banks were also no use, Anglo-India was up to the hilt . . .

'Wait a minute,' Mr Banerjee exclaimed. What was this? A sum set aside. For what? For payment to Swaraj. Who were they? They didn't appear to be suppliers. Sailen Sen explained. It was an advertising budget, Swaraj was designing billboards. Billboards? The accountant admitted he knew little about advertising but surely the traffic islands scheme would fulfil a similar function? Sailen Sen pondered this. Yes, he supposed it would. There it was then – here was the budget, already earmarked. All Mr Sen had to do was figure out how to divert it. Had he signed a contract with Swaraj? He hadn't? Perfect. Sailen Sen dithered, he did not like the idea but the accountant insisted. This was not time to be faint-hearted. Sailen Sen weakened, Mr Banerjee faxed him figures. Sailen Sen pored over them and gave in. There was nothing else to be done. He would have to drop the billboards scheme.

Chandu met Aziz at the clubhouse. The three friends had spent many an evening there. The mood was subdued. The news of the accident had not been long in getting to them. Sadan and his 'cadre' had returned the day after the event, having had to leave their 'work' unfinished. The secret cargo had been hidden, the mission (whatever it was) postponed. The news had spread like wildfire through the *basti*. Chandu had heard it at a card-game within an hour of Sadan's return, fifth-hand from a gambling partner. Throwing in his cards he had rushed to the party office to see what Sadan could tell him. The party man had not been keen to discuss details but had given into Chandu's insistence and had told him the story as he knew it. How Choto had left them the evening before and the next they'd heard of him he was dead. The day after the accident some villagers had helped Sadan and his boys cremate what remained of their driver. They had done all they could – Sadan had even sent one of his men to break the news to Choto's mother. And that was all. Now, if Chandu would excuse him, he had things to do, he said, ending the interview. To emphasise the point, he summoned two of his cadre to escort Chandu out.

Aziz listened to Chandu's version of the story. Then he told of how he had heard the news. He'd been in the company of Nawab, the *mastaan* holding court in a shop, when Kanchan burst in. Sobbing. Nawab's 'boys' had been all for throwing the child out but their leader had stopped them. The child might have something interesting to say. If not, they could throw him as far as they wanted. They liked the idea and Kanchan was bidden to speak. He told them, weeping copiously, that Choto was no more. Nawab shook him and demanded to know – what of the Trekker? Kanchan told him it was gone too. Nawab was outraged. His vehicle destroyed. Unpaid for. He cursed every ancestor of Choto and everything and every-one connected with him. Aziz had been horrified. Nawab had no loyalty – no word for Choto except to describe him as a misbegotten fool who had reduced the Trekker to nothingness!

Aziz remembered the days the three of them had spent together. The card games – including the last one where Choto had lost more than he had ever earned. The football games, first as children when they both played on the junior club team (in the days when the clubhouse actually housed a youth club) and the impromptu matches in the rain. The many evenings they had spent together, discussing football and films, telling tall tales of their exploits, comparing notes on women. Aziz and Chandu remembered Choto as the one more likely to talk than to act. Choto had been the naïve one, the one they could endlessly exploit for fun. And they remembered, with a twinge of guilt, how often they had taken advantage of him.

Chandu was conscience stricken. After all, had he not encouraged Choto to continue with the Trekker? Worse still, hadn't he been the one who had taken him to Sadan, got him the job that had ended so disastrously, so finally? He was responsible for the death of Choto, their friend, the one who tried to avoid drinking because he did not want to upset his mother and could not afford it, though he always maintained it was because he preferred *ganja*. Just a few days before he died, Choto had told him of his dream of the day he would own his own taxi. Now it was all over. He was dead, just like that. If only he, Chandu, had not told him of Sadan or his trip. Choto would then still be around, smoking his *bidis*, getting annoyed with that child, Kanchan, chasing the girl, Gowri. But he wasn't and here they were, Chandu and Aziz, two of a group that so recently had been three.

'Aziz, what if I had never taken him to see Sadan?'

'If you hadn't, he might still be alive.'

'Why did I tell him? Why?' cried Chandu.

'Because, you fool, that was all you could do,' Aziz shook his companion roughly. 'You did your best.'

'No, I could have stayed out of his business, couldn't I?'

'But you would not have thanked yourself for that either, *shala*! He needed the work, you found it for him. It's as simple as that. Get out that bottle, let us drink to his memory at least.'

'You think we can?'

'Of course we can! What else can we do? Can we bring him back to life?' Aziz snatched the bottle from Chandu's unwilling hand and drank straight from it. He thrust it back.

'Drink!' And Chandu drank deep. They drank together, to forget. And for one night at least they did. Others in the *basti* did not. A mother sat stony-faced, silent, a girl wept inconsolably.

CHAPTER SEVENTEEN

Durga was uncharacteristically late. It was almost welcome. It gave me something to talk about. I tried to lighten the atmosphere, to joke about it but the mood at the breakfast table remained steadfastly sombre. Dada had left for his office without eating, as he had begun doing the morning after his surprise announcement, and both my parents were still too pre-occupied to talk much. With hindsight, it was perhaps just as well – no speculation on our part could have prepared us for what we were about to hear.

The storm – if I may call it that – broke around eleven. Disappointed by Durga's absence but still unwilling to discuss it or any other matter, Ma had begun preparations for the day's cooking on her own. I tried to help but she impatiently sent me away. I was more of a hindrance than a help in the art of routine preparation, she said. It was a comment worthy of the cheerful mother I was used to and I began to smile, hoping for a break in the tension – but just then Durga appeared.

I was horrified. The small, tidy woman we knew was transformed into a dishevelled, wild-eyed apparition, her sari torn, as though someone had tried to rip it off her. She looked more like a vagrant than our familiar Durga. My mother and I both stared, aghast.

'Durga?' my mother asked. Instead of answering Durga collapsed in a dead faint.

We laid her on the mat kept for her afternoon siesta. Ma ran for water as I fanned her. She opened her eyes weakly, made as if to speak but was unable to. My mother wiped her brow and, cradling her head in her arms, gave her to drink – the first time that Durga had been fed by one of us, rather than us by her. After some ten minutes she was strong enough to sit up – we would have kept her resting longer but she insisted. She wanted to tell us something. We listened.

The words came first as a trickle, then a stream, finally a flood. It was the story that we had lived beside for years but had never heard, except for little snippets – the drought ridden village on the banks of the wide, sandy-bedded river, the son, nothing else. But that morning she told us the whole sad tale. She told of her childhood, of being a girl in a family where the father owned no land, a father who hired himself out for a few coins or a measly measure of rice. Her mother worked in the fields too, for less than half the pay, if you could call it that, then came home to their tiny dwelling whose thatch was so worn that the sun shone through it, so worn that it leaked even in the slightest drizzle. They had nothing, let alone for repairs. She told of how she tended a sickly brother barely two years younger than herself and learned to work young, younger than I was when I learned my first letters. She told of the burning heat of the summers, the hard cracked unyielding soil, the long journey to the water. Smelly, brackish water. Her little brother was fed the best morsels but he did not grow stronger, he sickened and he died. Of a fever. There were no doctors they could afford, not even the nearest dispensary. When he died, her father begged and borrowed wood to burn the body – but it was not enough and a half-consumed body was consigned to the shallow, pitiless river. When she came of age, she was given in marriage to an equally unfortunate young man. A man who spent the tiny dowry her father mortgaged his life's labour for in no time at all. There was no work for either of them in the barren fields so she and her husband worked for some time on the road that was being built – until the money ran out and the work stopped. The entire community, and they with it, was left with no money, no work and no road – only a dusty track that started nowhere and ended nowhere. Her husband took to drink, where he found the money she did not know, and took to beating her. Then, in one of those showers that promised the rains that might make the crops grow but were always false, he contracted a fever too. No longer did he beat her, he had not the strength for it. Instead, he swore at her, cursed her and blamed her for the evil fate that had befallen him. Then, one night he had stopped cursing her and quietly passed away. She had not had the chance to tell him that she was with child. Perhaps it was just as well, because he would probably have cursed her for bringing another mouth into the world for him to feed. As she sat alone in the dark hut beside the body, she remembered that someone had once left the village and travelled to the far-away city. That traveller had never returned but had sent a letter, which, for a fee, the post-office *peon* had read out, telling of the wealth he was accumulating, of the food that was to be had on the streets. With nothing but a dead husband and a baby growing inside her, she decided to follow. She dug out her secret store of money and walked out, leaving the body on its mat. She crossed the river at dawn before the sand was too hot to walk on and from there had made her way, she hardly knew how, to a railway platform in the city.

Alone and lost she had wandered the streets, bewildered by the traffic, the cattle, the dogs, the crowds. Soon she too fell sick, and was wracked by fever. Another woman, a refugee from floods elsewhere, took pity on her and took her into her own shack and nursed her till she was well enough to sit up and drink a little water on her own. Her benefactress had then found her work as a servant, introducing her as her sister – the employers cared too little for dialect to realise that they were not even from the same district, let alone of the same parents. But that first job had not lasted long because she did not know how to look after city people's things and had beaten a shirt to shreds. Her protector then found her another job, which she kept until it was time to have her baby. Soon after the child was born the flood refugee left, saying she was going to visit her village. She did not return and Durga found herself alone. At least she had a roof over her head. She found another job and took the child with her – her new employers kindly allowed her to have him with her, so long as he did not make too much noise. They docked her wages for the time she spent with him. And, when he grew a little older, a friendly neighbour's daughter (a few years older but too young to work yet) became his daytime *ayah*. Several jobs later, she came to work in our house.

Over the years she had saved every coin she made for her son, once even lying to us about a wedding in the family so that she could buy him the clothes he was then old enough to demand. Determined he would escape the poverty that was her lot, she had sent him to school but he proved too slow to keep up and had dropped out. He had been apprenticed at a garage but that too failed. He failed at everything he turned his hand to. He was too weak, he did not apply himself, he made mistakes, he was careless. In the end all he did was hang around with friends, drinking tea, smoking *bidis*. She had been so pleased that my father had found something for him ... but it was not to be, he turned his back on it and instead took up that offer from the man no one could trust. A thug, no less. A man whom the entire *basti* feared, a man who stalked the area with his hangers-on, terrorising young and old. A man who sold his services to the highest bidder, who, when required, would do the bidding of the landlords or the parties, who 'convinced' voters, who 'encouraged' settlers to move on, who provided goods that were otherwise unavailable. Her son had chosen to work for that man. And that had brought disaster.

We did not understand. She told us brokenly and the full horror dawned upon us. He had died in a car accident. The car that belonged to the *mastaan* he had been hired to drive to a village far away. Sonapukur. I heard my mother draw breath sharply. Durga had heard it the day before – one of the party boys he had been ferrying had told her and then a good for nothing called Chandu had confirmed it. And then she had received a visit from the thug himself. He had expressed shallow sympathy and reminded her that there was money owing. Money that he would expect paid. Not immediately, but soon. He was not a heartless man, he said, so he would give her a month to recover, then he would expect the first payments. Naturally, he said, if she was unable to pay cash, he could make arrangements for other forms of payment. Her shack for instance, though not worth much, would, he said, serve as part payment. He would help her to find alternative accommodation.

We listened, stunned, not daring to say anything – her son was the driver of the vehicle whose accident threatened Raja Mama's investment, and nearly proved the downfall of Sailen Sen. How close it was to us.

Putul was in his office. Well, not really *his* office, but the office that had been assigned to him for the duration of their stay in Delhi. In spite of his reservations about the trip and about getting involved in the business, he had to admit that he liked this office his uncle had assigned to him. To begin with, it was properly air-conditioned and the chair he sat in was leather-upholstered. Not Rexine, but real leather. And the desk was modern. Really modern. Unlike the offices in Calcutta, this one looked like it had been designed and maintained for an important person. A real VIP. He even had a secretary to field his calls. Only there weren't too many – the only calls that came in were from Sailen Kaka and from his friends, school and college friends who now lived in the capital. Pity they were all so busy. Still, the view of Connaught Place from ten stories up was spectacular. The cars below were matchbox toys. A short lift ride down there was everything he could possibly want: shops, restaurants, places to meet, entertain and be entertained. It was such a pity that John's itinerary had not included Delhi. He would have been impressed, very impressed. Quite a change from the barren empty lot that their tiny flat in Glasgow had looked out on. This was life, and real luxury. A buzzer sounded. He swivelled round in his chair. The discreet little light on the console was flashing. A call, perhaps? Someone free for lunch or dinner? He activated the intercom.

'Yes, Miss Kohli?'

'A call for you, Mr Sen.'

'Who is it, Miss Kohli?'

'A Mr Ghosh, Mr Sen.'

'Ghosh? I don't think I know him – did he say anything more?'

'Said he was a friend of yours, Mr Sen. Mr Dhiren Ghosh.'

'Oh, Dhiren. Put him through, put him through!' He picked up the receiver and leaned back. Dhiren came on the line.

'Putul?' The telephone crackled.

'Dhiren. Where are you? This line is terrible.'

'Sonapukur. Where did you think I was?'

'Delhi. Or Calcutta. What on earth are you doing in Sonapukur?'

'What the hell do you think I am doing in Sonapukur? This is where I'm posted!'

'Yes, I know . . . but . . .'

'Shut up, Putul,' Dhiren interrupted, 'I need to talk to you.'

'In the line of duty, I hope' Putul stretched his legs under the smart desk.

'Just listen, you idiot,' Putul stiffened. 'Putul, listen – do you know a John Stewart?

'John who?' He was genuinely hurt by Dhiren's brusqueness.

'John Stewart, a Britisher, you idiot!'

'There's no need to be rude, Dhiren. Yes, I do know a John Stewart. He was in Glasgow with me and is visiting India. I was going to introduce you but then Sailen Kaka dragged me here.'

'You sitting down, Putul?' Dhiren's voice softened.

'You don't think I take 'phone calls standing up, do you?' Putul retorted.

'This friend of yours, Stewart – he's dead.'

'WHAT?'

'He's dead, that's all. An accident, near here on Sunday night.'

'Near where?'

'Here. Sonapukur.'

'Sonapukur? Sonapukur! What was he doing there?'

'Visiting his grandfather's last posting. Didn't he tell you? We checked up on him and all we found was your name,' Dhiren lied. 'I called you in Calcutta, only you turned out to be in Delhi,' Dhiren was determined to stick to his side of the agreement. For now at least.

'What happened?'

'I told you, he died in an accident,' the policeman said patiently. 'Now, can you get back to Calcutta soon?'

Putul, still in a state of shock, racked his brains. He remembered. 'His grandfather!'

'His grandfather?'

'Yes, yes, and his great-grandfather!'

'Putul, get a grip on yourself. This fellow dies on the Sonapukur road and you are babbling about his ancestors.'

'No, no,' Putul said slowly, 'his grandfather used to be in Sonapukur.'

'Yes, Putul.'

'His grandfather was a policeman in Sonapukur before Independence.'

'That's just what I needed to know.' Dhiren sighed. 'Look, can you get back to Calcutta today?'

'Calcutta?'

'Where you live . . .'

'Where I live?'

'Putul,' Dhiren said firmly. 'Get a grip on yourself. I'd like you to confirm identification of the body, so you'd better get back to Calcutta quickly. The sooner it is sent to Britain the better.'

'I've got an address, a telephone number . . . I suppose it must be family?'

'Never mind that, just get back to Calcutta. I'll get someone to pick you up at your house.'

Dhiren was as good as his word. A policeman was waiting at the house and, before he had time to explain to his aunt, Putul was whisked away to a *thana* in a jeep complete with armed bodyguard. Dhiren wasn't there but a smartly-dressed inspector was.

'Mr Sen?' Putul nodded and was waved to a chair. He sat down.

'Mr Sen, I believe the deceased, John Stewart, was a guest of yours?'

'Not a guest, not really. Though he would have been if I hadn't been called away to Delhi. Business, you know.'

The inspector was scribbling in his notebook. He looked up. 'Business? What kind of business? Was this John Stewart a business associate?'

'Business associate? No.' Putul did not understand. 'No, he wasn't a business associate. Just a friend.'

'Friend? Where did you meet him?'

'England. Not that it is anything to do with you!' Putul was getting annoyed.

The inspector shook his head and closed his notebook. 'Mr Sen, I have reason to believe your families were connected. Business, as you say.'

'What if they were?' Putul responded belligerently.

'Mr Sen, your uncle is a partner in Anglo-India, is he not?'

'Yes.'

'And, Mr Sen, surely you are aware that Anglo-India is a joint-venture?' the inspector continued sarcastically.

'Naturally!'

'And you know who the British partner is?'

'Of course I do! John Stewart's father. Though I don't know what business that is of yours!'

'Plenty. You are named as Mr Stewart's sponsor in India.' The inspector didn't like these rich types. Too bloody self-important for their own good.

'So what? So bloody what?'

'Mr Sen, I just needed to confirm the facts. That you are a close associate of the deceased.' He snapped his notebook shut. 'You come with me now, Mr Sen.' Putul followed in a daze.

No fan of the four-wheel drive, Putul felt particularly uncomfortable in the back of his second jeep that day as it bounced along the pot-holed road to the hospital. The mortuary was tucked away deep inside the building. Putul followed his guide down the maze of corridors. Confirming identification of the body, it turned out, was a formality. The police and the embassy official had already satisfied themselves that it was that of John Stewart. It could have been of any European – it was charred beyond recognition. However, the forensics men had examined the teeth and they matched the dental record sent over. Putul was none too keen to stay and got out as quickly as he could, holding back his nausea. The cold, clammy damp, the smell of preservatives . . .

Back in the jeep, he accepted a cigarette from the inspector who seemed to have softened. Death was hard, even for the rich. Putul puffed hungrily, feeling progressively more light-headed, then sicker than before. As soon as he reached his uncle's house he fled upstairs and flung himself over the bathroom sink. He stayed there for a good half-hour, ignoring the entreaties of his aunt to come out. Finally relieved, he washed his face, then stripped and stood under the shower, eyes closed, waiting for calm. It came after his aunt retreated, leaving him to step out of the bathroom into his own space. He towelled down and put on fresh clothes – loose white kurta, pajamas. He did not go down.

He lay on his bed, staring at the immobile fan on the ceiling for what seemed like a long time. His mind remained steadfastly blank. Gradually consciousness returned. John Stewart was dead, a body on a slab. He did not wish to return to Delhi. He did not wish to stay where he was. He could go away. Where? Far away. Where? He knew. He would go to Britain, accompany the body there, carry his uncle's condolences. Maybe he could do some work for the firm there. That's what he would tell his uncle. He could stay there for a while. He was decided. He descended the stairs to make his announcement and arrangements.

I desperately needed to get out and left the house soon after lunch and headed down Rash Behari Avenue. I had no fixed plans, I just wanted to get away from the stresses of home. I wandered down past Gariahat Market, past Triangular Park and Lake Road, towards Deshapriya Park. Suddenly I saw Ratna, crossing at the Lansdowne Road junction. She did not see me, did not hear my call. I dashed after her, ignoring the angry shouts of braking drivers. She was moving fast, wending her way through the crowd, so that I had a hard time catching up.

'Ratna!' I shouted. This time she stopped and saw me.

'Ratna, I thought I'd never catch up with you!' I reached her. 'Where are you going?'

'Home.'

'Home? This way?' She was headed in the wrong direction.

'I have to pick up something along here. A book . ...'

'A book? That's a coincidence, I was thinking of shopping for books too. But can we stop for a minute? Have a Limca or something?' Ratna looked uncertain. I pressed her, I wanted company, someone to talk to about something, anything. To take my mind off recent events.

'Are you meeting Rasheed?' As soon as I said it I could see it was the wrong question.

'No.' There was a flat finality in her tone.

'No?' Confused, I dug myself deeper into the hole. If only I could have thought of something else to say.

'No. Not now, not for a while, maybe never!'

'What?!' I couldn't believe my ears. 'Maybe never?' I repeated foolishly.

'No.'

'Ratna, what's going on? No, don't tell me here on the street, let's get in somewhere.' And I half dragged her across the road to a sweet shop.

Once we were seated I asked again, 'Ratna, what's happened between you and Rasheed?'

'Nothing.'

'What do you mean, nothing? Have you had a fight or something?'

'A fight? No, not a fight. Nothing's happened between us, nor is anything going to, Meena. That's the problem.'

'I don't understand. Everything seemed so . . . so,' I searched for words, '*good*, the last time I saw both of you.'

'It's all off,' she repeated.

'But why, Ratna, why? What's happened? Please, please, tell me!' I begged.

It poured out. 'Rasheed's lost his job. The contract fell through. I don't know what or why. Something to do with money, Rasheed had to go. He has no other prospects right now. So we have decided it's best to part. He has no job, we have no future. I don't really want to talk about it. I must go . . .' She had left before I even had time to say good-bye. I just watched her go.

At home things were not improving, no one spoke to each other and Dada spent more and more time in the office. The day after her outburst, Durga came in to say she was leaving. I was alone in the house and tried to dissuade her, to get her to continue with us. I even offered to ask Ma to let her have the room at the bottom of the stairs rent-free. But she was adamant.

'I lived for my son. Without him what is the point? Why should I go on living here, working as though there were something to work for? Now I am not only a widow but childless too. I have no one to look after and no one to look after me in my old age. Why then should I labour in this city which is not my home? You have been very good to me, you and your family, and you and your brother have been almost as my own children. But you are not, and now you are grown you have less and less need of your parents, forget me. The one child – of the three I have helped raise – for whom I was entirely responsible, whose entire childhood was dependent on me and me alone, he is gone. Maybe it is just my fate. Now all I want is to return to the village of my husband, of his father and of mine, and to spend the rest of my days there.'

She insisted there was nothing left for her – the child she had brought into the world on her own was gone. All that was left for her was to return – to nothing, she knew. But that was all she wanted. There was no point staying here, she said, the *mastaan* would make it impossible, he would hound her. And why should she allow it? If her son were alive and the car destroyed then she might pay for it, but now? It was nothing to her, she would not, could not stay.

I tried to reason with her, I told her how important she was to me, I pleaded, I begged. But to no avail. On the verge of tears she told me that she cared for me almost as much as she had for her own child, but that I had my own life, I did not need her. And she was right. I gave in – what else could I do? I promised to tell my parents of her decision and advanced her, out of my own limited means, her outstanding pay. I tried to press her to accept an extra sum but she would have none of it. The last I saw of her she was walking slowly down the street, away from our house on her way out of the city, out of our lives, never once looking back.

EPILOGUE

The morning arrived. There was no fog, the sun shone brightly in a clear blue sky. In his room, Putul checked through his suitcase, making sure he had everything he needed. Warm clothes, suits. Shaving cream, soap, shampoo, razor, toothpaste, toothbrush. And in his hand-luggage his passport, ticket, traveller's cheques. Letters for Sailen Kaka's business contacts. The duplicate death certificate in an envelope with the Stewart address on it. Everything present and correct. And a packet of cigarettes. He'd taken up smoking.

Breakfast was on the table. His aunt, red-eyed from crying, served him herself. His uncle sat silent, ostentatiously concentrating on his food. When he finished, he rose slowly, touched Putul on the shoulder, cleared his throat as if to say something, thought better of it and left the room without a word. Putul tried to drink his tea but gave up and pushed it away. Without a word his aunt cleared the table and sat down, not looking at him but at the table surface, playing with a crumb. At precisely half past ten the driver appeared and the servant carried the bags down to the car. Putul *pronaamed* his aunt, she raised him up and embraced him. Neither spoke. Then he was in the car pulling out of the driveway. He looked back, catching sight of his aunt at the window, her shoulders shaking.

The road to the airport was clear. Out of the city onto the Eastern Metropolitan Bypass, past the tanneries, the huge festering dumps of Dhapa, the flooded wetlands of the sewage-fed fish farms. And along VIP Road, with the lorries, bullock carts, cyclists. The driver left him at the entrance – Putul forbade him to enter so he hung around on the other side of the barrier, watching till he could see his employer's nephew no more.

Durga shouldered her bundle, raised it to her head and walked out of the station, barefoot. She threaded her way through the crowd outside and found the bus was outside. A mass of people blocked the entrance, the conductor pushing, sweating, swearing as he organised the loading of bags and livestock. She forced her way through, the conductor made as if to stop her. Then he saw her face, her demeanour and let her pass. He could collect her fare later, he would remember her. Someone cursed under his breath as her bundle swung round. Oblivious to the effect she was having, Durga clambered aboard, storing her own small bundle under the seat. The bustle outside continued for at least twenty minutes but she sat quiet, not joining in the growing grumbles. 'What are you waiting for?

How many more do you want to squeeze in here?' The conductor slapped the palm of his hand on the body of the bus and yelped the command to start.

The bus rattled over ruts in the town road, past the markets, the houses, the tea-shops, the diminishing road-side vendors, out, out onto a half-built road. Gradually the town faded and fields replaced the buildings. Flat, dry fields dotted with small huts in a burning sun. No green except high in the coconut trees and in the occasional eucalyptus plantation, no animals except for scrawny dogs and goats and the occasional chicken pecking at hard earth. Durga watched for a while, then tiredness overtook her and she slept. Slept every mile of the four-hour journey, not even waking when another woman pushed her so as to make space to sit. Not waking when a squalling child threw up over its mother, hot dry vomit onto a bony lap. Not even when the bus came to its final destination. All the other passengers had disembarked and the conductor came up to scold her, then remembered. He shook her gently by the shoulder. Startled, she awoke, and paid the demanded fare out of the almost empty knot in the corner of her sari. The conductor helped her out with her bundle and pointed her in the direction she wanted. She had been away so long she had forgotten. Besides, things had changed, the bus had brought her a few kilometres closer, right up to the banks of the river. Ahead of her lay a long walk across the sand. But this time she had footwear. Old footwear, but footwear all the same. She put on her slippers and began to trek.

Somewhere in the middle of the riverbed she became conscious of a dull pain in her skull. Shading her eyes, she tried to see the far bank. She stopped. She could see the village. She could distinguish figures. Children, adults. She looked at them and saw the distended bellies of her childhood, the ribs of the dogs. Around her the land was brown, parched, clean. Silent faces watched her walk down the street. The few children who ran up behind her, curious, tired of following in her silent wake. She walked past the temple, the old tree, along familiar paths. Up ahead stood the hut she had left that fateful night, the hut that had been her last home here, her husband's hut. It crumbled into four roofless walls, drying mud sinking back into the land from which it had risen. She moved on, further into the drought-stricken village, to where she knew her father's house would still be standing. *It* would be there, she knew . . .

A man on the distant shore thought he saw a human figure stumble in the golden sand. It did not rise again. Maybe he had been mistaken – no one would be fool enough to cross the river when the sun was so high. He looked away and saw a company of crows quarrelling over the carcass of a bird. One of their own? He shook his head – it must be the sun. It was hot for this time of the year. The drought wasn't over yet.